the CURIOUS CASE of the MIDNIGHT SPECTER

Also By Moriah Chavis

Thorns of Winter (Twenty Hills Publishing)

Heart of the Sea (Quill & Flame Publishers)

Sea of Sorrow (Self-Published)

The Curious Case of the Midnight Specter

MORIAH CHAVIS

Twenty
Hills

PRAISE FOR
THE CURIOUS CASE OF THE MIDNIGHT SPECTER

"From the very first page, I was captivated by the gripping mystery that had me hooked until the very last page. The characters are vibrant, complex, and utterly engaging. Moriah Chavis has crafted a story that's both chilling and enchanting, making me an instant fan of her remarkable storytelling. I can't wait to see what she writes next!"

– Natalie Walters, bestselling and award-winning author of the *SNAP Agency.*

"A languid romp through Victorian society, with a zesty dash of murder and mayhem!"

– April J. Skelly, author of *A Lethal Engagement*

"An adventurous romp with a spunky heroine reminiscent of Enola Holmes. This mystery with a touch of magic is full of delightful characters, unexpected twists, and a whodunit that will keep you guessing until the page-turning end!"

– Lorie Langdon, author of the *Disney Happily Never After Series*

"Clever and charming! Chavis's heartfelt ghost story will keep you on your toes and entertained from start to finish. Both life and death play a vital role in the tale, and you'll never look at either of them quite the same way again."

– Rachelle Nelson, Christy & Carol award winning author of *Sky of Seven Colors*

"Moriah does it again, but this time with a mystery wrapped in late 1800's England. Her story follows a young girl, Leighanna Pauley, touched by life and death and given a second chance. Moriah wastes no time and throws you into a tale of twists and turns that leave her readers connecting dots and questioning everyone Leighanna knows. I loved diving into this story. The mystery, the drama, the questions, and the tension left me turning the pages faster than the hands of time herself. This is a story I know I'll be revisiting and sharing with my kids."

– Kimberly Byrd, author of Door of Keys

"For fans of Enola Holmes or any good BBC mystery comes a murder mystery that will keep you hooked from the first page. With the personification of death and life, this book brings a whole new perspective to the detective mystery genre."

– Amanda Auler, author of The Mothmar Trilogy

"*The Curious Case of the Midnight Specter* is a riveting story. Full of mystery and intrigue and a chilling climax, this book is sure to keep you guessing and anxiously turning the page."

– Caitlin Miller, award-winning author of Our Yellow Tape Letters

"Move over, Sherlock Holmes—there's a new detective in town! Leighanna Pauley is fierce and unrelenting as she tracks a ruthless killer leaving a macabre trail of victims. With gaslamp intrigue, bone-chilling suspense, and a touch of the supernatural, this murder mystery grips you from the first page. Danger lurks in every shadow, and Leighanna's sharp wit and determination will keep you hooked until the very last twist!"

– Jenelle Hovde, author of No Stone Unturned, Tyndale House Publishers

"*The Curious Case of the Midnight Specter* by Moriah Chavis had me riveted to the page. This young adult Victorian mystery features a daring heroine with gumption and heart in equal measure. The clever plot kept me guessing, unraveling clue by clue until the satisfying ending. This gripping story will appeal to fans of Enola Holmes and any reader who savors a brilliantly penned whodunit!"
  – Rachel Scott McDaniel, award-winning author of *The Dreams We Knew*

"Chilling! *The Curious Case of the Midnight Spector* kept me up late turning page after haunting page. Fans of amateur sleuths like Miss Scarlet will love to follow Leighanna Pauley as she navigates her first case and a woman's place in polite Victorian society (with a cat in tow!). This series starter reminded me of the darkly romantic writings of Daphne Du Maurier and the haunting paranormal mystery of Erin Craig's *House of Salt and Sorrow*."
  – Adelyn Belsterling, author of *I Wish I May*

To my mother, who never let us win at Clue.

Table of Contents

PROLOGUE..1
   Between Life and Death

CHAPTER ONE..11
   The Invitation

CHAPTER TWO...25
   Whispers and Shadows

CHAPTER THREE..41
   Curiosity and the Cat

CHAPTER FOUR...44
   Midnight at Morven Manor

CHAPTER FIVE...55
   Miss Lavender Lemon's Tea Shoppe

CHAPTER SIX...71
   A Moment in Time

CHAPTER SEVEN...76
   The Rules of Society

CHAPTER EIGHT..90
   The Conservatory

CHAPTER NINE...103
   The Scene of the Crime

CHAPTER TEN..116
   The Clockmaker

CHAPTER ELEVEN...137
   Fight Club

CHAPTER TWELVE..156
   On the Other Side of Time

CHAPTER THIRTEEN...160
   Hunt for the Guilty

CHAPTER FOURTEEN.................................177
    The Evidence Thickens
CHAPTER FIFTEEN....................................186
    A Night at the Ring
CHAPTER SIXTEEN...................................194
    Secrets Between Siblings
CHAPTER SEVENTEEN..............................200
    Riding Pants and Writing Lists
CHAPTER EIGHTEEN.................................210
    Trying to Spill the Tea
CHAPTER NINETEEN.................................220
    In the Dead of Night
CHAPTER TWENTY....................................236
    Another Murder
CHAPTER TWENTY-ONE.............................241
    Thicker Than Thieves
CHAPTER TWENTY-TWO............................248
    Storm in a Teacup
CHAPTER TWENTY-THREE..........................256
    Like a Sneak in the Night
CHAPTER TWENTY-FOUR...........................265
    Trust, but Verify
CHAPTER TWENTY-FIVE.............................271
    Superior Evidence
CHAPTER TWENTY-SIX...............................280
    How to Catch a Killer
CHAPTER TWENTY-SEVEN..........................295
    The Beginning

Acknowledgments.....................................305
About the Author......................................309

Even Death
was tempted
by the sweetness
of Life.

PROLOGUE
Between Life and Death

Christmas 1889

L EIGHANNA PAULEY LAY SUSPENDED between life and death. Consumption wreaked havoc on her lungs, and each cough brought a new round of pain. Sweat coated her brow and soaked through her clothes. Though she was drenched with illness, she feared she'd never be warm again. The mattress beneath her felt too soft and the blanket over her too heavy. Everything was too much. The certainty of her expiration seemed to draw closer with every rattling breath, each cough adding more blood to the cloth clenched in her fist. She wanted, more than anything, a reprieve.

Voices assaulted her ears, and a groan passed her lips. Someone asked her a question, but the words mixed and twisted together in her mind. She thought someone said her name, but she couldn't be sure. Then cool metal touched her inner arm, and she heard ". . . a small cut below the elbow."

The bleeding. They were bleeding her. Her heart raced, as if wanting to push the blood out of her faster. They would have called the doctor. Was that who spoke to her now? Some of the fog lifted, and she heard him tell her, "You must grab the metal pole, Miss Pauley. The bleeding will help."

She weakly grabbed the metal pole to help rush the blood from her veins. It was to help her, not hinder.

But Leighanna felt like nothing would help. Of all her seventeen years on this earth, nothing had ailed her like this. Fire thrashed inside her chest as another cough worked its way up her throat. She plastered her uninjured arm over her mouth as she heaved. When she pulled her arm back, bright crimson speckled the white sleeve of her nightdress. Another wave of exhaustion overcame her as the doctor wrapped her fingers around the metal pole. She stared into his eyes, the only part of him visible besides his dark brown hair. The rest of his face was hidden behind a white fabric mask.

"Squeeze the metal pole, Miss Pauley, to get the blood to flow from the wound," he said, voice slightly muffled, and assured her once more it would help, but she didn't have the strength.

Black spots speckled Leighanna's vision. Her arm flopped back down on the bed. Warm blood trickled from the cut and stained the sheets. Her mother's sobs echoed in the room.

Leighanna felt a cloth wrap around her elbow to halt the bleeding. Her sleeve was tugged back down to her wrist before the covers were pulled up and tucked beneath her chin.

In the distance, she heard her mother asking the doctor questions. He pushed her mother outside to answer them.

Leighanna was now alone with her thoughts. They spun as she wavered in the space between sleep and awake. Time passed, but it had no meaning behind it. A part of her knew her mother came in and out of the room. Another part suspected the Christmas holiday was near. Her mother wouldn't let her brother visit, and her father couldn't cross the sea in time—that elusive substance she was quickly running out of. Only the cat hung around at the foot of her bed, until her mother made him leave, too.

Suddenly, she heard new voices. One of them was familiar in the way you recognize an aunt or uncle you haven't seen in sixteen of your seventeen years of living. No matter; she had heard it before.

"One of us is not supposed to be here," it—*she*—said. A woman —a woman in white.

Who are you? Leighanna tried to ask, but the words wouldn't fall from her lips.

Then Leighanna heard no more.

Death wore a top hat. When he entered the homes of the living, he always took it off out of respect. He did the same when he entered the residence of Leighanna Pauley. The society girl lived on the outside of Stornshire, a modest town between London and Bath, in an equally modest townhome—like those he didn't visit often. Death rarely saw homes as nice as this one, not until Age had trickled through many years of laughter, tears, and wrinkles. No, by then, welcoming smiles greeted Death when he visited.

People always spoke of being too old. Men and women did whatever necessary to fight off Time. What they didn't understand was that aging meant living. Not aging meant Death came to their door, wearing his top hat, with a heaviness in his chest.

More often than he'd like, Time called him to a home before the person had a chance at a full life. Those moments he hated the most, no matter the condition of the residence.

He stepped over the threshold and into the warmth of the

fireplaces that spread to even his most chilled corners. He almost didn't see Life until he'd reached the top of the staircase leading to the second floor.

"You shouldn't be here," Life said, crossing her arms over her chest. Her gown of white shone against her tanned skin. Her long, curly white tresses looked as if the wind from the winter storm fought against her presence.

Death met her on the landing. "I come when called," he said.

She huffed. "As do I." A piece of her always hung around the living, but when she felt the tug on her strings, that was when people needed all of her. In those moments, she gave them the burst of life they needed.

Death peeked over Life's shoulder. The shadows danced around his suit, and he straightened it in an effort to still them. "Is she through there?" he asked.

Life arched a brow. "You don't know?"

"I do, but I was being kind enough to ask," he said.

"I'm supposed to be here, which would mean you are not." Life's warmth caressed the coldest parts of him, where the shadows never went away. He moved closer; even he was tempted by the sweetness of Life.

He placed his top hat on the knob at the top of the banister. It hung there in the silence, a few of his shadows wrapping around the brim. Life glanced at it before walking into the bedroom. Death followed her, trailing on the scents of honey and spring cascading behind her.

But unlike his beautiful counterpart, the room smelled of indecision, with an undercurrent of sickness. The essence of Life and the undertone of Death mixed together. The honey danced alongside the bitter bite of frankincense. Death didn't know what to think of it.

The blue walls of the high society home near Stornshire's edge hadn't seen the sunlight in days. Velvet curtains brushed the floor. The older woman in the chair near the bed walked over to the window and peeked through the drapes. A sliver of moonlight stretched over the large rug but ended before it reached the canopied bed where a girl slept with breaths coming in harsh gasps.

Leighanna Pauley.

"One of us is not supposed to be here," Life told Death, her voice soft and melodic, like the tinkling of bells or the sound of a child's first laugh. But the words tasted like a lie on Life's tongue, bitter and sharp. She remembered Leighanna's birth, like she did every life she welcomed earthside. This girl had been a spark from the start, even in her mother's womb, and her first cry had nearly broken windows with its sharp zing.

The girl groaned from the bed. Her lips moved as if trying to form words, but no sound came.

Death glanced toward Life. His dark shadows penetrated every corner of the room. "But I—"

"Yes, you've said," Life said.

"Maybe it is you who should not be here."

Life pursed her lips. Standing here now, it felt like her place, but it looked like Death's.

"She isn't meant to join you," Life said. She didn't think so, anyway. Her threads hung around them like strands of silk. They didn't *feel* ready for his scissors. "Not yet."

They both glanced at the girl. The room stretched around them, bigger than many of the rooms they saw in this business. Not like the slums where Life rarely hovered and Death was a constant specter.

Leighanna Pauley rolled over in her sleep. The covers shifted on the bed and the top sheet fell to the floor. The soft rustling grabbed her mother's attention, and she rushed over to her daughter and placed the blanket back where it belonged. Her hand hovered above Leighanna's slowly breathing body, and she slapped the other hand over her own mouth to mute her sobs. The doctor walked in. The cloth mask hung from just below his eyes to his shirt collar. The space between his brows wrinkled.

"You should not get so close, Mrs. Pauley," he told the mother. "And where have you put your mask?"

Mrs. Pauley rushed over to her chair and retrieved an equally stark white face covering. She tugged the straps over her ears before turning to look at the doctor. A frown pinched the corner of her eyes.

"She's not getting any better. You said she would get better. The bleedings—"

"Don't work for everyone," he said, tone apologetic. "You must be patient. Why aren't the curtains opened?"

The mother fretted toward the window, making excuses about how Leighanna flinched at the light.

"Light is what's best for her," the doctor said, ripping the curtains aside. The moon shone down on the carpeted floors. The two continued to argue until a maid stepped in and laid a hand on Mrs. Pauley's shoulder.

"Ma'am, why don't you come have a lie down?" The maid had golden blond curls and a face covering hiding her younger features.

"I don't want to leave her, Etta." Mrs. Pauley rested her hand on top of the maid's.

"A cup of tea will do you good," the maid insisted.

The doctor nodded his appreciation to the maid as she tugged the lady of the house back into the hall. His nurse trailed in and checked on the girl, while the doctor gave instructions.

"Which of us do you think is mistaken?" Life said.

"I would rather not be here," Death said.

Life watched Death study the girl as another cough threatened to wake her. He took a step closer. "I don't relish this job," he muttered. "I pity the young ones as much as I do the ones who go below instead of above." He pointed at the ground to emphasize his point.

Life bit her bottom lip as she took in his words. "What of her afterlife?" she asked.

"She has a glow about her." Death cocked his head to the side. "Do you see it? I can't tell if it's the promise of goodness after life or if there's still *life*."

Life remained quiet because she couldn't either. It made her uncomfortable. The strings that only she could see appeared like twine around her. They had a faint golden glow that she could dim with a snap of her fingers. Now, she brightened them so they shone like shooting stars. Usually, the strings grew more taut the closer the person got to the end, but that wasn't the case here. Faint lines from other lives sprouted in every direction, but she narrowed her focus on those coming from Leighanna. Instead of stiff and sure, they were slack. They felt weak. Odd. They didn't seem expended. She plucked the nearest one and listened to the sound it made.

The note was flat, but it still had music left.

"This feels different," Death continued, breaking her from her trance. He drew nearer to the girl. Life noted his hand hovering near his scissors.

Leighanna's brown hair lay limply on the silken pillow, her body wrapped in a pile of blankets. Sweat plastered small brunette curls to her temple. A flinch contorted her features as the sickness rattled in her chest. Her cheeks reddened, though her skin had a pale sheen to it.

"This appears to be more of your place," Life said, but she

lingered near the girl. "I'd like to help her, but something feels off. Perhaps I'm not meant to be here."

"Can you see the years ahead?" Death asked.

Life's brow furrowed. "Almost? She's only seventeen. The years ahead are so fickle already."

"Maybe if we claim her at the same time—"

"And do what, exactly? One cannot be in two places at once, on this side and the other."

"I suppose you are correct," Death said. "Now is not the time to say I've missed you, is it?"

Life sighed, choosing to ignore his words but feeling a jolt of pleasure. Leighanna took a breath and saved her from responding.

They both moved closer.

"We cannot both claim her," Life stated. She glanced at the watch pendant pinned to her dress. "Either way, we're nearing the moment." From the corner of her eye, she noticed Death's pointer finger resting on the scissors hanging from his belt. "One minute— then *one* of us claims her."

Death nodded. "Very well. How would you like to decide?"

Life paced around the bed. "I do not know."

"Should we reconvene and come back?" Death asked.

Life shot him a glare. "We need to decide *now*." She glanced at her watch. "Thirty seconds."

"Maybe we'll know in the last second," Death replied.

They both looked at the girl and watched the seconds tick by. "Twenty seconds," Life said.

Death and Life, opposites in every way, should not think like one another. But when the moment came to claim the girl, Life and Death did the same thing, in the same moment. They both lunged forward, fingers grazing the girl's skin. The girl took a breath, her soul splitting in two, part of it going to Death and the other to Life.

"No!"

The word was so loud that Life and Death jumped. "Was that the girl?" Life asked.

They looked at each other, both having released the girl as her soul hung between them. The echo of the word rang in Life's ears, the only evidence that she hadn't imagined it.

"I–I'm not sure. I—" Death's eyes widened. He shook his hand, as if he were a child who had touched a hot iron pot after being warned not to.

Life took a step closer to the girl, as did Death. They both reached for Leighanna's soul. Both their fingers grazed it, and—

For a moment, she hung between the two, but Life won.

This time.

A shadow passed over Death's face. "I must go. Immediately. There's been a murder." He vanished. Life watched, words lost, as Leighanna's soul stitched back together. The room felt larger without Death at her side. Or maybe it was the girl. A shudder ran through Leighanna's body, and she leaned over the side of the bed, a cough ripping through her. The doctor rushed in.

And in the shadows, a little bit of Death and a little slice of Life hovered in the corner, attached to the girl on the edge of both.

CHAPTER ONE
The Invitation

THE INK SMELLED FRESH on the morning paper. Leighanna wanted to bury her face between the black and white lines, breathing in the stories. Just holding the morning newsprint calmed her nerves. However, reading the newest updates in police investigations and Paris's response to the consumption epidemic made her heart beat rapidly. Each day brought on a new revelation around the city—around the world. She felt lucky to have escaped her bout with consumption last month. Reading the paper was a small victory. A month ago, she hadn't been able to hold her head up, much less the newspaper. But Leighanna had lived to read the stories, whereas many of those in the paper did not. She'd always had a fascination with the world around her, and her dance with death had increased that. She yearned to understand. Why was she one of the few who survived when so many others had not?

Her mother would be aghast if she walked in to see her daughter sitting near an open window in her nightgown, her long, dark curly hair a mess around her face. She was a prisoner in her own home until Florence Pauley said otherwise, no matter how incensed it made her. Leighanna narrowed her brown eyes on the printed lines and continued to read. It offered her a bite of rebellion to get through another odious day of staring at the blue walls of her bedroom. She knew she would only have a few more moments of solace before her mother came to check on her.

A soft meow sounded at her feet, and her chest swelled with joy. She moved the paper to the side. "Do you need something, Stan?" she said to the male tortie who she'd named after Æthelstan, the first true King of England. She'd found him next to the modiste three years ago on the afternoon of her fourteenth birthday. Being the runt of the litter—half his face yellow and the other half black—the cat had been skinnier than a rose stem.

She'd earned his trust with a plate of sardines. After he had eaten, she'd picked him up, only got bitten once, and by the evening, he'd been bathed, washed free of fleas, and was dozing comfortably in her bed. Since that day, he had been her constant companion.

Now, Stan took her attention as encouragement and jumped up into her lap. He did his little circle dance until he settled into a purring, mottled lump of orange and brown and yellow on her lap. The warm tangerine light of the incoming dawn shone down on the pair from the partially opened windows, warming Leighanna's nightdress and rushing away the slight draft pushing through the crack.

Snow had fallen the night before, painting the world white. The only ones awake besides her mother were the house staff, newsboys, and lamplighters snuffing out the gas street lamps.

She was alone with her thoughts, the cat, and the dying embers of her fire. She raised the newspaper back up and continued reading by the light of the rising sun.

"Leighanna, I've told you!" Mrs. Florence Pauley pushed into her daughter's room. "The neighbors can see you!" Leighanna rolled her eyes and stifled her irritation before yanking the paper down. Stan made a grunt of protest but didn't move.

"No one is awake yet, Mother."

"Katrina is here to see you, but you are not to receive her in your nightgown. I had Etta clean your dress. She's had to continually keep Stan from laying on the other laundry."

Leighanna ignored the jab toward Stan and asked, "Why is Kat so early? She couldn't have let me sleep in?" But she didn't mind, not really. It had been weeks since she'd seen her friend, and happiness flooded her veins.

"You weren't sleeping, dear. She knows you too well, I suppose," her mother replied. Her eyes flashed to the cat in her lap. "That cat needs to be outside."

"*Animals* belong outside," Leighanna said, frowning. "Stan's family. He hasn't marked his territory or infected the neighbors' cats with kittens—"

"Leighanna!"

"It's true, Mother."

"Don't speak of cats' spawning tendencies." She waved her hand around as if to brush the words from the air.

"*Spawning?* He isn't a fish."

"Leighanna." Her mother said her name in that way that made her head bow in prayer, as if it was the only way she would survive with a daughter like her.

Leighanna rolled her eyes again but said no more. Her mother's threats had begun as soon as Leighanna brought home the injured kitten years ago, but she'd yet to force her hand and toss the cat into the street. Luckily for Leighanna, Stan loved to take baths, unlike normal cats. Once a week, she washed, brushed, and dusted him in pyrethrum to keep away any pests. Stan never marked his territory. While her maid said it was because of the citrus cleaner she sprayed, Leighanna believed he didn't need to tell anyone what they already knew. He ruled the house. Exactly like the king he was.

Mother shivered, and her eyes landed on the open window. "Good heavens, you need to close that window before you catch your—" She stopped. "Close the window, Leighanna."

"Cheerio to you, too, Mother."

Mother ignored her, sauntered toward the draft, and yanked the window shut. "If you're not going to send him outside, he at least needs to get moving, as do you. I told you to be ready by nine if you insist on going out in this weather." She yanked the paper from Leighanna's hand.

"I wasn't done reading that," Leighanna fussed.

Mother propped her hands on her hips, drawing attention to the bright blue dress she wore, something new by the looks of the fabric. The collar was framed in lace, and Leighanna's neck tickled just looking at her. She scratched the phantom itch and glanced at her mother. A strand of hair fell in Mrs. Pauley's eyes. She brushed it back with the paper she'd stolen from her daughter, a sharp gaze settling on the girl still not dressed for the day.

"Well? Get up! Get dressed! Katrina will not wait all morning."

Leighanna picked up Stan and placed him on the floor. Stan made a disgruntled sound in the back of his throat and dashed from the room. Etta's soft voice floated through the doorway as the maid cooed sweet words to the cat from the hallway.

"Fine," Leighanna said, even though she relished the idea of seeing her friend after so long. "But I want the paper back, please. I wasn't done reading that! I was about to get to the article about the police's recent investigation—"

"What have I told you about reading those stories?" her mother said, but she relinquished the paper. "They fill your mind with drivel."

Leighanna hugged it to her chest. Her mother motioned toward the wardrobe, and Leighanna jumped to her feet with pursed lips. Etta walked in the room with Stan on her heels. He jumped on the bed, and the maid shooed him away from the navy skirt spread out on the crisp bedspread. Leighanna's feet squished in the patterned rug covering most of the bedroom floor. She folded the paper and set it on the table next to her bed.

"Are you ready to change, miss? Your hair . . ."

A laugh bubbled in Leighanna's chest, and she ruffled her out-of-control curls. "My hair is the least of my worries. It's only Katrina. Help me into this dress."

Etta tied her into her stays and the navy skirt, before buttoning the vest over the striped blue and white shirtwaist with its puffy sleeves. Leighanna wanted nothing more than to escape into more comfortable clothing, like the loose-fitting men's shirtwaist and trousers she had hidden at the back of her closet for the springtime when she worked in the garden. But her mother demanded she dress like a lady, so she let Etta help her become what her mother desired.

"When do you think these sleeves will go out of fashion?" she asked Etta, waving her arms as if she were a bird about to take flight.

The maid tried to hide her smile, but Leighanna saw it in the looking glass's reflection as Etta attempted to do something reasonable with her hair. "You don't like the extra volume they add to the ensemble, miss?"

"I look like I belong on top of a wedding cake."

This time, Etta did laugh. Leighanna eyed Etta's outfit, a simple tan skirt and vest with a cream shirtwaist beneath. The sleeves didn't have the same level of poof as hers. "You look more agreeable," she said.

Etta rolled her eyes. "Miss—"

"Mother isn't here. You can call me Leighanna, like I said last month. Almost dying gave me a new view on life, and I can't believe I didn't suggest you call me Leighanna sooner. Or Leigh, if you prefer. How long have you been my companion now?"

"Maid, miss," Etta corrected with a grin.

"Semantics. Has it been seven years already? Seven! Time does fly, does it not?" Leighanna continued.

"And your mother would end my employment if she knew we spoke so informally. She already didn't take kindly to the change in my working wardrobe."

"You looked like a ghost in black. I mean, what a dreadful uniform! You should have demanded a wardrobe shift at least by year three."

Etta affected mock outrage.

Leighanna smiled. "Mother would never end your employment. You help me take care of Stan. You bathed him most of December when I was so ill," she said, picking up the cat and hugging him to her chest. "Do you know how difficult it is to find a saint like you?"

In front of polite society, her maid was wise to attach the "miss," but it still made Leighanna feel uncomfortable, especially after surviving death. They were all equal at the end, so she didn't see why it mattered in the middle.

Stan rubbed his head against Leighanna's chin. His purrs could be heard all the way in London. She plopped him down on her naked toes to straighten her top.

Etta started pinning Leighanna's hair to the side to accompany the small navy hat that would sit on the side of her head. Leighanna leaned down and picked up Stan as soon as the last pin was in place. Curls were organized to the right and the hat perched on the left of her head. Stan laid his head on her shoulder with the tip of his soft nose buried in her collar.

"My paper, please," she said.

Etta handed the newspaper to her.

"Thank you," Leighanna said with a nod and began walking out of the room.

"Miss, your shoes! Leighanna, your stockings!" Etta called after her. But Leighanna was already moving toward the curving staircase with a cat in one arm and the paper tucked under the other.

"I'm in my own home, Etta! I don't need stockings!" She rushed down the stairs before Etta could catch up to her.

Katrina Murray waited by the window in the parlor. Unlike Leighanna's dull ensemble, Katrina was a bright burst of red. It perfectly matched her bronzed skin, a rare sight but a gift from her American—deceased—mother. Her ebony curls were plaited down her back, the end of the braid brushing the bustle on the back of her dress. A hat with a feather that was damp from falling snowflakes sat on the side of her head.

"I'll leave you to your visitor, Miss Pauley," Etta said, disappearing around the corner.

"Hello, Kat. It's been too long," Leighanna said, smiling at her friend.

Katrina jumped with a start and rushed over to her. She buried both Leighanna and Stan in a fierce hug, choking on a sob. "Dear Lord above," Katrina said. "I thought I'd lost you! Your mother wasn't allowing visitors until she knew for sure you were completely healed, even though I did come every day to ask after your health."

"I threatened to tell the neighbors Mother was holding me

against my will," Leighanna said between the tight embrace before she pulled back. Stan wiggled from his owner's hold with a hiss.

Katrina laughed and brushed the tears from her cheeks. "It was not the same without you at the Bartons' New Year's Day banquet. There was no one there to critique Casper's top hat!"

Leighanna squeezed Katrina's arm as a rush of kinship flooded her chest. "I'm well, and upset I missed the event myself. Nothing as trivial as consumption can faze me."

She held up the newspaper, thoughts turning to what she'd read this morning. "I am but one life, and still living! I was just about to read the news when Mother informed me of your arrival. The newsboy told me it's quite a story." Leighanna sat down on the fainting couch next to the window and tapped the spot beside her. "We can read it together. Or if you'd rather I read it aloud, I can do that, too." They used to love reading the articles in the paper with one another, and joy engulfed her at enjoying the hobby with her friend once again.

"That would be fine, but I have something to tell you first."

Leighanna hardly registered the words. More excitement rushed through her as she flipped through the paper to find the article, one the *Gazette* had put on page three, most likely to hide the seriousness of the event. Katrina obviously didn't want to hear the story, so she read it to herself.

THE RIPPER COMES TO STORNSHIRE?

Has the infamous Jack the Ripper come to Stornshire? Since the events of Mary Kelly's death on 9 November 1888, there have been no murders associated with the killer who terrorized London streets. Is it because the murderer has slaughtered his last victim or because he sits behind bars? Or has he moved to our quaint side of the world, a mere dozen kilometers from his previous domain? The murder of Jessilyn Cane at Lord Marcus and Lady Adelia Carmine's Morven Manor begs these questions to be answered. However, the police—

"Leighanna," Katrina said, interrupting her reading. "I need to speak with you about something that happened while you were ill. It's important—"

"Did you read this, Kat?" Leighanna asked, looking over the paper. "I'm sorry. I don't mean to interrupt, but have you heard? *This* is important. They haven't caught Jessilyn Caine's killer yet. The *Gazette's* reporter has been keeping the public aware—"

"Leighanna, you almost died—we almost lost you—no one wants to talk about what happened at that party," Katrina said, voice stiff and mood instantly shifting. "What has come over you? Why do you want to speak of such things?" She looked at Leighanna as if it had been closer to three decades since they had seen one another rather than a few weeks.

Irritation prickled Leighanna's skin, but she set the paper down. She'd been excited to share the story with her friend, but Katrina didn't seem to care in the slightest. "It's important to Jessilyn Caine's family."

Katrina's cheek tightened with a forced smile. "I'm not saying we ignore it, but—"

"You have something more important to tell me? What could be more important than this?"

Hurt flashed across Katrina's cheeks, but Leighanna straightened her shoulders and stood by her words. Katrina used to care about these things. They used to see eye-to-eye. Had a handful of weeks really changed her that much? Leighanna needed to know the truth. Her mind whirled with all the possibilities, completely consumed by the case.

"It isn't more important, but it is pressing." Katrina rubbed her gloved hands together.

"I'm sorry, Kat. I didn't mean for it to sound like that." Worry scrunched Leighanna's brow. Leighanna and Katrina had been friends longer than she could remember. Her friend always erred on the side of caution. Leighanna understood why she acted as she did. Worry and whispers threatened to trail after Katrina Murray wherever she went. She spoke and acted like a proper lady to lessen the blows.

Leighanna was one of the only ones who knew Katrina's lineage, though as they didn't live in the city, Leighanna didn't anticipate many would mind that she wasn't fully European.

Those in America were more concerned with her formerly enslaved mother's status, even though the woman who gave birth to Katrina died before her friend had the chance to know her. Leighanna's father was fierce in his anti-slavery stance, even though it had been a while since it had ended in America. It made him less popular with some of his clients, but it made Leighanna all the more proud to call him her father.

Katrina took a deep breath. Before her lips formed words, a knock sounded at the door. Jeremiah, their friend since childhood, rushed in, and a burst of warmth spread through Leighanna's middle. His brown eyes matched the wild waves of his hair. He held a letter in his perpetually charcoal-stained hands.

"Slow down," Katrina said. "You're breathing as if you've just run a race."

"I came as soon as my cousin received word from your brother that you were receiving visitors," he said. "I see you fare well, Miss Pauley."

Leighanna nodded and smiled. "Quite well! Kat was saying something . . ."

Katrina waved off her concern. "It can wait."

Leighanna motioned to Jeremiah. "Well, are you going to tell us which race you've been part of?" Her grin widened. She could never imagine Jeremiah running for the joy of it. Flecks of paint commonly appeared on random parts of his person. He had the thin and tall frame of a starving artist, but the bank account of one who never struggled. His clothes, though of the best quality, were wrinkled as if he threw them on in a hurry when he had awoken that morning. His shoulders were speckled with melting snowflakes.

It reminded Leighanna of how she had insisted she didn't need stockings in her own house. She did her best to hide her lack thereof under her dress, but unlike Katrina, she didn't have the advantage of a short, petite stature. The tips of her toes still stuck out. She hurriedly slipped her feet under the end of her skirt. Her hands ruffled the fabric in an effort to hide the tips of her toenails.

"They're going forward with the party at Morven Manor, Lady Carmine's estate," Jeremiah announced.

Leighanna's jaw dropped, and she jumped to her feet. "You're kidding! After a girl was murdered?"

"Doesn't society think it's too soon?" Katrina asked.

Leighanna felt her friend's eyes on her, but she didn't budge. She rushed over to Jeremiah and took the invitation from his grasp. He shrugged off his overcoat and hung it next to the door.

"It's an early Valentine's celebration," he said, the deep tenor of his voice dancing over her skin.

Heat blossomed on her cheeks. Her hands shook as they unfolded the invitation. "Did you steal this from our post box?" Leighanna asked, arching a brow.

He rubbed the back of his neck and shrugged. "Your postman was just dropping by. Saved him the walk up the steps."

"How chivalrous of you." Leighanna scanned the invitation.

Surprise sparked in her chest as she read the next line. "A masquerade?"

Katrina gasped. Leighanna turned to look at her. "They wouldn't!" her friend said. "That's macabre. To hold a party so similar to the night . . . No, I can't even speak it."

"Just because she died at a masquerade doesn't mean anyone else will get hurt." Jeremiah walked around Leighanna and took a seat in the parlor.

"Well, I, for one, don't wish to attend," Katrina said.

"Not all of us were able to attend the original party," Jeremiah said.

Katrina sighed. "Yes, because you weren't even in town and Leighanna was too sick to move. Either way, that party is not this one. I don't want to be part of it. It's not only bad taste, but it has the inklings of a bad omen."

Leighanna's attention flicked back to the invite.

"The event was preplanned," Jeremiah said. "It's been in my aunt's diary since October. According to Casper, anyway."

Leighanna tried not to think of Casper Barton when at all possible, so she brushed possible conversation of him to the side and said, "You know the Carmines. They never cancel a party. It says they're honoring her at the dinner, Kat. It might be nice."

Katrina threw her a disbelieving look. "You just survived death. Now you want to visit a place where a girl was *murdered*? Are you forgetting they haven't caught the killer yet? What if he comes back?"

"The killer will not come back," Leighanna said. "They drew too much attention to themselves by killing her on the biggest estate in Stornshire. Even the commissioner mentioned the unlikelihood. It's probably the safest place for us to be." She picked up the paper from the table and held it out, pointing at a line near the bottom.

Katrina yanked the paper from her hands and read the article. Leighanna sat back on the fainting couch.

But the killer might come back elsewhere.

No other killings had taken place—yet. Leighanna believed what the commissioner said, that the murderer wouldn't kill at Morven Manor again. Going to the party would be a perfect opportunity to visit the crime scene. She had an eerie, indescribable draw to where it happened that she couldn't explain. She hadn't been at the party that night, but that made her almost more curious to figure out the events of the evening and what happened to Jessilyn Caine. Even thinking such a thing would cause her mother's blood to curdle, but she couldn't help it. It interested her.

"I think it's nothing but a show, and a distasteful one," Katrina said, breaking Leighanna from her thoughts. "You're not considering going, are you, Leighanna?"

Leighanna placed the invitation in her lap and smoothed out the wrinkles in her skirt. "I would like to attend. I wasn't able to go to any of the Christmas parties—"

"Because you lay dying," Katrina interrupted, and Leighanna's irritation spiked. "You've only just gotten well! Your strength would leave you again, and we don't need to go to this party."

"I'm not weak, Kat. I'm perfectly agreeable," Leighanna said. "My brother will be putting me in the boxing ring next to win him some coin."

Jeremiah sighed. "You're thinking too much, Miss Murray. This party is a chance to change what happened at Morven Manor's Christmas event."

"You can't change what happened. Someone died!" Katrina said.

Before Jeremiah could say anything more, Leighanna said, "I nearly died myself. I think it's high time I begin living! Don't act like we haven't gotten into our own bout of mischief before. Remember Boxing Day last year and the litter of puppies?"

Katrina's cheeks heated, but she wore a slight grin. "This is not a litter of puppies, Leigh."

Leighanna waved off her concern. "Either way, I would like to honor Miss Caine, and this seems the perfect place to do it. What better idea would there be than to show her murderer they cannot take away our spirit!"

Katrina's brow furrowed. She opened her mouth to reply, but Leighanna grabbed her hand and said, "The party isn't for another week and a half—and I will be attending, with *you*."

"No, I don't think it's a good idea. Who's to say I want to go?" The line between Katrina's brows deepened, and her mouth parted slightly. She looked at Leighanna like she didn't recognize her.

"Who else will make sure I don't make a fool of myself and ruin any and all marriage prospects?"

Jeremiah smiled, running his hand across Stan's back. Leighanna patted the seat next to her for Stan to join her. The cat jumped on the fainting couch and rubbed his side against her thigh before settling down and beginning to purr.

Her mother had locked her in this house long enough. She needed to get out. The party was the perfect place to go. While the others danced, she would search for clues in the best place she knew: the scene of the crime.

CHAPTER TWO
Whispers and Shadows

FOR THE NEXT WEEK, Leighanna was forced to listen to Katrina's list of reasons they shouldn't attend the party. It surprised Leighanna more than irritated her. The friend who used to be willing to get into a little trouble seemed so prim and proper lately, and Leighanna didn't know what to do about the shift in her friend's demeanor. Especially when her refusal to go to the party started with, "It's the scene of a crime," followed by, "This speaks ill of the dead," and finally, "What if something else were to happen?"

But Leighanna remained resolute. She would attend the masquerade at Morven Manor, and no threats of the macabre were going to stop her.

Katrina even tried to entangle Leighanna's mother into her schemes, but for once, she agreed with her daughter. Not for the same reasons, though. Seeing her daughter healthy enough to run barefooted down their stairs with Stan in tow meant she was well enough to attend a ball. In her mind, not attending would show society there was something seriously wrong with her daughter. Fear of rumors being spread lit a fire beneath her mother enough to ignore Katrina's well-intentioned meddling.

The afternoon of the party, Katrina's badgering had gone from pleading to fussing as they sat with their needlepoint in the parlor. She hadn't been able to convince Leighanna's brother, August, to her side, either. It seemed to have angered her even more. But Leighanna still enjoyed spending time with her friend, despite her soured mood.

"You care nothing for your own health," Katrina said as she punched the needle through the tapestry. Katrina's dress acted as a blue exclamation mark on the subject, just bright enough to hurt Leighanna's eyes if she looked too long. Leighanna's ensemble, on the other hand, was a muted brown. She liked to think it made her warmer, or maybe it was the continued conversation boiling her blood.

"Why don't we go out today and get some air? The snow is beginning to melt." Leighanna rose to her feet to look out the window, wishing thoughts of the weather would successfully change the subject. Any hope of that happening was stomped on when she turned back and saw Katrina's glare. "If you look at me too long like that, your face will get stuck," Leighanna said.

Katrina ironed out her frown and looked at her needlepoint with no expression at all. "I'd like to stab you with this needle," she muttered.

Leighanna laughed, amused more than frustrated.

The bell rang, and the butler, Miles, rushed to welcome the visitor. Leighanna pushed away from the window to peer around the parlor's open doors after a quick glance at the carriage outside, biting back a curse. Casper Barton, Jeremiah's slightly older cousin and the one in the family who would inherit the sizable Barton estate, stepped into the foyer. Fresh snow rested on his top hat and shoulders. Leighanna barely contained the scowl that the sight of his smug and too-perfect face called forth. He'd been her enemy since childhood when he used to pull her braids and comment on how she towered over all the boys her age. He'd changed his tactics since then. Now, he always had to have the last word and picked arguments with her over the silliest of things, like the price of tea in China. On top of his other transgressions, she would never forgive him for the comments he made about Stan when she got him three years ago.

He removed his hat, only enraging her more. His dark hair was expertly styled, curls perfectly tousled, even after wearing a hat to fight the winter wind wafting from the Thames. Someone as irritating as Casper shouldn't be allowed to look so . . . rakishly presentable.

"Are you here for my brother? I don't know if he's bothered to rise yet," she said in a stiff tone. The clock on the mantle said twelve in the afternoon, but her brother had come in past four in the morning smelling of booze and bad decisions.

"Good afternoon, ladies, and yes, I am here for Mr. August Pauley. We said we'd meet at noon. He and I have business to discuss concerning the club," he said, speaking of the warehouse that was part boxing club and part bar that Casper owned. "Surely he's caught up on his sleep by now!" His eyes scanned her, which caused her to bristle where she stood. "I'm glad to see you're faring well, Miss Pauley. I should have known nothing as trivial as consumption could claim victory over your pure stubbornness."

She gritted her teeth and clenched her gloved hands, cheeks growing warmer with each word. "You think you would be as worthy of an opponent?"

"I've never been defeated by you," he said, flashing her a grin.

"Leigh," Katrina said warningly, and Leighanna shut her mouth before she could say anything else, returning to her seat beside Katrina and taking her frustration out on her needlepoint.

Casper and his cousin looked like caricatures of each other. The two lived together, but they acted completely different and looked different, too. Where Jeremiah was lean and trim, Casper was broad and muscled—crisper and haughtier. Even with his wild locks, he carried himself like a man with divine purpose. When he wasn't traipsing around as the "perfect" gentleman, one was more likely to find chalk or blood splatter on his person earned at the boxing ring. His time there caused the fabric of his coats to stretch tight over his arms. Leighanna thought the muscles might do a better job of chasing away the wrinkles than laundering ever could. Many of the ladies in Stornshire enjoyed the view whenever he was around. Leighanna couldn't get past his superior attitude to care what he looked like.

"My cousin said you're planning on attending the masquerade at Morven Manor," Casper said, and Leighanna plastered on a grin.

"Mr. Pauley is almost ready, sir," the butler said to Casper before Leighanna could respond.

"Good man," Casper said with a nod.

Leighanna put down her needlepoint and picked up the paper.

"Yes, we are going," she said behind the newsprint.

Katrina continued to grumble under her breath as she worked her needlepoint.

"Do you still have two left feet or will you grace me with a dance, then?" Casper's fingers curled around the top of the paper and he pulled it down, his mischievous eyes gleaming at her. "To celebrate your miraculous healing."

Leighanna slapped his hand away and said, "If I stepped on your toes, it wouldn't be because of my left or right foot."

He winked at her, and she scowled. But instead of continuing to pester her, Casper turned and chatted with the butler as he waited for August. Her brother arrived a few moments later, buttoning his coat.

"Mr. Barton, my friend," August said, lumbering into the room. He was nearly the same height as Casper, though her brother's acquaintance had a few inches on him. There was no denying August and Leighanna were related. They had the same dark brown hair and eyes like their father, brown and sparkling.

They even shared the same nose, long with a bump at the center.

On her brother, people called the bump rugged. On Leighanna's face, her mother called it churlish. Her mother's upturned button nose was preferred, but Leighanna was never bothered by the look of her nose or what her mother had to say about it. Accompanied by the look —sharp eyes, slightly narrowed—she *had* inherited from Mrs. Pauley, Leighanna rarely encountered problems in society. The combination always stopped all unwanted comments or questions.

"Nice of you to finally grace us with your presence, brother," Leighanna said behind her paper.

August pulled it away from her face and ruffled her hair. "Good morning, sister!"

She yanked the paper back and stuck out her tongue at her brother. "Sometimes I wish you'd gone to America with Father," she said. "Don't you have business things to learn? If not with father then beside your friend here?" August only laughed.

"He didn't want to miss your lovely face before we left," Casper said. Leighanna ignored him and narrowed her gaze on the paper in her hands.

The anonymous zealous reporter had published another article on page three.

HIDDEN TRUTHS IN OUR SMALL TOWN

It's been over a month since Jessilyn Caine was found murdered on the Carmine estate, Morven Manor, and still the police refuse to release a statement concerning their position in the case. When asked for a statement, Commissioner Lewis responded with a dour expression and ordered a band of his merry men to remove our lead investigator from the premises.

Rumors of Scotland Yard's involvement in the matter have begun to circulate among those more socially involved than this reporter, though sightings of any constables from the nearby city of London have yet to come to fruition.

However, I am one who keeps my promises. You are owed information—information not awarded to us by the officials but by the rumors among the streets of our small town.

Jessilyn Caine was found in a similar state as many of Jack the Ripper's victims, though her internal belongings remained intact. However, not for lack of trying! Slices were found near her abdomen. Most likely the killer was interrupted by the stablehand who found Miss Caine that night. Is this the infamous Ripper interrupted, or do we have an imitator on our hands? The answers to our questions, unfortunately, remain in the minds of those most unwilling to share information the public thirsts for.

Other earlier articles had also hinted at hidden information, and it piqued Leighanna's unyielding curiosity. It also told her the police didn't seem to think finding the murderer was their top priority.

The assumption infuriated her because it meant society wanted to forget about it like they had forgotten about the women from the lower class who had died by the Ripper's hand. This wasn't another Ripper killing, of that she was certain. She had studied the Ripper case on her sick bed, her nose stuck in between the newsprint as her lungs and mind cleared. The same thing that happened in London was taking place in Stornshire. Londoners blamed the Ripper for the new murders, but even authorities weren't sure. Leighanna knew Jessilyn Caine was left with all her vital organs still intact and was of high society, not a woman of the night like the Ripper's other victims. That's what made them—the Ripper and this killer—so different. Jessilyn's killer went after her, risking bringing attention to the crime because of her station.

The slash marks on her person were too hesitant, because an experienced killer would have been skilled enough to finish before being spooked off by a stablehand. A shiver worked its way down Leighanna's spine at the thought.

"They're leaving, Leigh," Katrina mumbled.

"See you tomorrow, Miss Pauley," Casper said. He walked up to her and bowed low to the ground, practically on one knee.

Leighanna pushed down the paper. She stared at him with pursed lips. When he came back up, he winked at her.

Stan waltzed into the room and rubbed against Casper's legs. He leaned down and patted the cat on the head. Irritation swelled in Leighanna's chest, and she glared at her cat. The cat had apparently forgotten Casper's rude comments when Stan had first joined the family. Rather than being bothered by the look, Stan meowed and lumbered over to her, hopped in her lap, and pushed at the paper in her hands with his head.

"You little traitor," she mumbled as the men left the women to their embroidery and questions.

"Miss?" Etta stood at the doorway. "Are you ready to prepare for the party?"

Katrina rose and began to store her needlepoint. "You're still going, then?"

Leighanna smiled and gave her friend a tight hug. "I'm still going," she said. "Are you positive you don't want to get ready here?"

"I only live two doors down. I'll walk back home and pick you up for the party." Katrina moved to leave, but paused by Leighanna. "You can change your mind at the last moment. There are still a few hours until the ball."

"I won't change my mind," Leighanna said. "Go. Your maid will be irate if I don't get you home in time."

"Very well." Katrina nodded. "I'll see you in a few hours," she said through a sigh and left.

Leighanna used the next few hours to recharge her mind and body. Her thoughts were a jumbled mess with all the information she'd read about the Ripper from old news articles, like where he murdered his victims, how he left them, and whatever else the police had told the public. But she knew without a doubt that the Ripper wasn't responsible for killing Jessilyn Caine. Not only was she high society and her case at the forefront of every newspaper, but the killer had not been successful in retrieving Jessilyn's vital organs. Leighanna shivered thinking about it.

She buried her face in every paper around the city. The newsprint was spread about her room as if it, too, were a crime scene. Her stockings even had the tell-tale sign of ink on the bottom of her heel from stepping on and around the papers. She had settled on her decision and felt strong in her assertion: the Ripper and the

Stornshire murderer were not the same.

While similar, the case wasn't similar *enough*. Her mind was so busy turning what she knew already about the killer, that she barely spoke a word until she stood in front of her mirror in her new golden party dress. Somehow, Etta had managed to wrangle her into it.

Because there was still one thing that bothered her. Why was society so determined to blame this death on the Ripper? As far as Leighanna could tell, it was obvious it wasn't him, so that meant the killer could be anyone. And this killer didn't care about station.

"Why the Ripper?" she whispered to her reflection.

Etta straightened from fixing the train of her dress. "Pardon, miss?" she said, squinting in the candlelight to find any wayward wrinkles.

"It's not the Ripper, but society would rather bury their heads in the sand than admit it was someone else."

Etta remained silent for such a long moment, Leighanna might have thought she had left if she hadn't seen her in the mirror's reflection fixing her medium puffy sleeves. Leighanna tugged at the high back collar and bothered with the long skirt that brushed the top of her brown boots. Even though the dress had a square neckline showing the top of her chest, the cream lacy top beneath hid her from impropriety. It mirrored the lace tickling the back of her hand. The matching mask was light in her fingers. The simple design, a white half mask with golden curlicue designs painted on, used a small ribbon to tie it into place. More lace decorated the outside.

"Etta?" she said.

The maid's hands froze in her hair. "I don't think it's my place to comment on that, Leighanna."

Leighanna shook her head, and one of her curls fell free from its pin. "It should be all of us talking about it. I lived, and people don't even like when I bring up any mention of death, including my own brush with it. And they get clammy when I mention Miss Caine. Do they want us to forget about her?"

Etta cleared her throat, their eyes meeting in the mirror. "If I could be so bold . . ."

"That's all I ask of you," Leighanna said with a smile.

Etta chuckled and continued to fix her hair. "Well, I do think they want to forget. It is quite simple for the commissioner to blame the Ripper and then say he went back to London, passing the case to the London police. Crime is rampant in London—a missing girl and a murdered father, to name a few cases—and it is easy to say that heartache will not return to Stornshire. Will not touch the upper class."

"They found that missing girl. She was dead," Leighanna said, speaking of Amelia Jeffs. They assumed she was another Ripper victim, but they closed the case without determining whether or not their assumptions were founded.

"Leighanna, it puts society's mind at ease to think that crime is what happens in London, not Stornshire."

The words made Leighanna's blood curdle.

"But I—"

"You are not like the others, Leighanna. However, when you *do* bring it up, you remind them there might be more to worry about."

"And if there's one thing society doesn't like," Leighanna finished for her, "it's to be reminded of their mortality." She huffed. "Thank you for speaking freely, Etta. I needed that. This is why I'm going to the party."

"Happy to help." Etta paused before adding, "And I think what you're doing is noble."

"Not noble, just what needs to be done. And I need answers."

She clenched her gloved hand. A sense of purpose bloomed in her chest alongside anxiety about attending her first party since she'd fallen ill. Something had changed in her since her illness, and she didn't fit the mold of society anymore. She didn't know where she fit at all.

Maybe after tonight she would know.

Leighanna stood and straightened her hat on her head.

The doorbell rang, and Katrina's voice drifted through the halls.

"Can you go see if she needs anything before we leave?" Leighanna asked Etta.

"Certainly, miss."

Leighanna's nerves were buzzing in too much anticipation to repeat, "My name is Leighanna," as Etta left the room.

She stared at herself in the floor length looking glass near the windows, glad at least the sleeves didn't have as much poof as some of the other gowns her mother commissioned lately.

She met Stan's eyes in the looking glass. "What do you think?" she asked, fingers looping the last few buttons on her top. The jacket dipped into a low V with only two buttons above the waistband of her skirt.

Stan cocked his head to the side.

"I agree. It needs more color. I look like a bride." Which was most likely why her mother commissioned the dress in the first place, even if it had yet to land her a husband or any suitors.

Stan purred and closed his eyes.

"Gold?" She chuckled to herself. "Then I'll be a golden bride, Stan!" It felt good to laugh after dwelling on the coming evening and the macabre setting she would be walking into.

Stan escaped into the hall before Leighanna could ask him more questions. Footsteps sounded in the hall. Etta's voice drifted through the crack in the door.

"Etta, have you seen my reticule?" Leighanna riffled through the bedside table in search of the small bag, but nothing but old newspapers and makeup she never used was stuffed inside.

She walked out into the hall, and Etta shook her head. "I haven't seen it anywhere, Leighanna."

Stan jumped on the edge of the nearest chair, poking his nose into Etta's elbow.

"Have you seen my reticule, Stan?" Leighanna queried the cat.

He meowed, tail twitching. Something caught his eye, and he glanced behind her. She looked over her shoulder, seeing nothing. Stan hissed, and jumped from her chair. He dashed past her legs as she took a step toward her room, and she almost tripped on him.

"Æthelstan Pauley!" she shouted, but he ran down the stairs.

"Are you all right, Leighanna?" Etta asked, lips pinched and brows turned upward.

"I'm fine." She waved her off. "Is Kat ready?"

"She said she'd wait for you downstairs. I'll search for your reticule and join you in a moment."

"Thank you." Leighanna walked down the stairs, but Katrina wasn't waiting in the parlor. With pursed lips, Leighanna wandered into the kitchens, knowing her friend had a habit of stealing the fresh biscuits when no one was looking. But when she went to walk through the dining room, low voices drifted through the cracked double doors.

"I tried to tell her," Katrina said. "She needs to know. I already feel awful how it all happened, and then—you know how she can be." Katrina took a deep breath. "We don't need to go tonight. She's obsessed with this case, and it's not good for her."

"If I thought I could stop her, I would. You know Leigh when she sets her mind to something, and the best we can do is protect her. I'm not allowing you or my sister to go to that estate without me, or without Casper."

Katrina huffed loudly. "Casper and Leighanna get along as well as oil does with water. Having him keep after her tonight won't end well. We don't need to go. She's obsessed with the Jessilyn Caine case. If we tell her—"

"Once Leigh puts her mind to something, she follows through. She doesn't need to know, not yet."

Know what? Curiosity bubbled in Leighanna's chest, and she leaned in closer.

Shuffling noises sounded on the other side of the door. Before Leighanna could push into the room to demand they stop speaking in code, Stan dashed past and into the dining area.

"Stan!" August hollered, and Leighanna trailed after him, frustrated that her cat had been the one to interrupt instead of her.

Leighanna stared at them, suspicion about what was going on between her friend and brother raising her brows. Why were the two of them alone with one another? Why had her mother allowed it? Katrina's hands gripped the edge of the table. August laid askew in the nearest chair.

Leighanna chewed on possible words, but settled on, "What were you both discussing?" The pair shared a glance. "Go ahead. Say it." She threw out her hand toward Katrina, clenching her teeth to keep her irritation from bubbling over. "Or are you too scared to say it to my face?"

"It's not—" Katrina started, straightening her skirt.

"Oh, stop being like that, Leigh," August said. He barely offered Katrina a glance. "You know you're obsessed with the Jessilyn Caine case, and Katrina thought if we told you we—"

"Heard more rumors," Katrina supplied. "At the club, August heard them talking about her death. We didn't need to give you more reason to go."

Leighanna narrowed her eyes on her brother. "What did you learn?"

August rolled his eyes and stood. "Nothing terribly new. She was a flirt, that's all. No one really knows who she attended the party with. She was seen on the arm of many men that night."

Leighanna pondered the words, but they didn't add any information to what she already knew. In fact, it would make sense why society wanted to blame the Ripper for the murder if Jessilyn Caine hadn't been behaving as a respectable lady.

But it still didn't give any reason for her to be murdered.

Pushing away her anger at her friend and brother, she asked, "Have either of you seen my reticule?"

Katrina sighed and shook her head. "No, where would you have left it?"

"I don't know or I wouldn't have asked you. If we want to be fashionably late, we need to find it within the next hour. If we want to be on time, we have a mere fifteen minutes."

The threat of being late seemed to bring Katrina to her senses. She pushed away from the table. Her hands flitted around the wrinkles in her skirt. She leaned down and tugged the bottom of her dress back over her heeled boots.

August straightened his vest, gold to match the white pants with a shimmering seam.

"We all look so festive," Leighanna said, partly to fill the awkward silence and the pure disapproval clouding the room.

Stan mewed from underneath the table, his eyes following something unseen. Leighanna frowned and leaned down to her cat's level to call him out. He trotted over and let her pick him up. He purred but then stopped abruptly and turned his gaze toward the doorway.

"What's the matter, Stan?" she whispered.

"Even he doesn't want you to go," Katrina said.

Leighanna looked toward the direction of her cat's gaze and saw nothing standing in the doorway behind her. No, maybe something. Goosebumps rose on her arms, and a chill ran down her back as if someone had dumped a cold bucket of water on her. Her eyes drifted to the base of the stairs. Something was there. A shadow of sorts. She closed her eyes tight and then looked again.

Nothing. She shivered, and the feeling finally went away.

"We're going," she said, continuing to stroke Stan's head. She didn't care if her brother and Katrina both disapproved. She needed to know more about Jessilyn's murder. If her brother was hearing things at the club, surely gossip would fester at a party. "Now, I'm going to see if the carriage has arrived. I've given up on finding my reticule. Are you two coming?"

As she turned to go, Stan growled and jumped from her arms. His back claws dug into the fabric of her gloves, and a cry of pain escaped her lips. She ran after the cat and watched him turn the corner at the staircase. Her heart thundered in her chest, but there was nothing—or no one—standing in the hall.

"What has gotten into that cat?" Katrina asked behind her. "He's never done that."

"You're too kind to that beast," August said. "He'll turn on you."

"Stan would never," Leighanna said with righteous indignation. "Mother never turned you out of the house for being a brat. Besides, something spooked him."

"Did he scratch you?" Katrina asked, grabbing the injured hand.

"Blimey," August said with an unamused laugh. "He got you good." The three looked at the tear in her glove and the red line on her palm. A hiss of pain escaped her lips when Katrina lightly touched the wound.

Leighanna yanked her hand away. "I'll be fine. We have a party to attend."

She turned on her heel and walked toward the door. August and Katrina trailed after her. She grabbed her cloak from Miles, the butler, her mind whirling with questions of the conversation between her brother and best friend, but more so the cat. What had gotten into him? A better question: what had he seen? Another cold chill ran through her, and the hair on the back of her neck stood on end. She rubbed the back of her neck and looked behind her. Stan's eyes met hers.

"What is it, boy?" she whispered. He flicked his bushed up tail and blinked. "*Hmm.*"

She looked back down the hall one last time before squaring her shoulders and focusing on the night ahead, telling herself she hadn't seen a shadow at the base of the stairs.

CHAPTER THREE
Curiosity and the Cat

DON'T LOOK AT ME LIKE THAT," Death said.

"The cat almost caught you." Life joined Death in the entryway of the Pauleys' home. "And you left this behind. I thought you might want it back." She handed him his hat, and a burst of warmth spread up his arm where their fingers touched. Her light brightened the room, whereas his shadows hung around the edge of the bannister.

"Thank you," he mumbled.

"She's interesting," she said. "I'm drawn back here. Something about her."

The cat sat on the carpet in front of the door, meowing for a few minutes as Life and Death watched.

"He's too busy lamenting his owner's absence to notice me now," Death said in a cool voice. He held his top hat in his right hand and tapped the fingers of his left hand against his thigh.

When Stan realized his owner was not returning for the

foreseeable future, he flicked his tail and turned back to face Death. The cat blinked at him, and the hair on his back stood on end. Death narrowed his gaze. Cats never took a liking to him. Maybe they could tell he would take all nine of their lives.

Death stepped toward the cat. He'd felt the call earlier in the evening, but when he had arrived, no one here needed him. Everyone was as right as rain.

Leighanna Pauley's maid, Etta, chose that moment to walk down the stairs. "Stan, whatever is the matter, darling?" she asked. "Leighanna will be back later this evening." She strode over to the cat and leaned down to pet him, but he let out another hiss and escaped into the parlor. "Quite cheeky tonight, are we?" she said to his retreating form and went about her duties of straightening the front hall.

Death walked past her and felt no tugging near her strands. Hers were woven around her and strong with the bright glow of life. The maid shivered. She glanced toward the door and checked the lock, but it wasn't open, not even a crack. She shook her head and busied herself as Death walked through the door and outside. He watched Leighanna arguing with her brother on the cobblestone street. August chuffed her chin. She stuck out her tongue at him before climbing in the carriage. After they settled in, the carriage broke away from the townhome and headed toward Morven Manor.

Death glanced over his shoulder; the cat was now staring at him from around the lacy curtains. It let out another hiss from behind the glass—which he couldn't hear—before Etta pulled him away. He went without complaint, most likely pleased Death no longer hovered in their home.

Life joined him.

"I feel a pull toward her, but not for her," Death said. "Does that make sense?"

Life straightened her skirt. She wore a fashion similar to the ladies of the evening, a white gown with puffed sleeves. Her hair was pinned on top of her head in a curly updo, though she had decided against a hat. "No," she said, "but not a lot has made sense after that night."

Life clenched and unclenched her gloved fist. If he wasn't mistaken, he thought he saw a little bit of a shadow on her palm. He blinked and it disappeared.

"Why are you here?" he asked her.

"Same as you, it would seem. Like the cat, I sensed something different." Her eyes sparkled with mischief. "I came to investigate."

Death placed his hat on his head and held out his arm. Life looped her elbow through his and smiled. "Should we follow the carriage, then?" he asked.

"I wonder if they'll have lemonade." Life snapped her fingers. If the cat had been watching, he would have seen a quick flash of light, and then an empty street. If Leighanna Pauley had been watching the front lawn of Morven Manor when she arrived, she might have glimpsed another shadow near the fountain as Life and Death reappeared.

CHAPTER FOUR
Midnight at Morven Manor

THE BALLROOM WEIGHED HEAVILY with whispers of ghosts and ghouls. Morven Manor was decorated with white drapes and gold ornaments in the style of vines, as if walking into a winter wonderland that had been touched by King Midas. Candlelight sparkled around the room and made the decorations seem larger and brighter than they were, adding a muted ambience that the Carmines intended to romance their guests. Instead, the murder from the last party still hung in the air, no matter how much the guests tried to ignore it. The muted light felt like a bad omen of more dangers lurking in the shadows.

Throughout the night, Leighanna followed the whispers of the crowd. She'd hoped for more concrete evidence about the murder of Jessilyn Caine instead of more gossip—possibly from someone who had an inside look at the police investigation. So far, all she had heard were whispers shared in the tea room and conspiracies when she had visited the wash closet.

Leighanna stood in front of the wash closet looking glass, pretending to fix the makeup she hadn't put on her face. Two other women stepped up to the looking glasses, and one said, "We all know the Ripper barely bothers high society, so the rest of us should be safe."

The other responded, "And I heard she was out alone! He must have assumed she was . . . one of *them*."

"Are you suggesting the women the Ripper murdered are less important than women in society?" The words were out of Leighanna's mouth before she could consider the consequences. Both ladies paused.

The first woman who spoke, a woman with blonde hair and a half mask colored gold, frowned. "We would never suggest such a thing."

Leighanna pasted on a grin that didn't match the fire in her veins. "You should rephrase your previous statement, because it *did* imply that we are somehow better than the lower class, which is why we shouldn't have to fear being murdered."

They looked at her with wide-eyed horror. The other girl, a brunette with a plain white mask with curved edges painted in gold covering one side of her face, looped their arms together. "We don't have to be spoken to like this," she sneered and tugged her friend after her as they left the room.

They didn't want to hear it because they didn't like the truth, the conclusion Leighanna had already gathered: society liked the idea of tragedy, but they didn't want any part of it. Instead of taking Jessilyn's death seriously, they hid behind their masks and smiles, treating the murder as nothing more than a scandalous article in the local paper.

The more the party dragged on, the more irritated Leighanna grew. Her blood threatened to boil in her veins with every new piece of hearsay or slander partygoers shared about the late Jessilyn

Caine. She hadn't always been like this. Prior to contracting tuberculosis, she'd never found herself this incensed over the divide between what society thought good and proper and what they deemed wrong and uncouth. Sometime between the moment the infection entered her body and the second it started to leave, she'd changed. Her life was a gift, and she needed to do something with it that meant something.

But now, her frustration overshadowed her best intentions. It worked at her sanity to hear and see no one else caring about the death other than the way it made *them* look. Not only did it wear on her mind, her body felt the effects. She fought the urge to slip off her shoes and massage her arches. Instead, she grabbed a glass of lemonade and headed to the corner, away from the melee. Possibly its bitterness would wash away some of hers.

"Is the party not meeting your expectations?" Katrina asked, joining her in the corner. Katrina fixed the full face mask where it had fallen slightly askew and glanced at the party. Leighanna's half mask didn't pose as much of an issue, and the velvet ribbon kept the golden ornament in place.

Leighanna took another sip from her glass. "One cannot gossip all night and expect to drink lemonade like a lady." Pinky up, she took a sip. "It's my first party since my untimely kiss with death."

And I don't feel like I belong. She didn't tell Katrina her whole thoughts, but it slipped in unbidden.

Katrina, finally having enough of her mask, ripped it off and held it in her hand. She turned to Leighanna. "The disappointment shows. What did you expect, to come and single-handedly solve . . ." Her voice trailed away. "You must remember your place, Leighanna. Ladies don't—"

"Some of us have interests outside of high society," Leighanna snapped, immediately feeling guilty for her tone. "I apologize, I shouldn't—"

"You've always been curious," Katrina interrupted. She fiddled with the ribbon of her mask. "And you have a propensity to take in strays. I only worry about you. You did not kiss the cheek of death, but you did tempt him. Please refrain from giving him a reason to return."

Leighanna took a sip of her lemonade without another word, eyes scanning the ballroom. She wanted to ask Katrina what had happened to the friend who liked scheming and getting into things they shouldn't. Since she'd gotten better, Katrina cared more about how she appeared outwardly than she'd ever before. Leighanna shook the thought away and focused back on the crowd. Two ladies walked by and blocked her view of the dance floor, but their conversation intrigued her more.

"I heard they found her in the stables out back," the first girl whispered. She wore a gold skirt, a white shirtwaist, and a decorative white and gold vest over the top. Black ringlets spilled down her back, and she smiled with a red-lipped Cheshire grin.

Leighanna's heart raced. *Finally*, maybe she would get some information beside idle gossip. She broke away from the wall.

"Where are you going?" Katrina asked, but Leighanna waved away her question as if it was a gnat in the summer buzzing around her head. She heard the squeak of Katrina's boots as she tried to follow, but she got lost in the crowd as another song flowed from the band in the corner.

Leighanna weaved through the crowd, eyes trained on the two women. She stayed close enough to the ladies to hear their conversation but far enough away to not arouse suspicion.

"My word," the other girl tittered. Her auburn hair was braided in a fanciful updo, the curls spilling from both sides of a white hat with a large gold feather sticking out of it. She took a sip of the champagne in her hand. "What was her name again?" she asked.

Bile rose in Leighanna's throat. She gritted her teeth to stop from shouting the answer.

"Heavens if I know. I heard the Ripper killed her."

Irritation rose in Leighanna like she had never felt.

It had only been a month and already people were forgetting Jessilyn's name—forgetting the details of the case. She refused to be like the women before her. She could do something besides talk about the case. Instead, she would focus on the facts, not hearsay.

Her lips parted, ready to tell the women they needed to only read their local paper to sort out their idle gossip, when one of them spoke.

"Dear me, is that the commissioner's daughter? Can you believe she has the nerve to show her face when her father can't even catch a killer? I've heard there's pressure to send the case to the London police and let them handle it."

Leighanna's gaze swung to the entrance. She caught a flash of red hair in a blue dress.

She took a step toward the retreating figure when a hand grasped her arm. "You can't run off like that, Leigh," Katrina fussed. "You don't know who else might be here. We need to stick together."

"Kat—"

"It's been nary two months," she said, a line between her brows. "Even less time since you woke up fully recovered. Stop running away."

"They still haven't found the killer. They've already forgotten her name!" She yanked her arm from Katrina's grasp. "I bet not a single person in this room can name any of the women murdered by the Ripper, but they sure can tell you all about *him*. It isn't right."

"It's not the same, Leigh. Those women were . . ." She glanced around the room. "They were of a different class than we are."

"Prostitutes," Leighanna said, and a few people glanced their way. "They might not get justice, but that doesn't mean Jessilyn Caine can't. It happened in *our* town."

Katrina grabbed Leighanna's wrist. "*Shhh*. Your mother might hear you," she said.

"Jessilyn was Scottish, Kat. Isn't your grandfather from Edinburgh? You two could have run in the same circles."

"It's not as if we all know each other." Katrina glanced behind her to see if anyone was listening.

Katrina's father was one of the kindest men Leighanna had ever met and—though *his* father had to buy his way into society—he was proud of his Highland heritage. And bought it, he did. He invested in America's railroading ventures and had enough to buy his own company by 1865. Now, Mr. Ian James Dougald Murray III owned three major shipping companies, and Leighanna's family had purchased half the stock.

"Don't you ever want to be something more than some man's wife?" Leighanna blurted. "To be known for our names and not theirs? Jessilyn's name will die with her, and only her murderer will be remembered. Does that not bother you?"

Katrina glanced around the room. "We can't afford to think like that."

"We can't afford *not* to."

"Leigh, you need to—"

"I need to go talk to Rosalind Lewis." She started walking toward the direction of the commissioner's daughter, Katrina on her heels.

Katrina grabbed her shoulder, halting her in the middle of the dance floor. "You must relax." She turned to the crowd. "Glaring at everyone and expecting them to tell you what happened or be privy to what the papers aren't saying won't give profitable results."

"Fine. I'll smile."

"And dance, at least once. Have you stopped at all this entire time to *enjoy* the party?"

"What is there to enjoy when a murderer runs free?"

Katrina flinched. "Leigh . . ."

"Fine! Fine."

Katrina nodded to where Jeremiah sat doodling in his sketchbook, a lock of curly brown hair falling into his eyes. "What about Jeremiah? He's been hiding in the corner all evening."

"Jeremiah's *just* a friend, as I've said a number of times."

Katrina rolled her eyes.

Casper stepped into Leighanna's line of vision, throwing her a devilish grin before winking. Her cheeks burned, and she tightened her hold on Katrina's arm.

"And definitely not *him*." Leighanna nodded to Casper.

Katrina let loose a very unladylike snort of disbelief. "Then who, pray tell?" she asked, eyes bright.

Leighanna eyed the room around her, the fancy decoration, and the men and women all wearing white and gold outfits and masks, some covering half their faces and some hiding every feature. It was easy to get lost among them. She hadn't allowed herself even a moment to enjoy the night—and hadn't planned to. How could she when there was a case to be solved?

But if Katrina insisted, the least she could do was humor her. She made her decision. "Well, if you demand I must dance, then my partner has to be someone who enjoys it."

"Naturally," Katrina said, and some of the levity returned to the conversation. "So, I ask again, who will it be?"

Leighanna took Katrina's hand and pulled her onto the dance floor. "You."

Katrina's face widened with surprise as Leighanna pulled her onto the dance floor.

She tugged her hand free. "Leighanna, stop. We can't just dance however we want in the middle of a party!"

Leighanna sighed. "Come on, Kat! Have fun! What happened to my best friend?"

Katrina chewed on her bottom lip for a moment as the next song started.

"Come on," Leighanna encouraged. "Have fun!"

"Fine!" Katrina said, trying to hold back a smile.

They clasped hands and held each other at arm's length, turning and dancing to the music. Each step brought laughter to their lips as they weaved between the partygoers, bumping into couples and causing mayhem wherever their feet landed. The room spun as they danced faster. The grandfather clock at the top of the staircase struck midnight, and the sound echoed through the room. Leighanna closed her eyes and looped her arm through Kat's as they swayed to the music.

Suddenly, all sound halted, and a chill ran down Leighanna's spine. The hair on the back of her neck stood on end. Her arms fell to her sides, empty, fingers shaking slightly.

The grandfather clock struck again, and Leighanna jumped. The chiming of the clock rang in her ears. The guests from the party were gone. She stood utterly alone in the center of the ballroom floor. Fear wrapped its tight claws around Leighanna's heart. "Hello?" The word came out in a puff of cold air, swallowed by the echoing timbre continuing to chime.

"You have to stop the killer," a feminine voice echoed from behind, sending a shiver from Leighanna's neck to her toes.

Leighanna turned around and choked on a scream. A girl swayed in front of her. A line of red wrapped around her neck, blood dripping from the open wound. It bled into her dress, turning the fabric a dark crimson, hiding even the largest detail of the gown. Shadows hung beneath her eyes, and the ghost opened her mouth in a silent scream. Stumbling backward, Leighanna tripped on the edge of her dress and fell to the floor, a sharp pain traveling up her hip as it connected with the cool granite.

The ghost took a step closer to her, and familiarity struck inside Leighanna. She knew that face—had seen it in black and white.

"Jessilyn . . ." she whispered, the name coming out in a puff of smoke.

The ghost's neck jerked toward her, eyes widening. "He'll kill again." Her voice shook as her eyes darted around the empty room. "He'll kill again. I was only the first, but he *will* come for her. You have to save her."

Leighanna's heart stuttered in her chest, and she struggled to catch her breath. Jessilyn took a step toward her. Leighanna pushed back, distancing herself from the ghost as much as possible.

"Kill who?" Leighanna asked, tears burning in the back of her eyes.

Somewhere in the distance, the clock struck once more. The sound was slow and melodious, burying in Leighanna's bones and rattling her teeth.

"Save her, Leighanna. You *have* to save her."

"Who?" she screamed, the words bouncing around the room.

"I don't know." The ghost shook her head. "He's getting anxious—ready to kill another! He—"

The clock chimed again. It drowned out Jessilyn's words, and she took another step closer. Blood dripped down her neck as she leaned over Leighanna. A drop hit Leighanna's skin and burned. Bile rose in Leighanna's throat as she scrambled back from the ghost bending over her.

"Watch and listen. Who knows how long you have—" Her

head jerked around as the clock rang out with its second to last chime—eleven now.

"What are you—"

"*Find* him! He did not show me his face, but he will come for another. Hurry before he ends her, too," she said, as midnight struck. "You have been this close to death before."

"Well, what do we have here?" said another voice. It reminded her of the feminine tone she'd heard during that time she lay dying.

Out of the corner of her eye, Leighanna spotted a burst of light. The world spun. A bout of dizziness overcame her. She laid back on the floor and squeezed her eyes shut. Blood rushed in her ears and nearly drowned out the sound of Katrina's voice. "Leighanna? Leighanna? Can you hear me? Leighanna?"

Her eyes fluttered open. Party guests surrounded her on all sides. The ringing of the clock still echoed in her ears as she was helped to her feet, a fresh glass of lemonade shoved in her hand.

"Are you all right?" Katrina asked. "You simply . . . dropped to the ground."

Jeremiah stood at the back, a worried look on his face. Leighanna averted her gaze and focused on her friend, embarrassment and confusion warring inside her. "It's nothing, just too much spinning, is all. I need some food in my stomach."

Katrina led Leighanna to the closest chair. Those surrounding her were shoved to the side as her mother pushed her way over to Leighanna.

"Do you think she's still ill?" someone whispered.

"Get back to the dance," her mother ordered, then leaned toward Leighanna. "Are you well?"

The sharp gold and white of the party decorations and goers' outfits burned her eyes. She blinked a few times to clear her head. "I'm fine," she finally told her mother.

Jeremiah joined her on one side, Katrina on the other. Katrina squeezed Leighanna's hand. A worried look furrowed her friend's brow. Leighanna pasted on a smile, pushing the picture of Jessilyn with the ring of red around her neck out of her mind.

"I'm fine, truly," she said. "The warmth of the night . . ." The words fell away, and she kept her eyes trained on Katrina. "Come. I think we've had enough excitement for the evening."

"Leigh—Miss Pauley," Jeremiah began, but she didn't hear what else he had to say.

Out of the corner of her eye, Leighanna caught sight of a flash of red hair and blue dress as Rosalind Lewis left the room. An echo of what she had seen moments before played in her mind. Jessilyn said she was the first, and Jack the Ripper was no amateur. This confirmed someone else had killed Jessilyn Caine, and he was anxious to kill again. Her killer was still out there, and Jessilyn was not just another name to be forgotten because of her untimely demise. Leighanna made a decision.

No one would forget the name Jessilyn Caine. When Leighanna solved her murder, she would make sure of it.

CHAPTER FIVE
Miss Lavender Lemon's Tea Shoppe

LEIGHANNA'S MOTHER CONFINED HER to their home for five days after she fainted at the party. Her menses had taken the perfect time to visit. It gave her mother further ammunition to keep her indoors. Leighanna had spent that time reading every article, tacking some of them to the wall behind her bed. Though most of the whispers she heard were useless gossip, she still recorded them all in a leatherbound notebook she kept on her desk. It made her feel like she was doing something, even amongst the harsh cramps twisting her middle the first two days. She couldn't help Jessilyn in this life, but she could ensure people remembered her name. And when she discovered the murderer, she would never let them forget whose life had ended.

The last day of her confinement, her mother came into her room, sighing at the state of it. Random clippings covered every inch of the wall behind her bed, but instead of lecturing, she had let out a breath that could cause waves in the Thames and said, "I don't know why we bother with fresh paint."

Katrina saved Leighanna from another day of obsessively staring at her wall and ignoring her mother's complaints when she invited her to go to the seamstress shop. However, Leighanna planned on making a stop on the way to the seamstress, and she didn't think Katrina would join her. Leighanna should go alone.

She would rather swim in the North Sea against the current than go to the seamstress after a bout of imprisonment, but the plan allowed her a dose of freedom from the walls closing in around her. She grabbed it by the reins and held on. When Katrina's carriage arrived, she didn't wait for her to come to the door. Her eyes had been on the street for a half hour. She was halfway down the steps with her carpet bag looped through her elbow by the time the carriage came to a halt in front of her doorstep.

Stan mewed from inside the bag. Leighanna paused a few steps away from the carriage. She peeked through the small opening and shushed him. "We can't let everyone know you're with me," she whispered.

He blinked up at her and laid his head down on his paws.

"Good kitty," she said and then turned her attention to the driver. "Hello, Samuel!"

He waved and offered her a friendly smile. "Hello, Miss Pauley."

Leighanna hiked her skirt above her ankles to avoid the muddied snow and slid into the waiting carriage, trying to think of a way to get Katrina to drop her off at the tea shop instead of going with her to the seamstress. Katrina sat across from her, wearing a long winter cloak that pushed back from her shoulders and revealed a dress similar to Leighanna's, except in a cool mauve. Leighanna's outfit had less puff to the sleeves, though, something she had pleaded for her mother to consider the next time they visited the seamstress.

But, if her pleading worked, she wouldn't be visiting the modiste with Katrina today. A burst of anticipation coursed through her.

"You look smashing," Leighanna said. She placed the bag in her lap and peeked inside. Stan stared back at her before meowing.

"No." Katrina's sharp reply took Leighanna back for a moment.

"You love Stan. I won't let him wander without asking—"

Katrina huffed. "That isn't what I meant. I've grown used to Stan's presence. You know what I'm saying no to."

"Do I?"

Katrina rolled her eyes as Etta joined them, the maid shivering slightly from a brisk wind hitting the side of the carriage.

"January is still biting at our heels," Etta said before Katrina could answer Leighanna's question. "February hasn't even had a chance. It'll be March before you know it." She looked between the girls. "Is something amiss, Miss Leighanna?"

Leighanna bit her tongue. Katrina wouldn't approve, and she'd already said no to a question that hadn't been asked.

"Nothing's wrong, Etta. But I would like to know what you're saying no to, Kat. I haven't even asked—"

"You don't have to ask," Katrina said. "I'm not partaking in your scheming. It's unseemly. I went to the party, but that was my last straw. And after you passed out? It's as if you have no sense of self-preservation."

"You used to be fun," Leighanna said. "What happened to the girl who would play in her mother's garden and create stories of adventure? We used to imagine a world we could explore, and now I'm doing it."

Katrina eyed her. "We have to grow up, Leigh," she said. "We're ladies now. We don't play in the garden."

Etta bristled in the seat next to Leighanna as the carriage pulled away from the curb, tension hanging in the air between all three ladies. Leighanna straightened her shoulders and gave Katrina the look Mrs. Pauley gave Leighanna. It was a simple tilt of the chin with her eyes staring down her nose, daring a challenge.

"I'll drop you off at the seamstress, then," Leighanna said. "I have a meeting with Rosalind Lewis, and I can't be late."

Meeting was a loose definition of the event. To have a meeting implied prior notice. Leighanna merely asked a few friends to find Rosalind Lewis's regular haunts. The most popular one being the tea shop across the street from the police station.

Luckily for Katrina, who'd been ardent in her disapproval of Leighanna's curiosity concerning the case, the seamstress's shop was next door to Miss Lavender Lemon's Tea Shoppe. Katrina made a note of turning up her nose and walking into Madame Celine's shop.

"Well, what do you say, Stan?" Leighanna looked at the opening in her large carpet bag. People stared as they passed, but she was used to it. She enjoyed taking the cat with her, and she wouldn't let their looks stop her. He blinked his yellow eyes up at her, and she nodded.

"Very well. Let's go."

Leighanna took in a cold breath of air before wrapping a gloved hand around the tea shop's handle. A blast of warmth and peppermint hit her as she walked in. The sweet aroma of tea washed over her skin, and her shoulders instantly relaxed. Popular because of its seasonal decorations and drinks, Miss Lavender Lemon's Tea Shoppe rarely had open tables. Leighanna struggled to find an open seat, especially one near Rosalind Lewis. With her flaming red hair and bright green dress embroidered with emerald vines, Rosalind stood out in the deep winter theme of the shop.

The white tables sported sheer blue tablecloths covered with lace place settings, adding an air of delicacy to the already feminine shop. Pastries all dusted in sugar behind the glass countertop at the front of the shop suffused the shop with an ambience of winter. Paper snowflakes hung from the ceiling on string. Glass vases filled with crystals and water sat at the center of each table. The light from the tall candles flickered off the stones, mixing with the low light from the sun streaming in the windows, throwing light around the room and on the faces of the patrons.

Of the ten round tables pushed into the small space, the only open area was the raised tables in the back. Three of the four square, two-seater tables were already claimed, so Leighanna rushed to the last open spot. Miss Lavender, whose true name not many people knew—even Leighanna, but not from lack of trying—had replaced half of the back wall with gilded edged looking glasses imported from France. It reflected the space around them, making the room seem larger as Leighanna sat in the blue velvet chair.

She placed her cat-filled bag on the floor next to her feet and dug into her reticule for the can of sardines she stole from the pantry that morning. She cracked it open, the sound drowned out by the echo of voices, took off her glove, and grasped a fish between her fingers. Stan's head popped out from the bag. She pushed him back in and dropped the fish inside.

An empty cup was placed in front of her, alongside a simple menu printed on a typewriter. Her fingers grazed the neat lettering, wishing she had a typewriter to call her own. Until then, she'd keep writing her notes. It would appease her mother's incessant nagging that she practice her calligraphy.

"Lovely to see you, Miss Pauley," Victor Edwards, the tea

server, said. He was around her brother's age, though he had more roughened edges than August's cushy upbringing allowed. "I see you brought a companion." He cocked a blond brow at Leighanna.

She tapped a finger to her lips. "Our secret, Mr. Edwards. He's happy with his sardines. He won't cause any issues."

Victor laughed and shook his head in a teasing manner. "What would you like? Fancy the new sandwiches the Lady has added to her menu?"

Leighanna eyed the meals written in paint on the glass behind the tables but shook her head. "I'd fancy a table in the corner. How long should I expect to wait?"

Victor smirked, a strand of dirty blond hair breaking free from its styling oil. He straightened his vest and nodded toward the right. "I saw Etta at the butcher last week. She told me you were itching for a meeting with Commissioner Lewis's daughter, Rosalind, since the constables keep ignoring your letters. Etta implied it's about that girl meeting her demise."

Leighanna stopped herself from flinging her hands in the air and breaking composure. "Her name was Jessilyn Caine. Everyone in society seems to have forgotten that, alongside any sensible ideas surrounding her death."

"Sensible?" He leaned against his palms on the table. "And what unsensible ideas do they have, pray tell?"

She struggled not to roll her eyes and instead embraced his joking grin. "That conversation is not appropriate, Mr. Edwards." She leaned closer. "But if you happen to know anything about the events of that night . . ."

He flashed a wicked grin and bent closer. "I don't know much, but if I hear anything I'll tell you."

She arched a brow, not expecting that answer—not expecting him to truly know *anything*. "Thank you, Victor."

Victor laughed and straightened. "What'll it be, Pauley?" he asked her.

"A seat next to Rosalind Lewis when it becomes available and a cup of your finest Earl Grey."

He saluted her with two fingers to his forehead and said, "Coming right up. But I don't think you'll have much trouble gathering her attention. She's with her mother's lot."

Leighanna glanced over her shoulder, noticing the grimace on Rosalind's face as the women laughed at a joke by Mrs. Lewis. Unlike her daughter, Mrs. Lewis had light brown hair and was shorter than even Katrina, who was only five feet and four inches. Rosalind towered over her mother when they stood side by side. Her freckled cheeks made her apt to embarrassment, which blossomed red.

Victor returned and placed a steaming pot of tea in front of Leighanna, pouring her a cup. "I might be able to get her to invite *you* to her table," he said. "Sip your tea and watch me work my magic."

This time Leighanna did roll her eyes. "We shall see."

He winked and disappeared, leaving behind the pot.

"He should know something about the murder," one of the tea girls said after waiting on the next table a few feet away. Leighanna turned to the girl in the white and blue dress.

"Pardon?"

"Victor, miss. He's trying to pay his way at the art institute. Did Jeremiah Barton not tell you? They spoke the last time he attended."

"He did not. I doubt Jeremiah would know much. He was out of town for an art exhibition. I saw him off before I grew so ill," she said, and her mind whirled. "What do you know about the party?"

"He was working the party to make some money to pay this semester's tuition."

"And he knows more than he's saying?"

She nodded, eyes flashing to where Victor was weaving through the tables to fill teacups. "Yes, I think so." She paused. "I was working that night, too, and when I looked out the window, I saw him going near the stables, not long before the time the papers said Miss Caine was . . . well . . . you know."

Leighanna nursed the cup of Earl Grey while watching Rosalind in the mirrored wall. She sat there for fifteen minutes, considering other plans besides trusting Victor to get the other girl's attention, when he walked up to Rosalind's table and leaned down to whisper in her ear. Leighanna's stomach turned as she watched him in the corner. Why wouldn't he tell her he had been at the party? Was there something he wanted to hide?

Before she could think about it too long, Victor came back over and said, "She'll see you now."

Leighanna froze, teacup halfway to her lips. She glanced at her bag and then her eyes found Victor's. She smiled. Between clenched teeth, she asked, "What did you say to her?"

"I told her you looked quite melancholy sitting all by yourself. Take the opportunity, Miss Pauley."

Victor took her empty cup and pot, whisking it and himself away before she could say anything else. She steeled herself and grabbed Stan's bag before walking down the two steps to the main level of the tea shop. Every eye turned toward her before returning back into their conversations.

Once she reached the table, Rosalind half rose from her seat and said, "Miss Pauley, why don't you join us?"

Rosalind sat back down. Her mother offered Leighanna a small smile. Two older women sat at the table with Rosalind—one who resembled the commissioner's daughter, with the same smile and hair—a cousin perhaps. The other was blonde and petite. Four pairs of eyes turned to look at her at once and offered not smiles, but something similar.

"Please, sit. I'm positive we could borrow a chair from one of the nearby tables," Rosalind's mother said.

Leighanna's mind whirled with ways to ask after the Jessilyn Caine case, but the eyes of the blonde woman and the other redhead burned into her skin. Leighanna's gaze drifted to the half-empty tea cups. To the tuna sandwich on Rosalind's plate. An idea struck.

Up for an adventure, Stan? If only she could speak to her cat and have him understand. She peaked into her bag. He blinked his yellow eyes.

"I couldn't," she said, looking back toward the women. "I really—" She stopped and hefted her carpet bag next to Rosalind's reticule. "Goodness. My arm is getting tired holding that heavy bag. I see you're in need of some more tea, Mrs. Lewis. Let me."

She leaned over her bag, knocking over Rosalind's full cup with it. Rosalind let out a small yelp of surprise when the warm tea hit her skirt. Leighanna allowed Stan enough space to squeeze through the opening and attack the sandwich directly in front of him.

Screams lifted. The three other women at the table pushed back their seats. The blonde woman's chair toppled over, and the redhead declared, "My word! Get that beast out of here at once!"

Mrs. Lewis moved toward her daughter, but the toppled chair was in her way. Rosalind's dress was soaked through. Leighanna moved toward her, also blocking Mrs. Lewis from reaching her daughter on the other side. Leighanna fretted with the napkins left on the table while Mrs. Lewis shouted, "Get this vermin out of here now, Miss Pauley!"

"I'm dreadfully sorry!" Leighanna said to Rosalind, still drawing attention away from the table and to her hands as she tried to dab the dress dry to no avail.

"Miss Pauley," Rosalind said, but Leighanna ignored her and kept mopping up the tea with the soaked napkins.

"I really didn't mean anything by it—"

"Miss Pauley—"

"Honestly—" Leighanna knocked Rosalind's reticule onto the floor at the same moment the commissioner's daughter grabbed her hand.

Leighanna grasped the napkins and met Rosalind's gaze. Her eyes flashed to where Stan was still eating Rosalind's—*his*—sandwich.

"I think you'd best grab your cat before you're booted out," Rosalind said.

Leighanna dropped the napkins, wrapped Stan in her arms, and slid Rosalind's reticule in the carpet bag. She ran between the tables with, "Oy! Girl!" called out behind her by a large gentleman who had come from the back. But she kept running until she was down the street and Stan squirmed enough in her arms to force her to stop.

He turned his head up at her before plopping down on the cobblestones and licking his paws free of the fishy remnants. Leighanna leaned down, the fresh snow wet on the leather of her shoes, and peered into the carpet bag. At the bottom sat her reticule. Right next to it, Rosalind Lewis's.

"How long do you think it will be before she misses this, Stan?" She clicked her teeth and patted the side of the bag. "This gives me the perfect excuse to see her for tea, don't you think?" Stan listened and climbed inside, hiding the evidence as she walked the back streets toward the seamstress' shop where Etta and Katrina waited.

The next day, Leighanna fastened the top three buttons of her cloak and walked in leather boots—an old pair of August's she thought she might need in situations like these—with Etta down the street toward the commissioner's home. Katrina had refused to go with her and participate in her "devilish schemes to trick an officer of the law or his kin!" and would not hear her protests that she hadn't stolen from anyone, only borrowed Rosalind's reticule.

Etta, however, would not let her go alone, so they walked down the street together in the snow and mush. Unlike Leighanna, Etta didn't have a sensible pair of shoes to take from an older sibling, and her shoes were soaked through.

"On the way home, we're hiring a carriage and stopping at the McFaddens' shop to get you a nice pair of walking boots. I won't have you losing your toes while following me around Stornshire," Leighanna told her maid.

"Miss—"

"Stop it. It's a gift. I was barely breathing at Christmas. I like to give things throughout the year, not only when they're expected."

Etta sighed like she wanted to argue, but when they reached the front steps of the Lewis' home, she clamped her mouth shut.

Before Leighanna could rap her knuckles on the door, it swung open. A maid stood on the other side, about Leighanna's height. Her brown hair was tied up on top of her head, and her maid uniform was crisp and clean like the rest of the home. Even with freshly melting snow and road mush, the front walkway was sparkling clean, and nary one spot of ice in sight on the steps. The bricks didn't have a patch of dead weeds or foliage, and even the empty planters were filled with fresh soil as if spring were around the corner. The windows glinted in the morning sunlight peeking through the clouds.

"Good morning, Miss Pauley," the maid said. "Miss Rosa saw

you coming from the library window. She wanted to invite you in for tea."

"I actually came to return her reticule, but I couldn't impose."

The maid smiled and took a step back, opening the door wider. "She thought you might. She said, 'Either I've lost it like I'd lose my head if it wasn't attached, or Miss Pauley accidentally grabbed it when her cat was dining on my lunch.'"

Leighanna wasn't sure how to respond, and her heart beat rapidly with a spark of indecision mixed with regret warring in her chest. Maybe she shouldn't have been so hasty, but the idea had felt right at the time, even though now she wished she could turn on her heel and depart. Leighanna had left Stan at home for this particular trip, which was a small reassurance. One thing she didn't need to worry about was Stan trying to find the nearest fishy treat while she returned the reticule she'd stolen. She glanced back at Etta, who gave her a smile a little too wide before going inside.

The maid walked a few steps in front of them. She led them up the stairs and to the end of the long hall. They turned right into a small library. Rosalind sat on a lounging couch next to a large window overlooking the street. She sipped a cup of tea and set it on the table next to her, loose strands of red hair tangled on the puffed cream sleeves of her shirt. Stocking clad feet peeked from underneath a velvet green skirt, and her bare hands showed trimmed and neat nails befitting for a commissioner's daughter.

"Miss Rosa, Miss Pauley is here to see you."

The girl looked over her shoulder and smiled. The green in her skirt brought out the specks in her eyes, but the grin didn't tug all the way upward. She stood and walked over to the two waiting ladies.

Rosalind Lewis looked down her nose at Leighanna. Even though Leighanna stood taller than many other women, Rosalind stood even taller. She might have even surpassed August, who boasted six feet. Her wild red curls framed her face, held half back with a ribbon that hung around her shoulders in green fabric to match her dress.

"Welcome to my home, Miss Pauley."

Leighanna straightened her shoulders under her cloak, but no matter how much she pulled at her spine, the commissioner's daughter still towered over her. "Thank you for seeing me. I believe there was a mishap in the tea shop. I grabbed your reticule by accident . . ."

"Thank you," Rosalind said. "Take a seat."

She did as Rosalind asked. Etta walked over and stood in the corner, hands clasped in front of her. Once both women were seated, Leighanna held out the reticule, and Rosalind took it from her, the chill of her skin reaching through Leighanna's gloves. As soon as Rosalind pulled back, a loud crash sounded behind her.

"Marie?" Rosalind called out, but no reply came. A wrinkle formed between her brow, lips parting. She stood. "If you'll excuse me, Miss Pauley, my maid—"

"Of course! I can come with you," she said, rising from her seat and taking a step toward the low hum of activity now coming from downstairs.

Rosalind waved her off. "No need. I'll only be a moment." She exited the room.

That's all I need.

Leighanna counted to ten.

"Stay here, Etta," she said to the maid.

"But, miss—"

"I'll only be a moment." The echo of Rosalind's words danced toward the ceiling. Leighanna ran into the hall and turned for the last door on the right—maybe the commissioner's study? She dashed toward the closed door, almost tripping over her skirt in the process.

A small gasp of glee escaped her when it opened without sound.

Inside, it smelled of cigar smoke and whisky, a scent that reminded her of her father and tugged at her heart. She hadn't seen him nearly as much since his business boomed years ago. He'd been in America for the last few months, with a return date far enough away to cause her eyes to burn.

Leighanna pushed through the familiarity and went to the large mahogany desk first. But where she had success walking into the office without a blockade, the locked drawers proved a challenge. She cursed under her breath, frustration furrowing her brow, and dropped to her hands and knees. She tugged her pin out easily, but it brought with it half her hair.

"A later problem," Leighanna muttered to herself, working the pin into the lock.

To no avail.

"Blast it all." She looked around the room, searching for a key to pop out of thin air. And while no key appeared, the briefcase in the corner looked promising. The medium leather bag boasted a worn handle and a zipper that stuck when she tried it the first time. The smell of ink and newsprint wafted from the inside when she finally jiggled it open.

It was stuffed with files.

"Bloody brilliant," Leighanna whispered.

She laid out as many papers as she could, glancing over her shoulder and listening for the sound of footsteps. Time was not her friend. She grabbed the first thing she could and skimmed the front.

Did someone really report their dog's collar being stolen? She shook her head in disbelief, skimming the first few pages. *And a vandalized bird bath—oh, blimey.* She read the words the perpetrator had carved into the bath and blushed at the detailed curse words.

She stuffed the useless reports back inside and continued her search when someone knocked.

"Am I interrupting?" a voice said from behind her.

Leighanna grabbed the next paper and jerked upright, hiding it behind her back, stuffing it under her jacket and into her skirt, all while having the decency to look embarrassed. "Rosalind—"

"I think it best if we stick to formalities," Rosalind interrupted in a clipped voice. "Did you find everything you were looking for?"

"Miss—" Etta came dashing into the room, knocking Rosalind's shoulder, but the girl didn't react to it. She turned her questioning gaze on the maid before looking back at Leighanna and arching a brow.

"I see the show you put on for us has come to an end. And it would seem I've lost two dresses because of it." She waved her hands toward her middle, where a large, wet stain covered half her torso. "My maid made a mess of the fresh tray for our afternoon tea. Instead of the floor, the tea fell on me. The scones had already welcomed their demise when I arrived."

Leighanna held in a wince, her grip tightening around the paper in her hands. "Miss Lewis," she began, but Rosalind raised her hand.

"I think you better leave, Miss Pauley. You are an unwelcome guest in the commissioner's home. I wouldn't want to have to contact the authorities."

Without thinking, Leighanna dashed from the room, grabbing Etta on the way out. Her maid didn't say a word as she pulled her down the staircase and back out into the afternoon sunshine.

A crowd of people covered the front walk, and Etta's hand slipped from Leighanna's. Leighanna reached back and grabbed the papers from the back of her skirt. The crowd gasped, and a sharp cry rang in the air. Leighanna's heart beat rapidly in her chest.

When she glanced back, she saw Etta had fallen to the cobblestones. The distraction caused her feet to stumble over the uneven sidewalk and into the middle of the empty road. People clustered around Etta, checking to see if the maid was injured from her fall. Confusion furrowed Leighanna's brow, heart thundering in her chest. She took a step closer to the crowd surrounding Etta. Their eyes met, and a look of horror passed over Etta's face.

"Leighanna!" Etta screamed.

But Leighanna didn't see the moving carriage until it was too late.

CHAPTER SIX
A Moment in Time

TIME STOOD STILL, as did everyone else in the crowd. Leighanna Pauley was in the middle of it all, the carriage only a foot away from colliding with her. The crowd all stared at the scene it was about to create. Life had felt . . . something that called her here, and she looked around for Death, finding him on the other side of the carriage, wearing his top hat. A look of exhaustion pulled down his cheeks.

"Does this girl have a death wish?" Time asked, hands on her hips and curly red hair hanging down to her waist. The top half of her outfit matched the people around her, fashion for 1890, but the bottom—

"What are you wearing?" Life asked.

Time glanced down at her outfit. "You don't like them?" She held out her leg, the wide expanse of denim hanging two feet in the air. "Got them in the 1970s. Way more fashionable than the 1570s. I still have nightmares about those layers." She shuddered. "They're called bell bottoms." She shook her leg as if it would ring. "I can get you a pair next time I visit. They have them in every color of the rainbow."

Life sighed. "Time—"

"You need to learn how to live a little," Time interrupted. She clapped her hands together. "Now, tell me why you wanted me to stop this moment. I was planning on visiting the early 2000s again before I took a trip backward." She pursed her lips. "You're not trying to cheat Death, are you?"

Life huffed. "Why do you assume I am the one who shouldn't be here?" She nodded toward Death. "It could be him that's not supposed to claim her yet."

"Have you considered maybe you messing with my job is why you're in this predicament now?" Time asked, looking at both Life and Death. Their eyes met, and Life's skin prickled with unease. She looked away.

Life thought about Time's question. But she was good at her job. She'd been doing this job since the first breath of air in man's lungs. Her instincts were correct. But Leighanna Pauley confused her, and she was starting to wonder if the girl really did have a death wish.

"She's a unique case."

Time sighed. "Well, I'm not one to question the Boss, so I'll take your word for it. If He says He isn't done with her yet . . ." She shrugged.

Death shook his head. "We follow orders, and we come when called. We cannot help it if we both respond to the same summons."

Life nodded, a sense of rightness settling in her chest at his words. "But we felt you might be needed for this incident," Life told Time.

Time walked around the frozen girl. Death hovered behind

her, too close for Life's comfort. Life noted the look of horror on Leighanna's face, almost as intense as the curiosity needling Time's brow.

Time glanced away and studied the rest of the scene in front of her. The horse's breath was inches away from Leighanna. Life wasn't sure how much time stood between her and the impact, but if the frustration wrinkling Time's brow was any indication, it wasn't long enough. The crowd of people hovered around the scene, looks of matching horror taking over all of their faces. In the second before everything froze, Etta had reached out her hand toward her mistress as if she alone could pull her back.

"*Hmm*," Time said. "I believe I can fix this."

Death crossed his arms. "We've been called to her together, so I'm assuming—"

Time waved him off. "Yeah, yeah. We all have orders. If it wasn't for His guidance, who knows where we'd be?"

"This moment is not Leighanna Pauley's last," Life said.

Time pulled her watch from the pocket of her bellbottoms. Life studied her threads that stretched between the watch and all the humans in the square, each of them a different level of rigidity depending on how long the people around the square had left. Life tried not to focus on the loose threads, only the one wrapped around Leighanna's wrist.

Death brushed back his coat, and a ray of sunshine caught the metal of his scissors that dangled from his belt. "Some lives are cut short, Life," he said.

"Not this one," Time said. "Give me a moment. We've got time to spare." She winked and snapped her fingers.

A mirage appeared. The semi-transparent clock ticked away, the size of a carriage wheel. Differing time-measuring instruments —a sundial, an hourglass, a candle clock, and an instrument Life didn't recognize with a rectangular shape with boxy numbers—shadowed the outside of the main clock. Sparks of gold and silver wove in and out of the constantly moving picture. Time gently lifted her hand toward the clock, fingers hardly brushing the surface. She tapped a section, moved a piece there, the constant tick-tock sounding in the otherwise silent square.

Death slowly pulled his jacket back around his scissors, and the absence of the blades allowed Life to breathe again.

Time continued to work. Sweat beaded her brow, and with one final change, the echo of ticking halted. The people around them moved backward. Etta's hand dropped a few inches, and the carriage moved more than a foot away from where it had been. Time's shoulders slumped, and she stepped back and spread her hands wide. Life watched as Leighanna's body sped forward while the others continued to go back.

"Three . . . two . . . one . . ." Time mumbled and then snapped.

The people froze. And the ticking picked back up. A smile broke across Time's face.

"Done. It wasn't too difficult, though I do see . . ." She leaned closer to the clock. "*Hmm*. Interesting."

Life peered closer. "What is it?"

Time pursed her lips. "There's a knot. Do you not see it in your threads?" She pulled her pocket watch back out. "Someone snipped her thread and knotted it back together. Who do we know who has scissors?" She arched a fiery brow. Death's hand hovered near the spot his scissors rested.

Life flexed her fingers. Time's gaze swung toward the motion.

"Thank you for your help, Time," Life said, hiding her hands behind her back.

Time snapped her fingers and the mirage of time elements disappeared.

"Yes, thank you," Death echoed.

Time snorted. "A pleasure, as always." She studied the pocket watch for a few seconds before snapping it shut. "Have a nice . . . whatever it is you two are up to."

And with that, Time disappeared and time picked back up where it had left off.

CHAPTER SEVEN
The Rules of Society

ONE MOMENT LEIGHANNA WAS STANDING in front of the carriage, her life and death flashing before her eyes, and the next she was down on the cobbles as the church bells rang at noon. Most of her body ached where it hit the ground, and the rest of her hurt where he—her savior—rescued her from her second kiss with death.

She opened her eyes and met a pair of dark blue ones.

"Mr. Barton?" she said, the breath catching in her lungs. Casper blinked down at her, as if he didn't realize how he'd come to be lying on top of her.

In front of all of Stornshire.

The carriage hadn't killed her, but mortification might.

A shadow passed behind Casper. She peered around him, and two figures—or was it three—stared at them, standing where the carriage had been moments before. Not moving, only staring. One, a woman with bronze skin dressed in all white; another, a tall man wearing a top hat and a suit of the blackest night; and lastly, a woman with wild curly red hair wearing trousers. Peculiar trousers with legs wider than the Thames.

She blinked, and they disappeared, leaving her with more questions than answers.

Am I going mad?

"Miss Pauley?" Casper's breath tickled her cheek.

She must be going mad if *his* was truly the voice belonging to the body on top of her.

They both seemed to simultaneously realize the precariousness of their position, and Casper jumped up, offering a hand to Leighanna. Her nose crinkled, and she dusted off her skirt, hands shaking slightly. The crowd of people clamored around her, crowding her. She had to reassure half a dozen people of her well being as Casper continued to hold her hand. It prickled beneath his touch, despite the gloves they both wore.

Behind Casper, Jeremiah pushed through the thinning crowd to get to her. "Leigh—Miss Pauley? Are you all right?"

They moved to the empty side of the street, near a bench, and she finally released Casper's hand. Jeremiah glanced at their freshly separated hands and blinked. A burst of warmth spread on Leighanna's face. Etta, having risen from her own tumble on the cobblestones, got rid of the few stragglers.

Jeremiah stood nearer to her. His warm brown eyes burned with concern. "One moment you were running down the commissioner's steps, and the next—"

Leighanna interrupted him with a glare thrown in Casper's direction. "I was being accosted by your cousin."

Casper let out a clipped laugh. "I see your appreciation knows no bounds."

She straightened her skirt. "Where did you even come from?"

Casper rolled his eyes in answer to her question. Jeremiah stepped up to her, fingers hovering on her elbow. Nervous energy prickled her skin, and she offered him a smile.

"You need to go home and rest. Why were you visiting the commissioner?" he asked.

"I needed to see Miss Rosalind Lewis." Shame flooded her at the memory of Rosalind's disappointed stare. Leighanna's mind flashed back to the borrowed papers, and she studied the road, noticing them lying near a puddle of water—and Casper reaching for them. She dashed over and tried to yank them from his hand, but he jerked upright and held them over his head.

"Remind me never to offer my assistance again, Miss Pauley," he said, a hint of a smile on his lips.

She pushed aside her dislike of Casper and held out her hand. "Thank you so much for getting these—"

"Now you're grateful, I see." He held the papers higher, and her hand itched to smack the grin from his face.

"Mr. Barton, if you would be so kind as to give me back my papers, please and thank you." She wiggled the fingers of her outstretched hand, and his grin widened. She glanced around at the street, but people were back to their normal business, not paying any mind to the girl who had almost been hit by the carriage now that her rescuer stood between her and death.

"And what will you give me for it?"

A ringing started in her ears, and her blood began to boil. She didn't want the papers back, she *needed* them. She placed her hands on her hips, indignant. "I will give you nothing! Those papers are mine—"

He leaned closer, enough for Leighanna to smell the leather and oak scent of his aftershave. A small shiver raced down her spine. "Are they?" he whispered.

She narrowed her gaze, ignoring the rapid beat of her heart. "I would be most appreciative," she began through clenched teeth, "if you would spare me the indecency of trying to jump in this skirt."

"Oh, but I'd like to see that," he replied, voice resuming a joking lilt.

Suddenly, Jeremiah ripped the papers from his hand and scanned the contents. "Leighanna—"

Her irritation with Casper forgotten, she grabbed Jeremiah's arm and leaned over so they could both read the papers. Etta stepped up to the group and cleared her throat. "We need to be going, Miss Leighanna."

"She's right. We should be off. The carriage?"

Etta handed Leighanna her fallen reticule, which Leighanna looped around her free wrist.

"It's just around the corner." Etta glanced at the men, worrying her bottom lip.

"Are you all right to fetch the carriage? You're not hurt are you? I should have asked before now."

"I'm quite well. I'll go get the carriage."

"Thank you, Etta. I need to speak with Mr. Barton and his cousin for a moment." Leighanna tightened her hold on Jeremiah's arm and pulled him down the sidewalk to the corner. "Jeremiah, could you please . . ."

He handed her the papers. Leighanna glared at Casper.

"Miss Pauley, did you take that from the commissioner's home?" Casper asked.

She shook her head as she folded the papers and stuffed them in her reticule. "Are you accusing me of thievery?"

Casper laughed. Concern continued to wrinkle Jeremiah's brow, but his cousin was aloft with amusement. "I would never suggest anything I wasn't certain of, Miss Pauley."

"Casper," Jeremiah warned. Jeremiah's cheeks bloomed red and a rush of kinship for her friend spread through Leighanna.

"Thank you, Jeremiah, but I can handle myself." She patted his arm. Her carriage came around the corner, and a sigh of relief escaped her lips. "That would be me. Jeremiah, thank you for retrieving this." She turned to Casper. "Thank you for pushing me out of the way, Cas—Mr. Barton."

He snorted. "A pleasure as always, Leighanna Pauley."

She forced back a sarcastic retort and only pursed her lips.

"We're going to be late, Casper," Jeremiah said. "Your mother told us to meet her at the tea shop by noon."

Casper dug in his pocket, cursing to himself. "Bloody pocket watch. I need to find another."

"Grandfather would be aghast," Jeremiah said, feigning disappointment. When Casper glanced away, Jeremiah slipped Leighanna a wink. A real smile took over her face.

Leighanna grabbed Etta's arm. "Well, if that's all . . . Mr. Barton and . . . Mr. Barton." She climbed into the carriage with Etta.

Jeremiah braced a hand on the doorframe. "I was working on some sketches and wanted your opinion before I take them to the university."

Excitement surged through Leighanna. Jeremiah always shared his artwork with her, but it had been awhile since the last time he had.

"I would be delighted. I have some appointments to attend to, but maybe Thursday afternoon you could come over for tea?"

Jeremiah nodded and smiled. "I'll be there promptly at tea time." He stood back and closed the carriage door. She waved at him through the window, the papers she had taken from the commissioner's office burning a hole through her reticule.

As soon as Jeremiah disappeared from view, she pulled the

papers out, straightened them in her lap, and began to read. Her eyes flashed over the page. With each page, the furrow between her brow deepened.

"Miss Pauley?"

Leighanna shook her head. "I can't— This list has clues and information about the murder."

Etta leaned closer. Leighanna couldn't believe it as she flipped the page and started reading the list. Why were they—

Her eyes skimmed the next line, breath rushing from her lungs. She knew most of the information already, except for one note circled in red at the bottom of the list.

The killer knew Jessilyn socially, it said.

Jessilyn Caine's killer was high society—one of them.

Leighanna hated how society insisted she separate herself from some people based on their status. But seeing with her own eyes how the police had hidden information from the community to protect the upper echelon made her head spin. She knew that if the suspect was lower class, they wouldn't hesitate to tell the papers. Her stomach churned at the thought.

When Jeremiah arrived at tea time two days later, Leighanna had pushed the thought of societal standards to the outskirts of her memory, not at all ready for a morning of tea with her friend. Instead of preparing for tea, she'd spent the morning pacing her bedroom floor and coming up with more questions than answers about the case. She hadn't even changed from her nightgown. When the bell rang, it shook the memory of the meeting free. She stuffed herself into a soft blue dress, a jacket with minimal sleeves to match, and dark navy stockings in record time.

"Miss?" Etta said, watching as Leighanna moved about the

room, cleaning up the mess she'd made of the last few days' papers. Her hair still hung around her head in a mess of brown curls, and she had neither the time nor patience to fix it.

"I can't believe I forgot," she muttered. Her wall of clues had grown to include the papers from the police and new articles about various crimes taking place in both London and Stornshire. She'd used red ink to circle pertinent clues, but so far what they'd found was more black and white than blatantly red.

Stan meowed in protest when she moved him off a stack of papers.

"Bloody brilliant," she cursed. "It'll just stay a mess."

"I can tell him you aren't ready to receive him—"

But Leighanna waved her off and headed to her wardrobe to grab her shoes. "No, don't do that. I—ah ha!" She dug to the back of her wardrobe and located a pair that matched.

Etta sighed. "Very well, Miss Leighanna. I'll let him know you'll only be a moment."

After lacing her shoes, Leighanna grabbed Stan and made her way down to the parlor. Sunlight shone into the room from the delicate white curtains, and her brother had moved the two sitting chairs to the center of the room, a small table between them. The fainting couch sat directly beneath the window, and when she put down Stan, he ran over and spun around until he found the perfect position to bask in the warmth of the sun. On the small coffee table sat a tray of tea, with half the biscuits already eaten, a few crumbs on the patterned carpet beneath August's feet as he sat next to Jeremiah, discussing his latest boxing match. Boxing was something their mother disapproved of with such vigor even the local parish envied her ability to scowl.

Irritation prickled under Leighanna's skin at her brother swooping in and boring her friend while they waited on her to get dressed—and eating her fresh biscuits. While her brother was sitting in black trousers and a white shirt, bottoms held up by leather suspenders, Jeremiah wore his best coat and trousers. His top hat rested on the small table next to him, with his portfolio in his lap.

August and Jeremiah couldn't have been more different. Her brother's interest in boxing started when he was only a school boy, and the thin, gangly creature he'd once been grew into a man of towering stature that rivaled even her father's height. The older August became, and the more time he spent with the likes of Casper and the other boxers, the more he looked like their father. An ache pierced her chest. She wished very much for her father's return from America, though it would still be a few more months.

August leaned nearer to Jeremiah, saying something too low for her to make out the words. Whatever he said, it caused Jeremiah's cheeks to burn red. Jeremiah glanced down at the sketchbook in his hands and back up at her brother.

Irritation prickled Leighanna's senses, and she cleared her throat.

"August, pull down your sleeves," she said, feigning her mother's stern cadence. She did it so well he turned to her with the expression of a little boy who'd gotten caught doing something naughty, at least until he realized his sister was smirking back at him.

August scoffed.

"Stay clear of me," she continued. "You reek."

August stood and rolled his eyes. Quick as a whip, he grabbed her, looping his arm around her waist and giving her a fierce hug.

"August!" she screamed, but he only squeezed tighter.

"What's wrong, Leigh?" he asked, and she tried to cover her nose.

"You smell worse than the Thames!"

His laughter rolled through her. Jeremiah stared at them, his cheeks a bright crimson, rubbing the back of his neck.

Leighanna pushed her brother away. "You know Mother

disapproves when you come home smelling like a sewer rat.”

August laughed and checked her cheek with the edge of his fist. Her eyes flashed toward Jeremiah. She wanted to ask what the two had been discussing so thoroughly when she came downstairs, but she held her tongue. The last thing she needed was causing a scuffle in the street with her brother and furthering her mother’s ire when it came to how Leighanna held herself in front of society. He stayed out of her business if she steered free of his.

“It’s only a little sweat, Leigh. Some women fancy it.”

She scrunched her nose. “No woman with any class.”

August chortled, rubbing the stubble on his chin. “That’s our Leigh.” He looked at Jeremiah as if they were sharing an unspoken joke. “Always speaking her mind.”

She gave him a closed-lipped smile. “You’re interrupting our tea, August,” she said.

He bowed. “Of course, dear sister. Wouldn’t want to interrupt your tea.”

With a kiss on her cheek, August left the room. Etta came in a few moments later with a fresh tea tray, and Leighanna took a seat next to Jeremiah. “Well?” She waved her hands in the direction of his sketches, arching a brow in anticipation. “Show me!” She needed a distraction from the newspaper articles and clues surrounding Jessilyn Caine’s murder. The information was missing pivotal points, like how they had come to the conclusion that the murderer was one in high society. The police may know the social class of the killer but they didn’t have all the facts. If she wanted more, she would have to go straight to the source.

The scene of the crime.

And she hadn’t figured out how to turn her path in that direction without embarrassing herself even further. Even now, thinking about how she left things with Rosalind Lewis churned the few contents of her stomach from her scarce breakfast.

With a nervous grin, Jeremiah opened his portfolio. Inside rested several intricate portraits of people in society—from the baker in town to ladies at parties.

"These are lovely, Jeremiah," she said, voice dripping with awe. She took the portfolio and placed it in her lap as Etta poured her a cup of tea and sat it on the table next to her. Her fingers grazed a pencil and charcoal sketch of a couple dancing. "Who is this?"

Jeremiah cleared his throat. "A couple I met while out of town for the art exhibition." His embarrassment only deepened. "I was glad you were able to see me off, but I felt guilty for not coming home when I found out you were so ill—"

She placed a hand over his, the warmth of his skin spreading through her veins. A flurry of excitement engulfed her. In her haste to come downstairs, her gloves were an afterthought, one she thanked herself for as Jeremiah's eyes met hers. "I did not expect you to pause your life for mine." She squeezed his hand to show her appreciation before letting go, drawing her attention back to the sketches in her lap.

"And this one?" She flipped to the next drawing, but Jeremiah ripped it from her hands. The edge of it caught the bend between her forefinger and thumb, slicing open the skin. A hiss passed through her teeth.

"I'm sorry, Leigh. I didn't mean to be a brute, but it's not finished," Jeremiah said, stumbling over his words. "That's the last piece I need to complete before I take my portfolio to the university —well, the conservatory. They moved the viewing. It's an invitation only party."

Leighanna shook her hand, trying to chase away the sting of the cut, but at the sound of his words, all thoughts ceased.

"The one down the road from Morven Manor?"

Jeremiah nodded, stuffing the papers into his portfolio and grabbing his tea. He took a long gulp. Jeremiah always acted like this when he had an art exhibition or gala coming up, like the one he had out of town when she was ill.

An image of the ghost girl popped into her head. She had seen her in the ballroom, but she hadn't seen where the girl had met her end. Fainting in the middle of the ballroom hadn't allowed her much time to explore. Leighanna was certain of two things: she needed to see where the crime actually took place and to see the ghost girl again. Maybe the ghost could tell her more about what had happened to her that night.

"May I accompany you?" Her cheeks flamed at asking to be his date so forwardly, but she pushed past her embarrassment and added, "August and Katrina can join us, as well as anyone else you'd like to invite."

Jeremiah's brow furrowed at first but he quickly recovered, his expression smoothing out and voice firming, "I don't know . . ."

She grabbed his hand again and said, "Your art is wonderful! You need to allow more people to see it. Please? It will be fun."

Jeremiah took a deep breath. "Okay, if you insist. I think I can secure a few last minute tickets."

Leighanna smiled. "This is going to be a night to remember!"

After tea with Jeremiah and a quick conversation with her mother about the upcoming event, Leighanna grabbed her things and rushed to Katrina's home a few doors down. Soon, they sat talking in the Murrays' parlor. It wasn't like her own. It held a warmth to it that Mrs. Murray, Katrina's stepmother, always possessed. The Highland Murray tartan of red and deep green curtains were pushed back to allow the light of the day. The furniture was the same green, and the carpets were plush beneath her boots. Leighanna sat with her feet tucked under her skirt on the couch across from the coffee table that faced two sitting chairs, one of them occupied by Katrina.

A half hour into the visit, she was no closer to convincing her to take part in her newest scheme.

"Please, Kat," she continued to beg. "I'm sorry for how things went about—"

"*Went about*?" Katrina demanded, springing to her feet and pacing around the room. "I don't even know what went wrong! Making scenes in the tea shop! Stealing from the commissioner!"

Mrs. Murray peeked in the room. "Do you girls need anything?"

Leighanna flashed a smile in her direction. Mrs. Murray's light brown hair was pulled back into a soft braid.

"We're fine, Mrs. Murray. Thank you."

"Thank you, Mama," Katrina mumbled, seating herself on the nearest chair. Her skirt billowed around her in a light blue fan. Their tea remained untouched on the table in front of them.

As soon as the door shut, Leighanna shifted in her seat and proclaimed indignantly, "I did not *steal* it. I simply borrowed it. I plan to give it back! Besides, I never make a scene unless necessary! You used to love things like this. Remember when we stole your French tutor's paddle because she kept hitting your fingers when you couldn't get conjugations?"

"My mother was furious when she found out. We should have just told her in the first place."

"But wasn't it fun to place it in your mother's bedroom and see the look on her face when she confronted Madame Moreau—"

Katrina scoffed, looking away. "What aren't you telling me?" she asked.

Leighanna fretted with the edge of her glove, frustration

boiling her blood. "My mother won't let me go unless you agree to it, but I also want you to be there! I want you to be by my side. Why are you so resistant?"

Katrina silently sipped her tea. She squirmed in her seat, her baby blue dress shifting to reveal her boots. She took a large gulp of tea, winced, and said, "I have no desire to go to any event near that place, and I won't be attending the ball in a fortnight either!"

"Kat, please! And don't think I will let you go without answering my questions." Leighanna rushed over to the empty seat next to her friend and grabbed one hand.

"We're growing up, and I have a reputation to take care of."

"What if I promise to not include you in anything that would tarnish it?"

Katrina sighed. "Leigh—"

"August said he will go, but only if he has someone to carry on his arm."

Katrina eyed their locked hands. "And he suggested me?" Her lips parted as if she was about to ask another question, but she sipped her tea instead, yanking her hand away.

Leighanna sighed. "I know you're . . . affectionate toward him—"

"Leighanna!"

"I'm not blind, Kat, but he refuses to court anyone, knowing it would bring my mother unfathomable delight." Katrina pursed her lips, so Leighanna continued. "He's much too preoccupied with his boxing endeavors to consider matrimony at present. But you are another story."

Katrina shifted in her seat. "Meaning what?"

"If he were to consider marrying anyone, you would be the most tolerable decision," she quipped. "But I don't think we have to worry about that. He won't mind escorting you because he sees you as my friend. A little sister." Leighanna leaned back, brushed the front of her skirt. "Besides," she paused and flashed Katrina a grin. "You're much too good for August."

Katrina's lip quirked, and she sighed. "Leigh . . ."

Leighanna grabbed her friend's free hand again, begging, "I'll buy you a new dress! Mother keeps telling me to use my clothing budget."

A laugh bubbled from Katrina's chest. She set down her cup of tea on the nearest table and eyed Leighanna's outfit, an older outfit she had already worn for two seasons. She had been the same size since the age of twelve, even though some people finally caught up to her height.

"Very well," Katrina said. Leighanna squealed, until Kat added, "But, you have to get a new dress, too. And if I want to leave, we will leave."

"Deal. You're making both my mother and myself quite happy."

"You might not like the rules of society," Katrina said, "but some of us like dressing like we're told."

"No one likes doing as they're told, not really."

"So if I tell you that you *must* go to the Carmine ball in a fortnight, you won't go?"

Leighanna pulled her hands free. "I can't promise you that."

CHAPTER EIGHT
The Conservatory

L EIGHANNA STOOD IN FRONT of the looking glass in her bedroom with a quirky brow and pursed lips. The Carmines' ball was still a week away. Before it commenced, however, was the invite-only party at the Conservatory. Leighanna had the misfortune of wearing the ugliest dress she'd seen. She refused to look at the reflection and focused on Etta's hands in her hair as she pinned it up before placing her hat on top. At least the hat wasn't the same shade of pink. It was a dark maroon like her underskirt.

Etta asked if she needed anything else before exiting and leaving Leighanna alone with Katrina.

Leighanna shouldn't have given Katrina so much control over her wardrobe. But when deciding between blackmail and which shoes to wear, only one of them was painful. She held the knowledge of the fun they used to have close to her heart and didn't use it against her friend again. Even considering the girls they were caused a knot to form in her chest. That Katrina *then* would have been up for her schemes and determined to find Jessilyn Caine's killer. The Katrina *now* worried more about what society thought of her.

A sliver of sadness wrapped around Leighanna's shoulders.

Their eyes met in the looking glass. "I'm not changing my mind," Katrina said. "You're wearing it."

Leighanna glanced down at her dress, the one her mother forced upon her last season. It was pink. It was frilly. It was atrocious. But the arms weren't as puffy as the newer items her mother had bought her, so Leighanna chose the lesser of evils.

She tugged at the sleeves, fine lace peeking out at the end. "I look like a piece of salmon," she grumbled.

Katrina rolled her eyes and turned around. "It's called blush, not salmon. The color is more orange than red."

"It's pink, all the same, and it's not my . . . well, I didn't pick the fabric. It has tiny white flowers on it." Leighanna held out her arm, face twisted.

Katrina grabbed her wrist and examined the pattern. "It's delicate, pretty."

"Casper will laugh." Leighanna wished her voice didn't carry a whine. Casper always had something to say when he saw she was in a bad mood. It irritated her to no end, and her skin prickled at the idea of being the punchline of his joke.

"Jeremiah will like it."

Leighanna knew Jeremiah only saw her as a friend, but the idea he might like how she looked—even in a ghastly pink—caused her heart to race. However, her mind was resistant. If he only liked her outfit, then he didn't like her. She would almost prefer he laugh like Casper would.

"I don't care who likes it," Leighanna said. "I don't like it."

"I like it. Besides, you have no choice." Katrina snatched up her reticule and walked toward the bedroom door. "Wear the black shoes."

After lacing her shoes, Leighanna followed Katrina downstairs to the waiting carriage. She remained quiet the short fifteen minute ride to the Conservatory, while her brother and Katrina kept up all of the conversation.

"Not in the mood to talk to us until our ears bleed?" her brother finally asked.

"The only bleeding that will happen is when I punch you in the mouth for that comment."

"Leighanna!" Katrina said through a gasp, but August only grinned.

The carriage came to a halt, and Katrina and August slid out first. Her brother turned around and offered Leighanna his hand, a smirk on his lips. Her cloak fell away to reveal the sleeve of the dress, in all its blushing glory. Lines of silver thread shined throughout it, and she cringed. Stepping down, she couldn't hide the dress if she wanted to avoid any puddles. Most of the snow from the week before had melted, and all that remained were muddied slush piles and a late winter, early spring bite.

"Don't," she said, extending a hand. "Or I will kick you into that mud puddle."

August glanced back at the mush, his perfectly messy hair blowing in the brisk breeze. Leighanna tightened her cloak around her and shouldered past him, ignoring his hand. He laughed, and she elbowed him in the ribs when he came up close behind her.

"Leigh!" August huffed. "Relax."

She glared at him, catching sight of the next carriage. Casper and Jeremiah would be inside. She bit the inside of her cheek to stop any ensuing arguments. She must not make any scenes if she intended to sneak away to Morven Manor, though she still hadn't planned out all the details. Getting to the party was step one. The rest would come as the night progressed.

As the carriage came to a halt and the cousins emerged, Leighanna turned to the Conservatory walk where Katrina waited. Behind her friend, the Conservatory rose high into the night sky. The building was lit with new gas lamps the town had installed, and an ethereal glow shown down around them. The front of the building consisted of hundreds of windows that let in the light for the multitude of plants inside. When the light hit the endless panes at the front entrance, it created rainbows of light around the foliage. It took Leighanna's breath away with its beauty.

Katrina motioned toward Leighanna's cloak. "You look lovely. The dress is very becoming on you—"

"I trust nothing you say. Everything looks good on you." Leighanna tilted her chin toward the hat on Katrina's head, peacock feathers and satin decorating it. "I would look like my grandmother in that hat. I look like her in this one!"

The maroon hat wasn't as bad as it could be, but it wasn't good either.

"You look more like Great Aunt Catherine," August interrupted from behind them. "But that's splitting hairs. After all, they were twins."

Casper's laugh danced across the stone toward Leighanna. The echo of party guests and music filtering through the open doorway couldn't drown him out. Leighanna turned to face them where they walked in front of the street toward the entrance.

If August was rugged in his appearance, Casper was a brute. His shoulders bulged against the constraints of his waistcoat, and he took off his hat and swept his hair to the side. He tucked one gloved hand in the front of his coat and smiled down at her. Jeremiah's face twisted, lips tilted downward, and he kept glancing toward the entrance. Leighanna tried to move toward him, but

Casper stepped up to her and blocked the pathway to Jeremiah.

"You aren't going to show us your new gown?" he asked.

"You're worse than the Cheshire Cat," Leighanna said. "Let me pass."

He only moved to block her path to her friend more. His smile widened slightly. "Miss Murray told me to insist I see your new ensemble."

"Katrina needs to keep her thoughts to herself." She waited for a breath and then stomped on his toes.

He yelped in surprise, but he moved out of her way. Jeremiah laughed and held out his arm. She looped hers through his as he said, "Not your color, is it, Miss Pauley?"

"Katrina decided on the dress."

"That would explain it," he said. "She fancies pink."

Leighanna held out her free hand, white glove shining in the light of the street lamps lining the walkway. Her cloak hid her dress. "I'm lit up like a Christmas tree as soon as I take this off."

Jeremiah smirked and pulled her closer to the entrance. The doors opened wide, and they were welcomed by spring. Flowers in full bloom, petals in every color, waited inside the conservatory. Between the rows of plants and foliage, artwork stood on easels of varying sizes—paintings, oils, and charcoal renderings next to sculptures and pottery.

"Where is your art?" she asked, feeling as if walking into the space was similar to walking into a church. The sudden change in temperature caused the cloak to weigh heavily around her, and she finally gave in and shrugged it off.

People whispered amongst themselves, carrying cups of warm tea and small hors d'œuvres on tiny plates. Someone reached out to take her cloak as they walked inside, and before she could stop them, she stood in her dress looking like a very tall piece of salmon.

She pursed her lips, but straightened her hat without another word.

"It's outside," Jeremiah said. "My art is unframed, so they want to keep it away from the plants."

"I'll need my cloak if we're going back outside," she said. Leighanna looked around for the person who had stolen it, feeling naked without something to cover her dress.

Casper, August, and Katrina walked in behind them. Katrina's hand rested in the crook of August's elbow, and Leighanna arched a brow. Her friend pretended not to notice and pasted on a wide smile. "It's not that cold tonight, Leigh," Katrina said.

"And the outside has a fire to keep it toasty," Casper said. He grabbed Leighanna's free arm and pulled her away from Jeremiah. She gasped, frustrated, and yanked it back.

"Keep your hands off me, you brute," she fussed.

"Have some fun, Miss Pauley," he whispered in her ear, the tips of his fingers brushing the back of her hand. "You must admit my cousin is a little bit of a bore."

She elbowed him in the side—or tried to. He dodged her blow. When he held out his arm again, she pursed her lips and took it. "Fine. If you must." They passed rows of sculptures and tables filled with pottery. Miniature art behind glass hung from strings attached to the ceiling windows, creating a maze she and Casper had to weave through to make it to the center of the Conservatory.

Two open doors led to the inner courtyard. A fire burned in the center of the circular area, paintings and charcoal drawings lining the outside space. Jeremiah stepped in front of them, face pinched and irritated.

"Are you going to continue to hang on my cousin's arm or are you here to see my work?" he asked. If it wasn't for the smirk he added at the end of the question, Leighanna wouldn't have bitten her tongue.

She yanked her arm free of Casper's grasp and took a step closer to her friend. "My apologies. Please, show me which ones are yours."

Jeremiah did a little mock bow and waved her forward. She followed the line of his hand and saw the first portrait. Of her. It showed her from the waist up, her gaze distant. She wore a crisp shirtwaist beneath a dark vest, and the way Jeremiah had drawn her, she looked as if she was in the process of walking away. He'd drawn her wearing a small hat, her messy curls trying to break free from the pins holding it in place atop her head.

"I apologize for being so forward just now, but I wanted to see your face when you saw it."

Leighanna's mouth hung slightly agape in surprise. Her gloved hand hovered over the image, not quite touching it for fear of destroying its beauty. "It's wonderful. This must have been the art you didn't want me to see the other day!" He laughed and rubbed the back of his neck. "You've drawn me better than I look in real life." A slice of affection spread through her middle, and she had the sudden urge to give Jeremiah a hug.

He smiled. "That's impossible. It falls disappointingly short, but my instructor loved it."

Leighanna beamed at him. "Very well. Since you've swept me off my feet with your lovely rendering of me, I accept your apology, but only if you show me everything else you've created."

Jeremiah smiled again and looped his arm through hers, guiding her forward. Leighanna paused to glance back at the rest of the party. August and Katrina stood near an oil canvas, heads bent together in a way that stirred questions in Leighanna's belly. Her brother had to stoop very low to be level with Katrina, and curiosity sparked. Did her brother fancy Katrina? She shook the thought loose. No, he couldn't. She might have joked about it, but she hadn't been serious. The last thing she wanted was for her brother to sweep Katrina off her feet, even if she was the best anyone, including her brother, could gain as a wife. A part of Leighanna didn't want to share her friend. She'd already lost her to society's ideas of how a woman should act. Seeing her brother so friendly reminded her of the childhood chum she had already lost. She didn't want to lose this new Katrina, too.

Jeremiah pulled her back to the present with a tug on her elbow and brought her in front of a charcoal rendering of a woman Leighanna did not recognize.

"It's . . ." Leighanna found herself at a loss for words. She studied the portrait, the tilt of the woman's chin as she gazed upward. Light, or the appearance of it, forever frozen in time, caressed her cheekbones and the gown of gray. Tendrils of hair hung loose and rebellious around her face, and a peacock feather hat rested atop her head.

"It's the perfect rendering of the human body," said a voice from behind.

Jeremiah's cheeks reddened, and Leighanna turned to face the speaker. The man stood no taller than she did, and if not for his hat, possibly even shorter. He took it off and bowed at the waist.

"Miss Pauley, this is Professor Dennings," Jeremiah explained. "He specializes in human anatomy."

The man smiled, and goosebumps peppered Leighanna's flesh. There was no warmth to his gaze. All she found in the cold, calculated stare was curiosity and configuration, as if she were a math problem to solve. Leighanna fisted her hands in front of her.

"Lovely to meet you," she said.

"You as well, though I've seen your face," the professor replied.

It was Leighanna's turn to redden. Embarrassment was the best way to describe Jeremiah using her as a model.

He turned to Jeremiah. "He refuses to tell us how he does it,"

Dennings said. "In all my years, I've never seen someone grasp the emotion so fully. Look here." The professor stepped up to the canvas. He pointed to the girl's chin. "See how he's captured the look of surprise and awe on her face. We don't know what emotion is going to come next, but we have the hope of something beautiful in front of her." He shook his head. "The hours of study this must have taken . . . He's one of my best students. His art has changed some, lost some of its less refined edges and more clearly labels what he's trying to convey." The man beamed at Jeremiah, and it caused confusion in Leighanna. She shook off the concern and turned toward her companion.

Leighanna opened her mouth to respond, but the words never came. The anticipation on Jeremiah's face doused her in awkwardness. She chuckled lightly and glanced around the room. "We're very proud of him," she managed to say. "Jeremiah and I have been friends since childhood, following his family's return from London."

"Ah, yes. I heard about your family's time in London," Dennings said, and remorse overtook his jovial countenance. "I'm dreadfully sorry about—"

But before Dennings could finish his thought, Leighanna was bumped from behind. The sudden loss of balance sent her careening toward the portrait. Her arms flailed, and her body pitched as she desperately tried to avoid punching a hole through the canvas. Her efforts weren't successful, and she landed in a pile across the cobblestones, hand in the artwork. A groan escaped her lips as she rolled over. People rushed toward her, and through the crowd, she saw the slack-jawed gaze of Rosalind Lewis.

Leighanna pushed upward and waved off the concern of those around her, though her arm did ache. She looked up at Jeremiah standing next to her, but his eyes were on the artwork she'd ruined.

"I'm so sorry—" she began, but he cut her off with a wave of his hand.

Her eyes flashed toward Rosalind's departing figure, before sliding back to Jeremiah's hunched form. "Jeremiah?" Leighanna whispered. He turned to her, features pinched, eyes shining with unshed tears. "Oh, Jeremiah. I'm so sorry!"

He forced a tight smile. "It's all right. I can fix it. Possibly create a better piece of art from its remains."

August and Katrina rushed over to them. August leaned down and picked her up in one arm, hugging her against him. She hung suspended in the air for a breath before he put her on her feet.

"Thanks, Auggie," she said. Katrina fretted with Leighanna's skirt, straightening the wrinkles and finding hidden dirt among the folds. "Katrina! I'm fine!"

Irritation swelled in Leighanna's chest, the same look mirrored on Katrina's face. "You're a wrinkled sight," she said.

She turned back to Jeremiah. He and Dennings, with a few of the people who witnessed her tumble, were focused on the destroyed artwork, murmuring over the torn canvas.

"Jeremiah, is there anything I can do to fix it?" she asked, stepping up to his side.

"No, it's all right." Awkwardness penetrated the space, and the room around her felt hot and stuffy.

Katrina placed a hand on her arm. "Are you all right, Leigh?" she whispered. "Do you need some air?"

Leighanna looked toward Jeremiah, but he turned away and paid her no attention. She wanted to apologize again, but feared it might send him to his breaking point. He and Dennings were already discussing possible ways to fix the artwork as people crowded around them. Whispers of her tumble assaulted her ears, along with her fainting spell at the Carmine party. Maybe she did need a moment.

"I believe some air would do me good," she said and sped through the crowd before anyone could stop her.

The cool late winter air filled her lungs, and Leighanna closed her eyes. Party sounds drifted past the open door, but other than that, she was alone. Some of the tightness and guilt in her chest loosened, and she opened her eyes to stare at the empty, well-manicured yard in front of the Conservatory.

A flash of red hair caught her attention. Rosalind Lewis was crossing the street and heading toward a waiting carriage. Leighanna glanced back at the party, but she held no desire to go back in. She had come with the intention of sneaking away, and now, when everyone was worried more over art than her, was the perfect moment. She didn't have long to change her mind before dashing across the street, calling out, "Rosalind! Miss Lewis!"

Miss Lewis had nearly reached her carriage when Leighanna grabbed her elbow, slightly winded.

"Miss Pauley!" she seethed, yanking away. A shot of pain ran up Leighanna's arm from her fall injury. "How dare you—"

"I want to apologize," Leighanna said. Her heart hammered against her ribcage, and she thought momentarily of the girl's face tilted upward in Jeremiah's drawing. A drawing she had just destroyed.

Leighanna felt anxiety curl down her spine, and she wanted nothing more than to crawl into the waiting carriage and pull away from the curb to escape Rosalind's inquiring gaze. Rosalind scrunched her face and narrowed her eyes.

"I'm afraid you will have to list what exactly you mean, Miss Pauley," Rosalind said. "You've continued to insult me; first, by breaking into my home and now grabbing me like an assailant."

Words tangling on her tongue, Leighanna took a step back. "I shouldn't have visited your home under false pretenses. I should have told you why I needed to visit instead of breaking into your father's office." She dug into her reticule and pulled out the papers. "I wanted to give these back."

"Needed?" Rosalind asked. She crossed her arms over her chest and steadied her gaze. "You didn't *need* to do anything. My father is the Police Commissioner. He reports directly to the Metropolitan in London. There is nothing you can find that he has not already discovered."

Shame and embarrassment washed over Leighanna, but she was used to it. Her mother had chided her about all her oddities—the cat obsession, her inability to keep her opinion to herself, and now her need to read the newspaper—all her life. The endless curiosity that accompanied her like a dear friend wasn't welcomed by the upper echelon.

Leighanna straightened her shoulders and stood as tall as she could, almost as if to reach Rosalind's height. Instead of allowing Rosalind Lewis to see her defeated, she forced pure will and determination to sharpen her gaze.

"If your father had done so well as Commissioner, then he would have caught the killer. But according to his papers, he's no closer to finding the culprit than London is to finding the infamous Jack the Ripper." Leighanna knew she was taking a chance not only giving Rosalind the papers back but also admitting to taking them. However, constables hadn't shown up at her door to arrest her since the incident.

Rosalind's jaw dropped. "Miss Pauley!"

"Do you think the Ripper killed Jessilyn Caine?"

Rosalind crossed her arms over her chest and said nothing.

"People are forgetting her name, dragging her memory through the mud," Leighanna continued. "Now, we both know where the crime scene is, and I'm going to do my part as a member of society and try to find justice for Jessilyn Caine. Because, as those notes stated, the person responsible for her murder is one of our own. Finding him is the best and only thing we can do. You didn't turn me into your father for sneaking into his office."

Rosalind shifted on her feet, pursing her lips. "There was—well, there was no point of you getting in trouble. I think, in your strange way, what you did was the means to a better end. Besides, my father didn't even notice it missing, which means it's not that important, or he doesn't seem to think it is. You say you want to get justice for Jessilyn Caine. I can stand behind that."

Leighanna swallowed the nervousness rising in her throat and asked, "Are you going to help me or not?"

"I never . . ." Rosalind fiddled with her reticule, continuing to stumble over her words. "My father doesn't believe that a woman's place is in investigative works." She studied Leighanna for so long, Leighanna started thinking up things to say to fill the silence.

"Miss?" The carriage driver came around to Rosalind's side.

"Miss Pauley—" Rosalind began, but she stopped and huffed. "Well, I'm tired of women only being victims. I suppose I can overlook what happened, since it was for a good reason, and I don't disagree with you." She let out another puff of air. "If you're going to be like this, then climb in. I know a maid at the Carmines' that owes me a favor. If you like, you and I can go to the scene of the crime and see if we can find justice for Jessalyn Caine."

CHAPTER NINE
The Scene of the Crime

They didn't enter Morven Manor through the front door, not like any respectable guests. Rosalind led her around the home and to the back entrance. Darkness cloaked the entire estate. Walking through the Carmines' shadowy grounds sent goosebumps over Leighanna's flesh, and she was grateful for Rosalind's presence.

She'd started her quest to solve Jessilyn Caine's murder so Jessilyn wouldn't be another soul forgotten. She didn't want society to remember the murderer over the victim. However, Leighanna did have to admit that she enjoyed the search.

A little too much.

She kept her mouth shut, though, as Rosalind led her to the back door near the kitchens and knocked twice.

A maid answered. "Good evening, Miss Lewis." Her face lit up with recognition. "We didn't realize you were visiting tonight. Lord Carmine—"

Rosalind stepped up to the maid and grabbed her arm, whispering fiercely in her ear. The girl's features schooled into a look Leighanna recognized from Etta that arose when two people were forced into each other's company and eventually found it pleasant. The girl gave a nod and smiled at them.

"Let me grab my coat," she said. She glanced at Leighanna's hovering form. "Are you sure it's all right she joins us?" The words were whispered loud enough to let Leighanna know where the maid's allegiance stood.

Rosalind glanced backward. "She's all right to know, Marie. She's a friend."

"Of yours?"

The allegiance teetered on the edge of fragility.

"A friend of mine is a friend of Lord Carmine's," Rosalind answered.

Rosalind's response appeased Marie. "I'll get Fergus," Marie said. "He can show you the stables."

Leighanna found her shoulders relaxing as the maid disappeared back into the kitchens.

"How do you know the staff here?"

"I used to be friends with the Carmines' son before he left for Oxford." Rosalind didn't seem like she wanted to talk about it, so Leighanna didn't say anything else. They stood in silence for what felt like hours, anxious energy running rampant through Leighanna's veins. It could have only been a few moments, though, before they were joined by Marie and another servant. The boy wrapped a coat tightly around his shoulders, tugging a worn cap over his head. He tilted it toward the ladies.

"G'evenin', misses. Name's Fergus." He held out his hand, and Leighanna took it. The rough calluses on his fingers suggested a hard day's work. "Marie tells me youse want to see the stables, yeah?"

His thick Scouse accent, less familiar in Stornshire, brought a smile to Leighanna's face, reminding her of the summers she spent with her aunt on the docks near Liverpool. The tightness around her shoulders lessened, and the man, only a few years her senior, smiled crookedly back.

"Indeed," Rosalind responded. "I trust you can keep this interaction between us."

"Yes, misses. Youse needn't worry about me speakin' to anyone 'bout it."

Rosalind huffed with a sharp tilt of her chin, but the servant didn't seem to notice. He walked in front of them, Marie following quickly behind. The ladies followed after. The night air sent a chill through Leighanna's blood, and she took the quiet, brisk walk as an opportunity to study the grounds. While most of it remained in shadow, the bright light of the moon highlighted the hedge maze of the back garden and an imposing fountain that continued to trickle quietly at the center. They wove through the low maze and back toward the smell of horses. The rustling of hooves awaited them at the back stables, an imposing building that rose high into the sky and was large enough to accommodate a dozen full-bodied horses and at least two carriages.

Though chilled outside, heat emanated from the stable. Horses hovered in the back recesses of the stalls in an effort to escape the cold. Unease curled in her belly, and she glanced back at Rosalind, finding her closer than anticipated.

Fergus walked into the stables, and the girls trailed after him. At their arrival, the horses awoke, knocking against the walls of their stalls. Leighanna jumped at the sudden noise, and Fergus turned to look at her.

"Ain't nothin' to worry about, misses. They're a little skittish since it happ'ned. Nothin' to worry about, though. They stays in their stalls, they do."

Fergus continued further into the stable. With each step, Leighanna felt as if more than her feet were traveling into the stables. An eeriness hung over the place, pulling at her soul and spirit and striking it to the bone. A girl had died here, and though there was no ghost in sight, the memory permeated the air.

"What do you know about what happened, Fergus?" Leighanna asked.

He stopped, leaning against the nearest stall. "Not much, misses. Youse know there was a party?" Leighanna nodded and he mirrored the motion, looking at her as he explained, "Then youse should also know that it was 'lot like the event they're havin' at the Conservatory, invitation only. Dancing but also 'lot of lounging. People 'neaking off together."

Leighanna's mind flashed to Victor at the tea shop. He'd been at the party, and he might have even spoken to Jessilyn. If Victor had spoken to Jessilyn, he could have been one of the last. Fear trickled down her spine at the thought that he *was* the last person to not only speak to her but to see her. She could hardly think it, but what if he had been the one to kill her? What other reason would he have to hide his presence at the party? He might have known Jessilyn from the tea shop. She turned to say something to her companion, but Rosalind remained at the entryway of the stables.

"Miss Lewis?"

Rosalind shook her head. "I told you I'd come with you, Miss Pauley. But even I know my limits, and stepping into a place where . . . where it happened is at the top of that list."

Leighanna swallowed the lump in her throat and continued forward past Fergus. Marie stopped a few stalls ahead, worrying her bottom lip. The nearest horse laid its head on her shoulder, and Marie rested a calming hand on its nose.

"Nothing to be afraid of, miss," Fergus said. "I'll show youse where it 'appened."

But his enduring insistence that she not worry only caused more worry to prickle across her skin. Fergus turned around and continued to walk down the long line of stalls before stopping at the last one.

"We 'ad to take the horse we 'ad outta here," Fergus said. "Kept getting spooked. Same time every night, that." He pulled out a pocket watch and moved it into the little light provided by the window above. "Around this time, that is. Midnight in a few moments."

"Do we need to leave?" Leighanna asked.

"No," he answered, but his gaze wavered, lips moving as if he wanted to say more but couldn't force the words to appear. "No," Fergus repeated.

Leighanna stepped into the stall. Ice ran through her, even colder than the wind from the winter remnants.

She leaned down and ran her hand over the hay.

"The hay still gets dirty, it does. Cann't explain it. Tried to leave it be for a while, but it kept getting some sort of gunk in it. Don't like to think 'bout it, so I replace it like the misses asks."

Leighanna picked up a handful of straw and sawdust and brought it to her nose. She inhaled the rich, earthy scent, almost more overpowering than the essence of horse from moments before.

Then time stopped.

She wasn't sure how she knew, but it did. Something about the taste of metal on her tongue, the way the wind died, whereas she hadn't known it was blowing before. The hair on the back of her neck rose, and she licked her lips.

Leighanna stood slowly, releasing the straw in her hand, and faced the ghost.

The same ghost who haunted her at the Valentine's Day party.

Before, Leighanna hadn't noticed what Jessilyn Caine had worn. Now, she looked like she wore only blood.

The sight stole the breath from her lungs, and Leighanna's head spun. Jessilyn's demeanor wasn't like that of the girl she had seen at the Carmines' party a few weeks ago. No, the ghost before her exuded fury. Jessilyn stepped up to Leighanna, face pinched. The blood continuing to pour from the wound in her neck was so red it was nearly black.

"Why haven't you caught him yet?" the ghost demanded, and Leighanna stumbled back, hitting the straw with a hard thunk. Fear consumed her and made it hard to think, to breathe. "He's going to kill again! He's growing impatient!"

Then, another figure joined them. This one a man. He took off his top hat and placed it on Leighanna's head. Leighanna stood to her feet. She felt safer wearing the hat, as if it was a shield rather than a hat. It smelled of cardamom and cigar smoke, a little like sitting in her father's office as he did business with his contacts from India. She held the edges of the hat, her hands as tight as the tension between her father and his associates before her father would say something against their current occupation. Before he would raise the profit margin and create friends continents away.

Jessilyn didn't want to be friends.

"Jessilyn?" Leighanna asked.

The girl cut her gaze toward Leighanna. "He's still in Stornshire."

The man, without his hat, stepped up to the ghost. The question of his origin dangled on the end of Leighanna's tongue, but she held back.

"Miss Caine," the man said and held out his hand. His long fingers reminded Leighanna of spider legs, and his skin was the same shade as the moon. There were bags under his eyes, but his face was kind, handsome, his hair styled messily on his head as if he ran his hands through it a lot. The rest of him, however, was crisp and neat, every fold of his suit precise. On his belt hung a pair of scissors with long, sharp blades. "She has agreed to help you. Maybe you should . . . clean yourself up a bit."

The ghost's face turned curious. Leighanna blinked and the blood disappeared, replaced by clean undergarments. The ring of red around her neck disappeared. Jessilyn looked back at Leighanna.

"What a sight . . ." Jessilyn said. "You . . . I remember you . . ." Her brows furrowed. "How can I remember you, but I can't remember him?"

Without warning, the ghost leaned forward and grasped Leighanna's arm. Ice rushed through her veins, and Leighanna's eyes widened. Fear rushed through her, and she tried to yank her arm away. The man echoed her horror, and he reached for Jessilyn before calling out. Whatever he said fell on deaf ears, and Leighanna couldn't make out the formation of his lips. His eyes, black as the night outside, shone with clear determination, though. In moments, a woman dressed in all white, from her hair to her heels, appeared next to him. Redness bloomed on the woman's tanned cheeks, and she yanked the top hat from Leighanna's head and pulled her away from the ghost.

Breath rushed into Leighanna's lungs as relief spread through her. She collapsed on the straw-strewn ground with a painful thwack. Voices assaulted her ears, and arms wrapped around her to help her back to her feet. Where the ghost had touched felt numb, and Leighanna searched for her between Marie, Fergus, and Rosalind's confused faces. Fergus offered her a hand, and she took it. He pulled her up so fast, her heart flew into her throat. The world around her spun as if she was on the edge of it.

"Miss, are you well?" Marie asked. "You were fine one moment . . ."

"You all right, miss?" Fergus asked, holding her face between his hands and searching her eyes.

"I'm . . . I'm fine."

Fergus released her face.

"Thank you," she muttered, dusting herself off.

"Of course, miss," he said.

"What happened?" Rosalind asked.

"I . . . did no one else see that?" Leighanna asked, at the same moment thunder rolled outside. Marie jumped, and Rosalind let out a small yelp.

"I didn't know to expect rain . . ." Marie mumbled.

"*Hmm*." Fergus made a noise in the back of his throat. "'Hat's strange, 'hat is. Didn't think we'd needa expect rain either, miss. Best be gettin' inside. The 'orses don't take too kindly to the storms. Give me a moment, and I'll be right out."

Leighanna turned to push open the stall door when lightning shot across the sky, shining into the windows and lighting the entire stable. She jumped at the sound, heart threatening to explode from her ribcage. Something caught in the corner of her vision, and she froze. A surge of fear danced down her spine, but it was chased by excitement. Leaning down, Leighanna dug through the straw and dust until she grasped something cool and smooth among the rough and scratchy debris.

She picked up an old pocket watch. The front was scratched, and the closure clasp was broken. It hung from a gold chain that had seen years of wear. She turned it over in her palm, looking for any indication of who the watch belonged to but not finding anything.

Rain peppered the roof, but not enough to force Leighanna back to her feet at Rosalind's insistence. Nothing could distract her from the pocket watch in her palm. She messed with the clasp, but it wouldn't come undone, and frustration burned in her chest.

The watch held no clues to who owned it, and the silence of

the moment swallowed her, until a loud bang and a scream sounded to her right.

Rosalind sat in the Carmines' sitting room with a bandaged wrist. Fergus hadn't been over exaggerating about the horse's fear of the storm. One had kicked open its stall door and ran at Rosalind. Thankfully, he didn't trample her and only her wrist was injured.

Leighanna had seen him again. As the horse threatened to take Rosalind's life, the man with the top hat shimmered nearby, his hand hovering over his scissors.

Leighanna's heart had lodged in her throat, and she'd been two seconds from shouting, "No! You can't take her!" Instead of running over Rosalind, the horse ran around, catching her wrist.

Rosalind and Leighanna's eyes had locked after Rosalind had fallen.

"Did you see him, too?" Leighanna had whispered as she helped her friend up.

Rosalind's brow furrowed. "See who?"

Leighanna's heart had sunk. She'd almost wished Rosalind *had* seen the man, then she'd have someone to discuss this whole supernatural business with.

What was so special about him? The man appeared at the scene of Jessilyn's murder, and he had communicated with the ghost, almost pleading with her.

Something akin to the feel of ice sliding down Leighanna's spine sent a shiver through her.

Death. The man in front of her had to have been Death, and the woman in white?

Life.

Leighanna shook herself out of the realization and focused on the Carmines' sitting room around her. After Rosalind's injury, Commissioner Lewis's private residence was phoned at once, telling him to come to Morven Manor. Once they arrived, Rosalind tried to get her mother to settle as she fretted over her, but whenever she spoke, Mrs. Lewis choked on a sob, and Rosalind would sigh and pat whichever part of her mother's back she could reach during the next bout of hugs.

Leighanna continued to hover in the corner of the Carmines' sitting room. It was larger than their entire residence, with windows that stood at least thirteen feet high and velvet curtains the color of spilled blood. The comparison caused Leighanna to shake her shoulders in unease, but she covered it by rubbing her arms as if cold. Candlelight flickered from the above chandelier, the gems sparkling with every movement of the light. She felt like a ghost would pop out at any moment, either from behind the curtains or swoop down from the light above. Morven Manor looked so similar to how it had a few weeks ago at the ball, she wanted to escape before time stopped again.

She hid her hands behind her back and fiddled with the pocket watch. Her finger worked at the clasp, but it remained shut tight. The relentless work caused an ache in her nail bed. She became so focused on the task, she didn't realize someone had spoken her name, until all eyes turned toward her.

"Miss Pauley," Marie repeated. The maid's hunched form hovered in the doorway. "Your brother is here, miss."

Thank heavens it's not Mother. Relief washed over her.

"Oh," Leighanna said. "Of course." She glanced at Rosalind, and the girl offered her a smile, more than what she could have hoped for. Something about the events of the night, both girls facing death in the stables even if Rosalind wasn't entirely aware of it, brought them closer.

With a final glance, Leighanna followed Marie out into the large hall. Their footsteps echoed across the marble floor. The home lacked any personal touch, mostly made of marble and stone. The absence of personality made the cool floor push all the way through the soles of her shoes. Marie led her out the large, oaken double doors, where her brother was pacing under the porch awning. At the sound of their approach, August stopped and looked up at her.

"Leigh?" August wrapped his fingers around her forearms, brow furrowed. "Are you all right?" Rain dripped down his hair and cheeks.

Leighanna pasted on a grin. "I'm fine." Then, not wanting to face further questions, she untangled herself from his hold, dashed around him, and ran through the torrent of rain and into the open door of the waiting carriage. Katrina jumped at her sudden appearance, and Leighanna perched on the opposite seat, shivering. August climbed in after.

"Blasted rain," he muttered, and hit the ceiling. The carriage lurched forward at his command.

Silence hung over the carriage, and Leighanna fidgeted in her seat, feeling the absence of her cloak. Her mind whirled with everything that had happened, and the pocket watch felt like hot iron in her clenched fist. She kept thinking back on Jessilyn, the look on her face as she demanded her killer be stopped before he killed again. Tension wafted from the other side of the carriage, and Leighanna averted her gaze, sneezing once as she remained sitting cold and wet. She wasn't sorry for what she had done, and she tried to ignore the look of hurt on Katrina's face. The disappointment on August's face was worse.

"What were you thinking, Leigh?" August whispered before they had dropped off Katrina.

"I was with Rosalind Lewis—"

"Exactly," he shouted.

Leighanna jerked in her seat. August had never sounded so angry. "Auggie—"

"Mother has not stopped worrying after you, not since you fell ill. She will be furious, and you don't even care. You know she doesn't want you being so reckless."

"I didn't mean—"

"What *did* you mean?" he asked sharply.

She and Katrina exchanged a glance, but her friend looked away.

"Why is it," Leighanna began in a whisper, "that you're allowed to do what you want to do, but when I have something that I want—*need*—to do, I'm the one who's a blight on the family? You traipse around Stornshire—no, you travel to London, boxing your way through all of society, and—"

August let out a humorless laugh. "Leighanna, you're a woman. You cannot understand."

"A woman?" Leighanna choked out a laugh. "You think I've no brain because I'm a woman? That I'm rash because I'm a *woman*?"

"You're rash because you're obsessed with this case!"

Leighanna gritted her teeth. "The only reason you get to do whatever you bloody decide to do is because you're a man, no matter how rash." She fisted her hands in her lap, wanting nothing more than to aim a good punch at his head.

The carriage came to a halt. Leighanna fumbled with her reticule and began sliding toward the exit.

"Leigh, I didn't—"

Leighanna stopped, pointing a finger at his nose. "No, I won't hear it. You're a hypocrite, August. If this was something *you* wanted to do, something *you* felt strongly about, no one would stop you. They can't stop me either."

With that, she slid from the carriage, leaving her friend and brother behind. The watch weighed heavily in the small pocket on the inside of her dress as she ran down the street from Katrina's house, up the steps of their own dwelling, and into the dry entryway of her home. She could already hear her mother's yet-unspoken complaints as she dripped all over the carpet, but she didn't have the patience to endure them, so she rushed up to her room, where Etta waited anxiously.

"Miss Pauley—"

"I'll get ready for bed on my own, Etta, thank you."

"But, Miss—"

"Goodnight, Etta," Leighanna replied, leaving no room for argument.

Etta chewed on her bottom lip, but Leighanna couldn't focus on her own discomfort for too long. Tears burned sharp and bright behind her eyes, but she walked into her room, the door shutting behind her maid. She stretched awkwardly, about to untangle herself from her dress, ignoring the tears until she lay in bed with Stan resting in the crook of her arm. Only then did she truly allow herself to cry.

CHAPTER TEN
The Clockmaker

E VEN THOUGH LEIGHANNA HADN'T STAYED at the party long enough to boast its guest list, she'd made enough of an impression that her mother had heard of her fall into Jeremiah's portrait. The tense conversation with August the night before still hung between the many plates and dishes spread on the mahogany table at breakfast. She was glad for the sea of cuisine to stand between her and her mother's yelling.

"You are a lady!" her mother said. Her face turned the color of an eggplant, and August continued stuffing forkfuls of pork pie into his mouth. "Not only did you make a fool of yourself and run away before you even properly apologized to Jeremiah Barton—"

"I apologized! And I did not run!" she said, but her mother ignored her and kept shouting.

"—but why in the blazes did you think it was a good idea to venture to Morven Manor?"

August stopped eating mid-chew, and Leighanna couldn't

think of what to say next. Her mouth hung partially askew. Finally, "Mother . . . I—"

But her mother raised her right hand and pinched the bridge of her nose with her left. "You have got to stop traipsing about Stornshire like you are . . ." Her mother took a deep breath. Etta hovered in the corner, and she and Leighanna locked gazes for a moment. "You are not a man, Leighanna, and you do not have the luxury of acting like one."

"Why do people insist on telling me that as if I don't realize it?" she mumbled, tugging on the bottom of her cream vest as if it was too tight.

Her mother either didn't hear her or pretended not to. "You will force my hand, if you do not. I would rather not send you away."

Leighanna's blood turned to ice. "You wouldn't! Father wouldn't allow it!"

Her mother glared. "Your father is not here, and if he was, he would support any decisions I make concerning your welfare."

A heavy silence followed.

"I'm sorry, Mother," Leighanna mumbled, though she didn't mean it.

Mrs. Pauley scoffed, but her shoulders slumped in defeat. "Your apologies will not be enough one day."

The front doorbell rang. They remained suspended in the uncomfortable silence until the butler appeared and whispered to Mrs. Pauley, "Katrina Murray—"

Leighanna jumped to her feet before the butler could finish his sentence and dashed from the room. Her mother's tired chastisement followed on her heels, but it lacked enough vigor to stop Leighanna's progress into the foyer. She gritted her teeth to avoid another argument falling from her lips, hands clenched and sweaty from the effort. Need her mother be so loud?

Katrina was crouched on the floor petting Stan when Leighanna spotted her, wearing a bright blue dress and a matching hat. She turned at the echo of Leighanna's footsteps, mouth opening with greeting, but she stopped at the sight of what must've been Leighanna's fraught expression. The same look of disapproval Leighanna had narrowly escaped at breakfast found a new host in Katrina. Her entire face looked pinched with irritation, and if it weren't for the glassy look in her eyes, Leighanna might have turned around and taken her chances with her mother.

"You don't have to look at me like that," Leighanna said, frustration causing a small headache at her temple.

Katrina sighed and some of her tension subsided. "I'm not looking at you in any sort of way other than concern, Leighanna."

Stan meowed at her feet, and Katrina wagged an irritated finger at him before leaning down and plucking him up, snuggling the cat into her chest. "Don't you start on me, too!" she cooed into the cat's ear. Leighanna heard Stan's purring from a yard away.

Rolling her eyes, Leighanna stepped closer and took the cat. Stan growled in protest and jumped from her arms. "Traitor," she said to his retreating form. He had always fancied her friend, choosing Katrina's lap over Leighanna's whenever the moment arose, at least until Leighanna's dance with death. Since then, Stan had stuck to her, but it appeared he was reverting to his old ways. She turned back to Katrina. "What brings you by so early this morning? We were sitting down for breakfast."

"Which is why I'm here." Katrina held out a folded piece of paper.

"To bring me a penny dreadful?" Leighanna unfolded the proffered pamphlet.

"That's no penny dreadful." Katrina rested her folded hands in front of her. "Open it."

Leighanna did, and it felt as if she was the one who'd been

knocked by the horse the night before and not Rosalind.

"It's—"

"Society doesn't like you at the moment, Leigh," Katrina whispered.

Leighanna's tongue stuck to the back of her throat as she read the article Katrina clipped from the morning paper. It had taken the reporter only a few hours to add the events of the evening to the gossip column, starting with her tumbling into Jeremiah's portrait and ending with her "shameful walk from Morven Manor and into the Murrays' waiting carriage."

"Bullocks," Leighanna cursed.

"Leigh—oh, hello, Kat—Miss Murray," August said, walking into the entryway. He looked at his sister, expression grim. "We need to talk."

"We talked enough last night, and I have things to attend to today. You can make an appointment with Etta, if it's important. She's in charge of my diary."

The maid in question came around the corner. "Do you need something, Miss Pauley?" she asked.

Leighanna smiled and said, "No, but I believe August does." She walked around her brother and up the stairs to her room, cream skirts swishing around her legs. "Are you coming, Kat? Or does whatever August has to say best it all?"

Katrina muttered something Leighanna couldn't quite hear before she turned the corner on the stairs.

Leighanna did, in fact, have plans for the day. Her plans involved opening the pocket watch with the broken clasp and finding out its owner. If she could discover that valuable piece of information, she would be one step closer to discovering who murdered Jessilyn Caine. Her mother's threat didn't worry her, not too much, anyway. Her mother would never send her away. She knew that in her bones. And her father would never agree. Besides, no trouble should befall her trying to locate the owner of a watch. If her mother asked, she could pretend she did it out of charity for the owner.

Katrina caught up with her.

Leighanna walked into her room with Katrina following behind. She grabbed her jacket from the back of her desk chair and slung it on, buttoning it over her vest.

"Where are you headed?" Katrina demanded.

Leighanna's shoulders tightened as she buttoned her jacket. "I have business across town," was the only reply she willingly gave.

"Business with whom?"

Leighanna bit the inside of her cheek. She opened her wardrobe and considered its contents, vaguely aware of Etta entering behind them. "Etta, have my—"

"Leigh, stop being ridiculous," Katrina interjected.

"—boots been cleaned?" Leighanna continued to talk as if Katrina wasn't in the room.

"Yes, miss."

Katrina stepped closer. "Leigh—"

"Could you request Samuel ready the carriage to leave in half an hour's time?" Leighanna asked. Katrina huffed and Etta exited the room.

Leighanna knew the more she ignored Katrina, the hotter her friend's blood boiled. They'd known each other their entire lives, and Leighanna had slowly witnessed Katrina's temper being stomped out, little by little, by lessons on how to be a lady. But every now and then, she saw glimpses of the feisty girl who had climbed the oak on Leighanna's aunt's estate because August dared her to. Leighanna missed that girl.

Something had wedged itself into their relationship following

Leighanna's sickness. The events she assumed should have brought them closer—for wasn't death always a unifier?—set their friendship to a discordant tune rather than a harmony. Leighanna certainly had her secrets, and she couldn't help but feel as if Katrina now had a few of her own. If she angered Katrina enough, maybe her friend would confess to them. Maybe Leighanna would feel comfortable enough to confess her own.

Silence hung over the room until Katrina said, "Are you really not going to tell me where you're going?"

"You don't have to come," Leighanna said. "There's no point in you knowing my destination." She reached up and grabbed a simple black bowler hat from the top shelf of her wardrobe and turned toward her friend. She caught a flash of hurt sliding over Katrina's face rather than the anger she'd expected. Regret wiggled under Leighanna's skin.

"You can't go traipsing around Stornshire alone."

Leighanna slumped. "That word. You and my mother love it, but I have done no traipsing. I'm walking with a mission." Leighanna had hoped Katrina might have asked to join her—demanded it. Asked because she had an interest in Leighanna's interests. Not for the sake of propriety.

Friendship was a complicated web. It survived on threads of events, emotions, and similarities. But when the wind blew, it lost a little of its strength, the emotions that carried each thread snapping and waving in the air.

"A mission *alone*. It's dangerous, Leigh. They haven't caught the killer."

"I won't be alone," Leighanna said, reticule now in hand. "Etta will be there."

"Etta is staff," Katrina said at the exact moment the maid walked back in.

Etta's face turned impossibly puce. "I will wait downstairs, Miss Pauley," she said and left Leighanna's shined boots just inside the door.

"You don't have to act like that," Leighanna said, scowling at Katrina as she shoved her feet into the boots.

Katrina straightened her shoulders, and Leighanna saw stubborn pride fall over her features. "I said nothing she didn't already know."

Fury rose inside Leighanna. "You're off your head!" She tried to quiet her voice, but even Stan jumped and ran under her bed. "You, of anyone, should know what it's like to be treated less than. She is my friend as much as she is my maid."

Katrina's eyes shone with indignance. "She wouldn't be here if she weren't being paid. I stand here trying to help you—"

"You stand here judging me like the rest of society! I have *never* treated *you* like that." Leighanna picked up her reticule from her desk, which held the watch, and then tugged on her gloves.

As if Leighanna had slapped her, a tear slipped down Katrina's cheek. She wiped it away with a gloved hand. An apology sat on the edge of Leighanna's lips. Katrina beat her to it, but not without an air of superiority.

"I'm sorry you feel that way," she said.

Leighanna was glad she kept her apology to herself. "As I've mentioned, I have an appointment across town." She fiddled with the strap of her reticule.

"You still don't need to go alone, unchaperoned."

"As you and my mother believe, no one wants to be seen with me. The absence of a chaperone is the least of anyone's concern."

At that moment, Leighanna's mother walked in with August at her heels. "Leighanna Pauley," she barked and gripped Leighanna's elbow, drawing her away from Katrina. "We can hear you all the way downstairs. Imagine if someone were to visit while you're screaming at our guest? Now apologize to Miss Murray."

Leighanna's jaw tightened and she begrudgingly mumbled, "I apologize."

Katrina, who stood off to the side near August, only nodded in reply.

"That's better." Her mother patted Leighanna's shoulder and let go of her. She straightened Leighanna's hat. "If you're leaving this house, you *will* take a chaperone," she said.

Leighanna gritted her teeth. "Mother—"

"I'll go with you," August offered.

Leighanna felt the fight leaving her body with each beat of her heart. "Fine," she whispered.

"If you will allow Katrina to accompany us," August added with a glance at Katrina.

Their mother nodded. "Splendid suggestion. Katrina will go with you."

"Mother!" Leighanna snapped.

Mrs. Pauley smiled. "The rumors around town are affecting the entire family. You need to be seen with your family and friends." Her gaze flashed toward Katrina. For a long time, the unsavory rumors—founded in truth—that had followed Katrina had led Mrs. Pauley to try to distance the girls, but that had changed years ago when their fathers went into business together. Even if business hadn't thrown them together, the girls had refused to be parted.

Leighanna wished they still had the same stubborn resolve toward their friendship. Once, they had been so close they would fall asleep holding hands, listening to August read the newest penny dreadful. She missed that friend more than anything.

"Fine," Leighanna told her mother. "But they have to stay in the carriage."

"Absolutely not," Leighanna argued, arms crossed as they stood outside the waiting carriage. "Mr. Barton was not invited." She pointed a finger at Casper who leaned against the carriage, arms crossed with an sly smirk only growing the more Leighanna protested.

"Leigh . . ." August groaned. "We have a match later, and if we take you all across town to drop you off at home after your outing, we won't have enough time to get to the—"

"Your intentions are quite clear! You want to tromp around Stornshire as much as I do, but you want to use me as your cover! I don't have that luxury because I am but a woman, so today, you do not have the luxury because you are with me."

Casper stepped away from the carriage and toward her, hat held to his chest. He had the decency to look contrite, but Leighanna doubted he wouldn't smirk as soon as her back was turned. "Miss Pauley, your brother is quite skilled in boxing. You wouldn't deny him a chance to bloody a brute, would you? What harm would it do to attend the match after your little mission?"

Leighanna glared. "Firstly, you own the business, which is the only reason no one snarls their nose up at your bloodied knuckles. Secondly, August's skill is moot. Thirdly, forgive me if I don't want your opinion on the matter. My *brother* didn't bother to tell me you would be joining us."

Casper laughed. "I am but the getaway carriage."

Leighanna's jaw dropped. "He is not driving us! You know what happened at the Spring Festival last year."

"'Twas but one table—" Casper began, arm thrown across his chest in mock outrage.

"One table of pies! Mrs. Wright was washing plums from her hair for weeks."

"Pure speculation. How are we to know the true length of time it takes a matron to clean plums from her hair?" Casper asked, leaning close enough for Leighanna to smell his cologne.

She pulled away. "You could've asked Jeremiah," she told her brother.

"Jer draws horses. He does not ride them. Or in the case of a carriage, hold their reins. When you're done arguing the particulars, we can be off." Casper put his hat back on.

Katrina stepped up from where she hovered near the stairs. "The faster you agree, the sooner you will get to where you're going. It's only a few hours," she was quick to add when Leighanna looked as if she was ready to say something else contrary.

The words rested on the tip of her tongue, but she swallowed them and nodded. If needed, she could slip away. She'd worn her running boots. She refused to let anyone stand in her way of her goal.

They climbed into the carriage. A pair of boxing gloves sat on the seat, and Leighanna picked them up and eyed the white strings and leather.

"Where to?" August said from the doorway.

Leighanna told him the address, and he repeated it to Casper. In a moment, they set off. The cobblestones bumped and moved beneath them.

"You can't be that good," Leighanna said, holding one of the gloves. "I see no blood on the strings."

August laughed. "They're brand new. I'm breaking them in today. They're from America. Father had them sent over. They've only recently adopted the rules we established back in the 60s."

"Fascinating," she said in a way that alluded to the polarizing belief.

"I like the rules. They keep the match clean," August said.

"And you, being the gentleman, are following them?" She quirked a brow.

He rolled his eyes. "I'm astonished you agree with Mother on anything."

"I don't agree—"

He halted her words with a laugh. "Mother made it clear boxing is not a gentleman's sport, Leigh."

"Oh, be quiet," she murmured and looked away. "Don't bring up what I said when under the influence of my own anger."

August snorted.

"We can go somewhere for lunch while the boys do their boxing," Katrina said. The mood in the carriage pressed on Leighanna's shoulders. Her frustration with August only worsened it.

"I'm fine, thank you," Leighanna replied. She didn't want to hear about tea and scones. Or little finger sandwiches. The roads became busier the closer they got to their destination. Anticipation built inside her chest, but she didn't want the others to notice. Knowing her luck, they would see the excitement as harmful and find some excuse to sabotage her plans. Pocket watches tell stories, if you know where to look. When she had lifted it up to her ear, she heard the passage of time. But the clasp had been broken, most likely during the night in question. She would wager August's entire boxing match on the hunch it had secrets to tell if it could only be opened.

"There's a lovely sandwich shop freshly open in the center of town. We could walk from the docks. I don't think it would be too exerting."

"We'll see," Leighanna said.

Katrina sighed.

August mumbled something to Katrina that sounded like, "You'll never thaw the ice with sandwiches and tea," but she pretended not to notice. "I have a friend at the seamstress shop across from the warehouse. If you want to change into something less conspicuous, you can come watch the fight," August said. "But you'd draw attention dressed like that."

"We'll consider it," Leighanna said and gazed out the window.

Katrina and August fell into a steady rhythm of conversation, and when, thankfully, none of it concerned Leighanna, she drowned them out with her thoughts, keeping her hands tight on her reticule. The pocket watch rested in its depths, ticking away, taunting her. Should she have given it to the police? Maybe. That's why she didn't want her friends to know she had it. Would that have gotten her anywhere? No. Besides, there was no definitive evidence the watch belonged to the killer. There was also no definitive evidence it did not. And until she knew more, finders keepers, as the Romans used to say.

"We're here," Casper called out, the carriage coming to an undignified stop.

Leighanna braced her hand on the seat, and Katrina let out a nervous laugh.

"I see your getaway carriage has eccentricities only a select few appreciate," Leighanna said, close-lipped.

"Don't be bitter, Leigh," August said. "It'll give you wrinkles."

Against every fiber in her being, Leighanna smoothed the wrinkle between her brow with two gloved fingers to the echo of his laughter. She slid from the opposite side of the carriage and stepped onto the crowded street. The brisk March air smelled of a coming storm, and people hurried past, trying to reach their destinations before the rain broke through.

"I'm fine on my own," she said as August climbed out behind her.

"No," August said.

"Auggie . . ."

"Look, let me walk you to the shop." He stepped closer. "This may be Stornshire, but every town has its rough edges."

She sighed. "Very well. But keep quiet."

August nodded, offering her his arm as Casper paid a passing pageboy a pence to watch the carriage while he and Katrina joined the siblings. The shop sat within sight of the parked carriage. Leighanna glanced back and watched the pageboy peer through the windows. As if he felt her gaze, he turned and blushed. She smiled, and focused back on the shop, pulling August to a stop.

"Here?" he asked.

"Interesting," Casper said.

"Why interesting?" Leighanna asked. Casper merely shook his head.

"Are we allowed to join you?" August asked.

"What business do you have with a clockmaker?" Leighanna asked, rolling her eyes.

"I could ask the same of you," her brother said, his hold tightening on her arm.

"I've got a watch that's only right twice a day. It needs some attention."

"Fine," August said. "Keep your secrets." He turned to Casper. "You should consider popping in, since you've lost your watch, Casper," August said.

Warning bells went off in Leighanna's mind. "You lost your watch, Mr. Barton?" The watch felt even heavier in her bag knowing someone in her presence was missing a watch. And she had one.

"Misplaced it is all," Casper told her. "Why?"

"Just curious," she said, tightening her hold on her reticule.

"Let's go, Casper. Let the girls keep their secrets. I'll pay the pageboy, Charles, to accompany you to the docks—no, don't fight me on this," he added when her lips parted to do just that. "Charlie knows his way around the place. I always buy my penny dreadfuls from him. If you want to come into the warehouse, go to the seamstress across the way and change into something less recognizable. Understood?"

"Very well."

August took Leighanna's hand and kissed the top, tipped his hat at Katrina, and slapped Casper on the stomach. "Let us leave them to their devices."

Casper bent over and blew out a puff of air. "If you insist," he said, straightening once more. He tipped his hat to Leighanna and Katrina and trailed after August, his brown hair shimmering obnoxiously in the midmorning light. Leighanna scrunched up her nose in disgust as she watched the boys walk away. The thought of Casper's missing watch wouldn't leave her.

"Are you ready?" Katrina asked, breaking her from her thoughts.

"You don't need to come with me," Leighanna replied as she walked to the door of the clock shop, shoulders straight and her head held high. Katrina trailed after her, mumbling her disapproval under her breath. Leighanna didn't bother to ask what she was complaining about this time.

Every tick-tock of the pocket watch incited her curiosity a little more, and she stuck her hand in the opening of her purse and wrapped it around the warm metal as she pushed her way into the clockmaker's shop. The smell of varnish and smoke hit her first. Gears and sockets covered every available space, and the only evidence of other life was the gentle cascading sound of metal sliding over metal as someone moved behind the wide oaken desk.

"Leigh, I don't think now is a good time," Katrina said.

Leighanna glanced back at her friend. Worry worked its way up Katrina's face as her gaze roved around the cluttered space. Katrina stepped forward, and her shoe hit a clock in a state of repair, half of its innards now underfoot.

"He seems a tad busy," Katrina whispered.

At that moment, a man popped up from behind the desk. Katrina shrieked. He wore a pair of goggles that made his eyes seem larger than his head, and his hair a mess of chestnut curls. Grease covered the front of his apron and his cheeks.

"How can I help you ladies?" he asked in a thick south London accent.

Leighanna and Katrina shared a look before Leighanna turned back to the man. She pursed her lips, feeling the heat of Katrina's body as she sidled up next to her. Leighanna wished she'd worn trousers for this encounter, to be more imposing like her brother. She wished that when people looked at her, their eyes widened like they did when her brother did business in town, his knuckles still bloodied and his brow wearing a fresh line of sweat, straight from the ring. Her brother did this without meaning to, but Leighanna had to force herself to stand straight and stare the man in the eye.

"Hello, sir. My name is Leighanna Pauley, and I was wondering if you could answer a few questions about a timepiece I found."

He lifted the goggles onto his forehead, pushing back his crazy curls and exposing a forehead wrinkled from studying small gears and knobs. "Do you have the timepiece with you?" he asked.

Leighanna nodded and pulled it free from her reticule. She stepped up to place it on the counter, but Katrina stopped her with a hand on her elbow. "Leigh," she whispered.

"What now, Katrina?" Irritation swirled in Leighanna's belly, and she half hated herself for it. Katrina had been her friend for as long as she could remember, but her constant correction was grating her last nerve.

Katrina's eyes flashed to the figure behind the desk. "Where did you get that?"

"That's unimportant. The owner is why I'm here."

Katrina's mouth opened and closed like a fish out of water, and her pause gave Leighanna the opportunity to turn back toward the clockmaker and place the pocket watch on the counter.

The clockmaker leaned closer, pulling his goggles back over his face and studying the gold outside. He turned it over in his palm and froze. He looked up at Leighanna, eyes impossibly round and wide behind the magnifying lenses.

"Where did you get this?" he asked.

"I found it," she said, voice trailing away.

"You don't just *find* a numbered pocket watch."

Leighanna's spine snapped to attention. "Numbered?"

She reached for it, but the clockmaker jerked it back toward him. He bent toward it, inspecting every inch of the watch and then doing it again. "Miss Pauley, you don't simply run up on a watch of this caliber. Do you know what brand of timepiece you possess?" The clockmaker leaned over the desk, but instead of feeling intimidated by his closeness, she bent closer. She placed her palms on the counter, the coolness of the glass top bleeding into her gloves.

"If I did," she began, "then I wouldn't be here asking you, Mr. . . ." She held out a gloved hand.

He grasped her fingers between his greasy, grime-covered digits. "Mr. Jameson, miss. Mr. Ronald Jameson." Mr. Jameson squeezed her hand before letting go. The small touch left a line of grease on the fingers of her gloves.

When Katrina stepped up to join her at the counter, she tutted her disapproval. Whether from treating Mr. Jameson as an equal or the grease he left behind, Leighanna couldn't be sure.

"If you'll allow me to take this in the back, I believe I have something you'll want to see." Mr. Jameson looked up from the watch as Katrina joined her.

"I need to keep the pocket watch, Mr. Jameson," Leighanna said.

He laughed. "I would never take such a valuable item without giving you a proper offer, miss."

"Five minutes, Mr. Jameson."

"You're not very trusting, I see."

"A woman can never be too careful."

He placed the pocket watch on the counter. "I think I can find what I need without keeping hold of your pocket watch."

Leighanna grasped the pocket watch and wrapped the chain around her wrist.

"This place is a mess," Katrina whispered when Mr. Jameson walked into the small back room. "*He's* a mess. How are you to trust his information?"

Leighanna held back a sigh and turned to look at her friend. "Why are you here, Katrina? You don't approve, so why do you insist on coming?"

"Because you're my friend, Leighanna." Her eyes softened, and a piece of Leighanna turned to mush as well. Moments like these reminded her of the Katrina who would have found joy in the search instead of questioning every turn.

She let out a tense breath. "Then why have you acted differently toward me since my illness?" Everyone treated her differently, and it hurt the most that her best friend was on that list.

Katrina took her free hand and squeezed it tightly. "I thought I'd lost you, Leighanna. I had prepared myself to lose you, and—" She paused and took in Leighanna's face. "And," she began slowly, "it feels like I did lose that friend. You're not who you used to be."

Leighanna couldn't deny the truth. She wasn't the same girl

she'd been before she fell ill. She'd seen things—people she believed to be . . . they couldn't possibly be Life and Death, could they? But who could they be if not them? It was the only explanation that made sense. She had been close to death back in December. Something—or someone—had pulled her back.

"I don't mean to push you away," was all Leighanna said, all she had time to say. Because she hadn't intended to push Katrina away, but she couldn't help but feel they were being tugged in opposite directions. Leighanna, in the direction of a killer and finding justice for Jessilyn Caine; Katrina, wherever society deemed her fit.

Mr. Jameson returned carrying a small photograph. Silence filled the room as Mr. Jameson placed it on the counter.

Leighanna blinked once.

Twice.

She held the pocket watch next to the photograph. "It's the same," she whispered.

"It's not just the same watch, miss. It's another Patek Philippe." His smile stretched impossibly wider. "There were only ten of these watches ever made, miss."

Leighanna looked over at Katrina. The same awe that Leighanna felt blanketed her friend's features. Mr. Jameson stared down at the watch in Leighanna's hand as if it was the most valuable thing in the room. Maybe it was.

"There are only nine more in existence," Katrina whispered.

"And only nine people this one could belong to, really," the clockmaker said.

"Oh?" Katrina asked before Leighanna could.

"The queen owns one of them."

"The queen?" Leighanna repeated, wide-eyed.

"She commissioned the piece."

"How did you get the photograph?" Leighanna asked.

"All clockmakers know Philippe's work. The pieces were all sold by Philippe's son, Leon, after he inherited the business. At least, all but the one belonging to the queen."

"Who did he sell them to?" Leighanna asked, leaning over the counter.

Mr. Jameson sighed. "I don't have records of those sales." Leighanna's hope deflated, but then he said, "The only person who would know is a clockmaker by the name of William Brown. He owns a shop near Hyde Park in London."

Leighanna held her watch to her cheek, feeling the ticking through the gold. Whoever had bought this watch paid a high price for it if there were only a few in existence—one of which belonged to the Queen of England. How much money did Leighanna hold in her hands? It made her skin crawl, worried she would do something irreparable to the piece that was already locked tight.

"May I?" Mr. Jameson asked.

Leighanna nodded and handed him the watch. He held it up close to his ear. His eyes closed, and the echo of the ticking seemed to fill the entire shop.

"It has a lovely heartbeat," he said and clicked the top. A frown tugged at the corner of his lips. "But it appears the face remains a mystery." He pursed his lips. "A piece such as this should really be better cared for," he said.

"Do you believe opening the watch would give us any insight into the owner?" she asked, taking it back.

Mr. Jameson shrugged. "Unless the owner engraved something on the opposite side, then no. But to do such a thing would ruin the value of the piece." Their eyes met. "You're holding a very special watch."

The way he said it made Leighanna's skin prickle with anticipation. Katrina looped her arm through Leighanna's and tugged her toward the exit.

She studied the watch in her hands and thought of the waitress at the tea shop, telling her Victor knew more than he was saying, that she had seen him near the stables. Is it possible he either saw the killer or was guilty? Could Victor's family afford such a watch? She believed the watch belonged to the killer, but her friend in the tea shop didn't come from money. Unless . . . he had stolen the watch. After all, anyone willing to kill would see thievery as nothing more than a child's game.

"Your brother will be looking for us, Leighanna," Katrina said, and Leighanna knew it was more for the benefit of the clockmaker than for her, though Leighanna didn't feel unsafe. No more unsafe than she did regularly while a killer was on the loose.

Leighanna forced herself to grin. "Thank you for your time, Mr. Jameson. We must be off before my brother sends someone after us."

"Of course. Thank you for showing me the rare piece."

Leighanna went to turn, but he pulled a book from below the counter. "Are you recording our visit?" she asked uneasily.

He glanced up and turned the book toward her. "I write down my customers' names and the service I give them, even if they do not buy anything or require labor." Leighanna's cheeks burned, and guilt washed through her. She'd asked for his time and offered nothing in return. Her hand itched to grab a clock from the wall and pay for it with the few coins she had on her.

"I wrote you here," he continued, "and what I provided along with the service fee."

"Would you happen to have information on the men who owned the other watches?"

Mr. Jameson paused, then began flipping back through the pages of his book. "One came about a year ago," he said. "I likely have his information, but there was a fire a few years back, after the first owner visited. It burned our books, though most of the clocks were salvaged."

"You don't have any record of the first man's visit?"

He tapped his temple. "Only what's up here, but he didn't tell me his name."

Leighanna tried not to scowl, her hope doused by his words, and merely nodded. "Thank you for your time. You've been very helpful."

"The clockmaker in London—"

"William Brown?"

"Yes, I can contact him for you, if you'd like. I can't guarantee he will give me the information you've requested, but I can at least phone him once I finish working."

A genuine smile crossed Leighanna's face. "I would appreciate it greatly, Mr. Jameson."

"If you write down your information, I'll send word tomorrow morning."

Leighanna scribbled down her name and address for the clockmaker on a scrap of paper, and Mr. Jameson placed it in the front pocket of his apron with a, "Speak with you soon, Miss Pauley," as she and Katrina walked back out into the cloudy day.

CHAPTER ELEVEN
Fight Club

W*ILLIAM BROWN.*

The name echoed in Leighanna's mind as she and Katrina walked the streets of Stornshire toward the docks, where the Thames River's stench rose above the clouds, but the smell of men's sweat and pride overrode even the river's odor. The same pageboy, Charlie, had been waiting outside the clockmaker's shop for them, and he walked behind them now. Leighanna glanced back, noticing the boy's head swiveling back and forth. He tipped his hat at her and said, "You're safe with me, miss!"

Since her time at the clockmaker had not taken as long as she thought, she decided they may as well go to the warehouse to see her brother in action. She was familiar with the place, though she'd only visited in men's clothing before now.

She turned back around, only catching the tail end of Katrina asking, "Are you listening to me, Leigh?" Katrina tugged on her elbow.

"I'm sorry, what?"

Katrina pulled her to a stop in the middle of the street. Leighanna could hear the river a few blocks away, and people passed them on both sides. Katrina let out a tense breath, and Leighanna gritted her teeth to stop herself from commenting.

"I don't think you should show the pocket watch around," Katrina repeated.

Leighanna frowned. "How gullible do you believe me to be, Katrina? I don't plan on advertising it around Stornshire." Katrina opened her mouth to say something, but Leighanna rushed to add, "Especially now that we know how rare an item I found."

"Not only rare." Katrina grabbed her wrist, yanking her toward the sidewalk from the street.

"Be careful!" Leighanna chided, the bottom of her dress muddied as she stumbled into a puddle while following her friend.

"Misses, wait!" Charlie called, running to catch up to them.

Katrina did not answer. She dragged Leighanna two blocks down the street and into an alleyway. Charlie stood at the edge, a look of concern pinching his features. "Misses, I don't think Mr. Pauley would like this."

"Kat, wait—" Leighanna called as Katrina continued to drag her through the alley until they couldn't see the street anymore. Charlie hovered at the entryway, hands in his pockets. "We're almost to the boxing house—"

Katrina stopped short and turned on her then, gesturing sharply toward Leighanna's reticule where the watch now resided. "Do you realize what you have there?" she demanded.

Leighanna shifted on her feet awkwardly, frustration swirling in her gut. "It's a pocket watch—"

Katrina laughed sharply and huffed. "Don't act daft. Where did you get that watch?"

"I found it," Leighanna said, working hard to keep her tone

calm, normal.

"Where?" Katrina demanded.

Leighanna considered lying, but Katrina would not believe anything but the truth. "I found it at Morven Manor."

"You stole from the Carmines?" Katrina balked, eyes wide.

Should've lied. Leighanna straightened her shoulders, shaking her head. Irritation wound its way across her back. "No, I found it in their stables where Jessilyn Caine was murdered. And before you say I should have given it to the police, neither you nor I know if it was the killer's or not. But I will find out who it could belong to. You don't have to be a part of this, and frankly, I don't know why I have to keep reminding you of that."

"I don't understand why I have to remind you we used to be friends," Katrina replied.

Leighanna stepped back as if slapped. "We're not friends now?"

"Leigh," Katrina sighed. "Since you got better, you've changed. I'm worried about you, and not because of what society thinks but because I don't want you to get hurt. You keep pushing me away, and that's the last thing I want."

"I don't know why I have to keep defending my actions when they don't have any effect on you." Hurt laced up her spine, but she pushed it and the tears away, swallowing the sadness rising in her throat.

"Can I not be worried?" Katrina took a deep breath. "Look, I'm sorry I have not been very . . . understanding of what you're doing by trying to . . . come to terms with Miss Caine's death—"

"Unmasking her murderer."

Katrina waved a hand in front of her face, as if swatting away a fly. "Whatever you wish to call it."

"Katrina." Leighanna paused, chewing on her words before continuing. "That's what it is. Do you not understand why I'm doing this? It is not enough for you to apologize for your behavior toward my pursuit of justice."

"Do you want me to understand—"

"Yes! You are a woman! Do you realize that everyone knows the name given to the butcher of London, but very few know the names of his victims? If this killer were to come after us—"

"Leigh!"

"—they would be more inclined to talk about the man who killed us than the life we lost. I will not let that happen to Jessilyn Caine. I won't."

Katrina stared at Leighanna for a long time, gaze glassy.

"Leigh," Katrina said slowly. "You are not Jessilyn Caine. You are alive. You don't need to dwell on what happened to the dead as penance for living."

"That's not what I'm doing," she argued, but even she wasn't convinced.

Katrina took a deep breath and let it out slowly. "Then I won't let you do it alone."

Leighanna took steadying breaths. The fight left her, and she reached out and took her friend's hand. "I always hate when we fight."

Katrina laughed. "It seems like all we do nowadays."

Leighanna choked on a laugh. "Then let's stop. Please? Let me do this. I will try not to risk my life."

Katrina nodded and let out a tense breath. "Very well, but with me by your side. Deal?"

Leighanna grinned. "Deal." She looked over her shoulder at a pacing Charlie, letting Katrina's hand fall and feeling the shift in their friendship.

"You ready to go, misses?" he asked.

"Come on," she told Katrina. "We have to change. Where was that dress shop, Charlie?"

Charlie led the way to the small shop. Last season's dresses were in the window, and the interior of the shop didn't allow for much light. A woman sat at a desk in the center of the shop with her hair pulled into a fancy updo and a frilly dress on her person. At their entrance, she gave them a dimpled grin. Leighanna, comforted by the woman's presence, gave her a smile in return.

"My brother August Pauley sent us," Leighanna explained.

The woman jumped from the stool. "Of course! Right this way." She led them to a changing room with a curtain pulled back to reveal a large room with a floor-length looking glass. "You can change here. He bought you these."

"I don't know about this," Katrina said, eyeing the clothes as Leighanna changed out of her dress and into the simpler skirt and women's shirt, a dark brown skirt and pale blue shirtwaist with puffed sleeves.

"It looks nice," Leighanna said, buttoning the shirt. "Less conspicuous than that." She motioned to her fancy outfit. "Hurry up, and I'll help you with your hair."

After she had changed, Leighanna helped Katrina switch out her hat for a simpler one. Katrina frowned harder, then nodded, and Charlie led them the short distance from the dress shop to the warehouse where the next boxing match was being held. The large building used to house shipping crates until Casper bought it and turned it into a gentlemen's fight club and bar. The roar of voices reached their ears before they even made it inside the building, showing that business was booming. A man with half an eyebrow and a crooked nose waited at the double doored entrance. Leighanna squared her shoulders and adjusted her reticule.

"Hello," she said.

His eyes roved up and down her body, and Leighanna repressed the urge to shoot him a glare. "No ladies allowed," he said.

"My brother is August Pauley," she said, as if the words did not apply to her. "He was supposed to leave my name on the list."

The guy pulled a folded piece of parchment from his pocket and scanned it for half a second. In a low south London drawl, he said, "Then that's a problem, innit?"

Leighanna refused to cower and arched her brow. "The only problem I see is you denying a lady and her friend entrance into the warehouse."

He coughed, but Leighanna surmised it was supposed to be his version of a laugh. "You're not on the list, love," he said.

"Check again." She took a breath. "Try Leigh Pauley. He probably didn't think when putting my name down."

He sighed and checked again, his half brow quirking upward when he found her name. "You don't look very much like a Leigh," he said and moved aside.

"And you don't look like you can read, but we've all been proved wrong today."

Katrina's hiss at her back almost distracted Leighanna from his cracked smile. "You should sign up for a fight. Might have a chance, love."

"I fear every other opponent would face me ungloved and willfully unprepared."

His laughter trailed after them as they entered the warehouse and into the raucous noise of the fight. Men were everywhere, the stench of body odor rising above the stale scent of the Thames through the cracked windows. Katrina clutched Leighanna's hand tightly as Leighanna navigated through the crowd. She was grateful her brother had had the foresight to get her more accommodating clothing.

"Where are you taking me?" Katrina asked, raising her voice to be heard over the din.

Before Leighanna could reply, a loud voice rose above the

melee. The entire warehouse quieted. They turned their heads to the center of the room. Muted sunlight from the ceiling windows pierced through the glass and illuminated the boxing ring. Men hung on the rope barrier, sweat and anticipation thick in the air, and fists full of pounds and notes drew the attention of the bookies and gamblers in the shadows. Katrina's face radiated disgust, but excitement ran through Leighanna's blood. The fight was wild, and it invigorated her in a way that it shouldn't have. Katrina grabbed her arm and pulled her back from the men, but they didn't have eyes for any of the women in the room.

The scene was the ring before them.

"Our next fight is between our reigning champion, Sir Oscar Alford, and rookie, August Pauley!"

A roar shook the room around them, but at that moment, someone leaned in close, whispering "Hello," in Leighanna's ear. She reared her elbow back and landed it in the assailant's stomach. She turned and saw Victor. He coughed through his apology, bent at the waist.

"Victor!" Leighanna's words were drowned by the crowd as her brother climbed into the ring. Her head ached from the rise in sound.

Katrina tugged on her sleeve. "Leighanna, are you all right?"

"Yes, he just scared me." Leighanna worried her bottom lip between her teeth, and her gaze flashed to the ring.

The men bounced on the balls of their feet in undershirts and old trousers. Their hands were padded in white gloves. Sweat dampened the hair near August's scalp, and his cheeks shone with pockets of red.

"What were you thinking, showing up here, Miss Pauley?" Victor asked, staring up at her in shock.

"I came to see my brother in action," she answered, the thundering of her heart in her ears almost drowning out the sound of her words. Was Victor the killer? Was she standing here with Jessilyn Caine's murderer? Or did he simply know more than he'd let on? He *was* seen near the scene of the crime, after all. "You made your bets?"

Victor straightened and stretched. "Not betting today, but it's a welcome surprise seeing you here."

The crowd cheered as the first punch was thrown. Blood splattered across the floor of the ring, and Katrina yelped in surprise and covered her mouth with her gloved hands.

"It's only a fight, Kat," Leighanna said. "He does this all the time." She turned back to Victor, even though the sight of blood had been a little jarring. "Were you looking for me?"

Victor reached into his pocket and then held out a slip of parchment. "I was. Got a special delivery for you. She asked if I could get it to you."

Leighanna unfolded the note.

Information for a cup of tea? - Rosa.

"How do I know this is from Rosalind Lewis?" she asked, struggling to be heard over the rising noise.

A question rose on Victor's lips, but the fight picked up pace and a loud thunk echoed around the room.

The crowd counted down.

"What's happening?" Katrina asked in a high pitched voice. She balanced on the toes of her boots, but she couldn't see above the crowd of men.

"Knockout," Victor said.

"Who?" Leighanna's eyes scanned the crowd and tucked the note from Rosalind in her pocket.

Victor glanced toward the ring and winced. That wince told Leighanna all she needed to know—August. Despite the danger of being crushed in the crowds, Leighanna shoved forward, dragging

Katrina with her, elbowing her way between sweaty bodies until she stood in front of the ropes. Katrina gasped and pushed past her and underneath the rope, scrambling onto the platform.

"Katrina, don't!" Leighanna cried out, surprise rushing through her. Her heart threatened to break through her ribs as she followed after her friend. Someone pushed her from behind, and Leighanna stumbled into the ring, shock and panic coursing through her. She caught sight of her brother knocked out on the mat, and her heart lodged in her throat.

Someone else pushed into the ring, colliding with her. Her reticule went flying, the tie loosening and the watch half-hanging out. A small scream escaped her. As the champion's coach and two other men stormed toward their winner, one of the three pairs of boots came down on the bag, including the watch. Leighanna stopped breathing. She saw more than heard the metal crack beneath his shoe.

"August, wake up!" Katrina's panicked voice rose above the crowd as a pair of hands scooped Leighanna up under the armpit and set her on her feet.

Leighanna swatted away the hands. "How dare—" Leighanna began, but her words were cut short.

"Now is not the time to argue, Miss Pauley. You should've waited outside." *Casper.* She glared up at him briefly.

"My pocket watch—"

Victor appeared in her line of vision, bending to scoop up the pocket watch before he grabbed her hand so tight the blood seemed to stop flowing, jerking her beneath the ropes and through the crowd. Casper shoved her from behind and latched onto her other hand.

"Come on!" one of them shouted at her. She only had just enough time to see someone picking her brother up to carry him to the side before he was lost from sight. Katrina was nowhere to be seen.

"A knockout!" The words echoed to the rafters, and the displeasure from the fight's outcome was evident in the crowd. One man started fussing at Casper and asking why he'd put a mate that couldn't fight in the ring. Casper started to say something, but the guy threw the punch before Casper could finish his sentence.

Leighanna shrieked before covering her nose with her hand, the same hand that Casper had been holding. Casper turned to the man and landed his first blow. The man shouted words Leighanna could not understand. Casper's face shifted. Gone was his resolute jaw and determined set to his brows. In its place was fury—red, hot, and violent. He took the man by the shirtwaist and punched him once. Again, and then another time. The crowd parted slightly, and Victor yanked Leighanna through them, but not before Leighanna turned and saw the man fall in a bloody heap on the floor. Horror struck her from all angles.

Someone pulled Casper away from the man, and he seemed to come to himself. Victor was yanked from Leighanna, and the crowd surrounded her. She searched the faces, looking for someone familiar and landed on Casper. Their eyes locked, his a blue so dark they were almost black, his hair a tousled mess. Flecks of the other man's blood dotted his collar. When he saw her, Casper elbowed through the crowd toward her. His warm hand wrapped around her gloved one, before he dragged her to the back of the warehouse where Victor waited.

Leighanna caught sight of Katrina, who was shoving toward the doors. Leighanna grabbed her friend's hand. Katrina jerked in her grasp and started to shout before recognition spread across her features.

"Stay close," Casper said above the noise, casting a look at Victor. Victor nodded. Leighanna dropped Casper's hand. She and

Katrina hurried after them toward the back of the building, safe in the gap the two men's bodies made. Casper pushed through a side door and into an empty hallway, and Victor moved aside, both men giving Leighanna and Katrina room to catch their breath as the heavy door clanged shut behind them. Leighanna placed a hand over her racing heartbeat, counting each breath until the rush of blood settled back into her veins. Taking one last breath, she stood up straight, mind flashing with the images of the fighting men still racing through her thoughts.

"You dropped this," Victor said behind her.

Leighanna slowly turned to face him. The pocket watch, broken as it was, lay held out toward her in his open palm. Leighanna looked down at the watch, then up at him, studying his features. She held her breath, waiting for a look of recognition.

But not an ounce of recognition for the watch shone on his face.

"Victor . . ." Leighanna took the watch from him, noticing the trampling underfoot had unleashed the broken clasp. She didn't dare open it yet and instead glanced at Casper briefly before she focused on Victor once more. "Why didn't you tell me the whole truth about your time at the party where . . . Miss Caine died?"

Casper hovered behind her. Katrina's anxious breathing seemed too quiet. Leighanna's heart thundered against her ribs.

Victor shifted awkwardly from one foot to the other. "Why does it matter?" he asked.

"Someone died," she hissed. "And you didn't tell me the whole truth!"

"Listen," he said uneasily, his gaze darting to Casper. He started to back down the hall, away from the other man, beckoning for her to follow.

"Leighanna—" Katrina protested, grabbing her elbow. Leighanna tossed a glare over her shoulder at Katrina before continuing after Victor. Katrina didn't release her.

When Victor came to a halt, Leighanna and Katrina standing close before him, he lowered his voice and said, "I was being paid to . . . keep an eye on some people."

"What do you mean? Like gossip?" Leighanna asked.

He swallowed, and Leighanna swore she saw a bead of sweat form on his brow. He glanced toward Katrina. "Lady Carmine hired me to gather gossip throughout Stornshire."

"Did you talk to Jessilyn Caine that night?"

He shook his head. "She was dancing most of the night until she . . . disappeared. By that time, drinks were flowing pretty heavily, and I was occupied."

"Doing what?"

He let out a humorless laugh. "Following someone who wasn't supposed to be with someone else. And before you ask, I can't tell you, but I can tell you I was inside the house on the third floor at midnight. But a killer? What must you think of me, Miss Pauley?"

She rolled her eyes. "I'm glad you aren't, but what information did you find for Lady Carmine?"

Victor licked his lips. "I'm afraid I can't tell you that."

"Can you at least give me a hint?"

He rolled his eyes. "It's best if I tell the information I find only to my employer."

"And if I were to pay you?"

Victor shook his head, rubbing his chin. "I still can't tell you what I've learned for Lady Carmine. I'm sorry."

Leighanna huffed. "Very well. But you were at the stables that night," Leighanna said.

Victor nodded. "Only because . . . the information I needed was in the stables, but I was not there when Jessilyn Caine was killed, like I said. You can ask the stablehand, Fergus. I think I saw him here tonight. He saw me come back into the house. And—"

Relief spread through Leighanna's chest, and a laugh escaped her lips.

Victor's frown deepened. "Why are you laughing?"

"I thought you were a killer!" Leighanna whispered with a smile. "But you're just a pageboy for a rich woman."

"I can take it from here, thank you," Casper said. Both Leighanna and Katrina jumped at the sound of his voice as he moved up behind them.

"Let the man speak," Leighanna said. The threat in her tone was shy after she'd seen him drop that man with a few punches, but Casper didn't seem to notice. She wanted to ask him where he'd learned to be such a brute, but something about the watch in her hand made her stop.

Victor laughed and rubbed the back of his neck. "Sometimes you forget you're one of them, don't you, Miss Pauley? One of society's pretty play things?"

Victor's cool tone turned her veins to ice, but he wasn't wrong. She didn't want to align herself with people who would so carelessly forget about Jessilyn Caine because it was easier than acknowledging the truth.

"One of them?" she said.

He rubbed his first two fingers and thumb together in the universal sign of money. "You got it whereas some of us don't. Doesn't mean I don't respect you, but you might be able to get more information than me when money does start talking."

Since she woke up on Boxing Day, it seemed Leighanna had indeed "forgotten" she was part of high society. "I forget," she said, looking up at Casper, "but there are others who know exactly where they stand."

Casper grimaced, his gaze locking with hers. "We are sometimes burdened by the memory, Miss Pauley," he said.

Do you think Casper more apt to murder than Victor? the voice in her head inquired. Anger, yes. She'd seen the evidence of that in the room just beyond. He didn't look dangerous now, not even with blood on his collar. But murder? Was her brother's friend truly capable of *murder*? Only evidence and time would tell.

Without the smell of the fight in her nostrils and the men's roaring in her ears, a kind of courage filled her. Leighanna took a deep breath, her jaw firming. "Victor has treated me more kindly than you ever have, Mr. Barton. And he was good enough to save my watch and try to pull me to safety, even when I thought the worst of him." Not that she was fully convinced of Victor's innocence either, not until she spoke to Fergus.

"Treating you kindly does not make him your friend!" Casper shouted, brow furrowed as his voice echoed down the hallway around them. Katrina flinched, and Casper's teeth ground. "You can't trust just anyone, Miss Pauley. *Victor* is not wrong. Money talks, and you don't know whose hands have been filled with a few pounds."

"I don't trust everyone. I just don't take very kindly to *you*. You beat that man—"

"What I did to that man was deserved," Casper snarled, his eyes narrowed. "He'll be fine and burdening people with his small mindedness, have no fear."

"Will you be waiting in the wings with fists raised high?"

"Leigh," Katrina whispered, tugging on her arm. "Now is probably not the time . . ."

"If he wants to argue, then it is the time."

"Your brother was hurt," Katrina said, and a bolt of surprise passed through Leighanna at the tears she saw pooling in Katrina's gaze. "We need to follow Mr. Barton to him, quickly."

"You're right," Leighanna said quietly. She turned her gaze back to Casper. "Mr. Barton, please show us to August and then take your leave."

Casper's jaw ticked. "Bring your *friend* along if you wish, Miss Pauley, but I won't be leaving your company."

Leighanna started to snap at him but Victor interrupted. "It's quite all right, Miss Pauley. I'll be needed back in the main room." She felt his warmth near her back as he bent closer. "Please, talk to Fergus so we can get this sorted out. And don't forget that tea, yeah?"

"I will, Mr. Edwards," she answered. "And, hold on one moment." She took the note from Rosalind out of her pocket. "Tell her I'll meet her tomorrow at the tea shop. Around tea time, yes?"

Victor winked and said, "Of course, miss."

"Ready?" Casper asked sharply as Victor disappeared. When Leighanna nodded, he jerked his head in the direction of the door they'd entered and the hallway beyond. "With your brother down, you are my responsibility, Miss Pauley. "

Leighanna laughed, the sound hollow. "Make no mistake, Mr. Barton, I can take care of myself."

August's laughter didn't match the growing pair of black eyes he sported. He sat on the edge of a straw cot in one of the back rooms of the warehouse, and Leighanna was amazed at how fast the skin around his eyes had turned a deep shade of red.

"Wait until I wake up in the morning," he told her.

"Mother will have a fit."

"If she didn't, I'd be more concerned."

Leighanna shared a smile of relief with Katrina. It would seem all was normal, with her brother at least.

Even knowing her brother wasn't at death's door, Leighanna did find herself looking around the room at large and waiting for the man in the top hat and scissors—*Death* himself—to appear, but all she could think about was the pocket watch ticking away in her reticule. She'd stuffed it back in her bag before Casper had led them down the long hallway and before he had even noticed it in her hand.

The scent of iron and sweat still lingered in her nose, especially here where it was so close. Katrina fought the smell with a perfume-covered handkerchief near her nose, but Leighanna didn't want to risk emptying the contents of her bag by pulling out her handkerchief, so she endured it.

Casper kept looking at her, as if he expected her to break. It amused her. Apparently even he wasn't privy to August's indulgence of her extracurricular activities.

"Why are they so upset?" Katrina asked behind her handkerchief.

"Sucker punched me," August grumbled. "His people know it, too. The house put the rule in place a few weeks back. An unfair knockout, forfeit the win."

"Lots of pounds invested," Casper mumbled. "Lots of money lost, on both sides."

August slid to the edge of the straw mattress and reached for his coat. Katrina jumped forward, as if to hold August in place. "Do you think you should be moving right now?" she asked.

He smiled up at her, the expression warmer than Leighanna expected. "I've done this before, Miss Murray. It isn't my first black eye. Right, Leigh?"

"I gave you your first," Leighanna replied, smirking. She flexed her fingers as if they were still sore from the punch years before.

Casper rolled his eyes. "Of course she did." He jerked a thumb over his shoulder. "I have the carriage out back."

August groaned. "Why would you do that, Casper? Now the men might follow us—"

"Follow us?" Katrina asked. "Wouldn't it be better to drive away then? Do you think the man you fought will be mad since he had to forfeit the win?"

Both Casper and August shook their heads, exchanging a glance. "It's not the fighters you have to worry about, Miss Murray," Casper answered. "It's the betters. While there are some angry *for* August, there are just as many who are upset his opponent had to forfeit the win."

"Lots of money lost," Leighanna agreed.

"You act as if you've been around this sort before." Katrina cast her a questioning frown, and Leighanna looked away.

She could almost hear the clock ticking in her bag, and she was happy the carriage awaited her. The sooner she returned home to her room, the sooner she could bring the watch into the light. Now that it was well and truly broken, she could hopefully study the inside.

"I'll go get the carriage ready," Casper said, promptly exiting the room. Leighanna said nothing, only went to her brother's side, intent on helping him.

August grunted as he stood from the cot, and the half exposed coils of the bed made the same disgruntled sound. Katrina moved to the doorway, watching August with a worried gaze. Leighanna looped his arm over her shoulders, but August wouldn't lean on her like she tried to encourage.

"I'll crush you," he protested.

"Nonsense."

"Did you fix your broken watch?" August asked.

"Unfortunately, no, but I have a lead for someone who might help get it ticking," she lied. "I also need to talk to Fergus, the stablehand at Morven Manor, before we leave."

"Leigh, you can't be serious. We need to go," August grunted.

Leighanna scanned the crowd of sweaty men. Her eyes landed on the same stablehand who had let them investigate the stables before standing near the exit. "It won't be long. He's just over there." She nodded in his direction.

August struggled to gain his footing and when Casper returned, he guided Leighanna aside and tried to take August from her. Leighanna's brother scowled and pushed Casper away, clearly intent on making the walk on his own.

Leighanna tucked Katrina's gloved hand into her own, and they followed August and Casper down the hallway toward a back exit. Behind tables to their right, men argued the bets. Casper took Leighanna's hand like he had before and whispered, "Stay close." She had half a mind to shove him off, but the look of rage in the men's eyes behind the tables made her reconsider.

Katrina looped her arm around August's. Leighanna assumed to both help him walk, and for protection as well. August didn't shove her off like he'd done with Casper. The group hustled toward the carriage, half obscured by the building next to them.

Leighanna spotted Fergus leaning against the wall near the exit. "Excuse me, sir?" Leighanna called out.

Fergus looked down at her, a piece of straw twirling in his lips. "Yes, misses?"

An elbow slammed into her back and she stumbled forward out of Casper's grasp, almost landing in the stable hand's arms. She needed to ask fast before she got overrun by the crowd or Casper pulled her away. "The night Miss Caine was murdered, did you see Victor in the stables?"

Fergus pulled the straw out of his mouth. "Victor? That I did."

"When?" Her heart thundered in her chest.

He spun the end of the straw between his thumb and pointer finger before putting it back in his mouth. She held her breath. "Before she died. Saw 'im head back inside. Victor's many things, but he ain't no killer, misses."

"Thank you, Fergus." Leighanna sighed with relief, mixed with frustration. If Victor wasn't the killer, she had more investigating to do. She pressed on through the crowd.

August staggered next to Leighanna, and Casper reclaimed her hand. Both men hovered so close Leighanna could feel their combined breaths against her back. The cacophony of the shouts pelting her was nearly drowned out by the roar of blood in her ears. Anxiety flowed through her, and the open carriage door was a welcomed sight.

A blur caught the corner of her eye. A knife glinted in the streetlights. "Look out!"

CHAPTER TWELVE
On the Other Side of Time

I T'S AMAZING THE SITUATIONS this girl gets herself into," Life noted, studying the scene before her with the curious gaze of an anthropologist.

Moments before, a disgruntled gambler had rushed at August Pauley with a crude knife, only missing him because his sister had noticed when others had not. She'd yanked her hand from the man escorting her and stuck out a booted foot.

The attacker went sprawling, dropping his knife far enough away that other bystanders could diffuse the situation and usher the Pauleys and their companions into the waiting carriage.

Death appeared beside Life. His top hat obscured an ample amount of his face so that the smile on his lips appeared more sinister than amused. But the last few weeks had taught Life a lot about Death, mainly that he wasn't all he appeared to be. He was more than the harbinger of the end, but a guide into the afterlife. With his guidance, what comes after didn't seem so terrifying.

"What are you doing here?" she asked. "No one died."

His face hardened. "I had an unfortunate case a few blocks away. I saw your light."

"*Hmm.* Care to join me?" Life asked, offering her arm.

"Are you following them around now?" Death asked as he looped his arm through hers.

"No, I come when called. August Pauley needed some assistance in the fight. That punch would have hit a particular part of his brain if I hadn't blocked the blow. Don't worry," she added. "I got permission. He should be right as rain now."

They didn't pass through the streets like the others. Time worked with them, even if she did sometimes get the periods confused. She had never flung them from one century to another, and being able to pass from one place to the next without having to use other means of transportation came in handy.

"Leighanna almost needed your interference," Death said in that same calm, cool way he always spoke. The words danced over Life's skin and reminded her why some people feared him.

They arrived back at Leighanna's home, watching as the Barton family carriage pulled into the alleyway between the Pauley's residence and the home next door. Casper still helped August climb down from the carriage, and they snuck him in the back door so Mrs. Pauley wouldn't see. Leighanna's friend, Katrina, followed after them, but Leighanna hovered in the backyard of her family's home.

"Are you all right, miss?" the butler said, coming out of the house.

A maid peeked through the back door, and Leighanna looked up and smiled at the girl. "I'm well, Etta. I'll be up in a moment." Leighanna looked back at the driver. "Could you grab my reticule for me? I left it in the carriage."

The driver turned and climbed into the vehicle as Leighanna

pulled the pocket watch from her pocket.

"Who do you think the watch belongs to?" Life asked Death.

Death unlooped his arm from Life's and took a step closer to Leighanna. A shiver visibly ran down Leighanna's spine as he drew nearer, and Life held her breath. Leighanna looked up and peered in Death's direction, eyes squinting as if looking through a layer of fog.

"Miss," came the driver's voice from the inside of the carriage, "are you sure—oh, I think I've found it. It's—" He cursed, and then promptly apologized.

With the driver out of sight, Leighanna looked down at the fractured watch in her hand once more and popped it open. Leighanna's shoulders rose with a surprised breath as she read the inscription inside.

Leighanna was too distracted by what was on the opposite side of the watch face to notice when Life and Death moved to hover around her shoulders.

For my grandson. - Papa B.

"Miss Pauley?"

Leighanna snapped the watch shut as the back door opened and Casper emerged. She turned and faced him with a scowl on her lips, the hand holding the watch hidden behind her back. "What is it, Mr. Barton?"

Life did not think Leighanna saw it, but she did—the moment of hurt falling over Mr. Barton's features before he schooled his emotions. "Your mother is looking for you."

"Has she seen August?" she asked.

A smile tugged at the corner of Casper's mouth. "That's why she's looking for you."

Leighanna hid the watch behind her back as the carriage driver finally appeared with her reticule in hand. "Here you are, miss," he said, wiping his brow. "It was jammed beneath the seat. It ripped slightly on the edge. I can pay for the damages—"

"You needn't do such a thing." In one motion, that even Life thought quite impressive, she slipped the watch into her pocket, the reticule around her wrist, and glided up the steps like the high society lady she was.

Chapter Thirteen
Hunt for the Guilty

WHAT WERE YOU THINKING?" Leighanna's mother asked as she paced in front of August and Leighanna in the parlor. The drapes were noticeably closed, and even the sunshine didn't dare join them for this conversation. One wore bruises and the other grime, and August would be lying in bed for at least a few days after he left the chair in front of the small center table. Leighanna bit the inside of her cheek as she sat on the fainting couch beneath the window to avoid telling her mother as much, thinking it best not to poke the bear when her cubs had done something she had ordered them against.

"You know what, please don't answer that," her mother continued with one hand raised in the air to stop any protests or explanations falling from her children's lips. "I've asked you that question too much lately, and I can tell you the answer: you weren't. Why were you over at the docks?"

"I went with August. You wanted him to be my chaperone," Leighanna said.

Her brother snorted and then winced in pain.

A disbelieving laugh escaped her mother's lips. Leighanna shifted in her seat as her mother hovered over her. She wasn't afraid to answer the question, but she knew if she told the truth, learning the watch could only belong to a certain number of people wouldn't help the situation with her mother any.

"There was a shop I wanted to visit," she answered, deciding that sticking to a half-truth was better than outright lying. Her mother had a way of finding out the truth even when she only had half of the information.

"What was so important that you *both* had to risk this family's reputation?" Her mother started to walk toward the exit. "And what happened to your clothes? What are you wearing?"

Tears burned behind Leighanna's eyes. "August didn't want me to stand out in the crowd. I'll go get my clothes next week," she mumbled, her mind already on something else, the least of which was her clothes.

She needed to figure out who killed Jessilyn, not only for Jessilyn and her memory, but for herself. She needed to prove to everyone in society that a woman could solve the mystery and give the girl—the ghost—rest. The girl hadn't just haunted the party that night, but Leighanna was now haunted by her, by the need to solve the case and to understand what had happened. Also that she, Leighanna Pauley, was as capable as any man.

"I'm sorry, Mother," she said in a small voice.

"I forced Leigh to go with me, Mother. I paid for her clothes," August said. He didn't rise from his seat. Leighanna wasn't sure he could without assistance now that he was sitting again.

Mother turned with her hand on the doorknob and peered

around Leighanna. "She is to blame for her actions, August, as much as you are for yours."

"She was covering for me, Mother. I told her to visit the shops, and she got worried when Mr. Barton and I were taking too long. It was my idea that she and Katrina change so she wouldn't draw attention. She was only there because of me. I didn't give her a choice."

Leighanna stared at her brother. He wouldn't meet her gaze, but he didn't shy from his mother's piercing stare. "The blame is on me alone," August said.

Leighanna turned her pleading gaze to her mother, the older woman's face pinched as she frowned. "If you go to the warehouse again without permission, I will call your aunt in the country," their mother warned.

"Yes, Mother," Leighanna said.

Her mother sighed, looking down. "What happened to your bag?"

Leighanna glanced at the reticule around her wrist. "It got caught on something on the carriage."

Her mother's eyes narrowed. "We're going to the modiste tomorrow. You can select another." Her mother waved her hand in dismissal, and Leighanna let out a breath of relief. "I'll send Miles to help you to your room, August, and I'll send some ice for your eye while we wait on the doctor."

"I don't need a doctor," August said. He rose from his seat, wobbling, and Leighanna rushed over to help him. Her mother wasn't far behind.

"Miles!" their mother called, and the butler rushed in and took her place.

"I've got him, miss," Miles said and Leighanna slowly let go.

"I'll get the door." Leighanna ran over and held open the door to the parlor. August and the butler limped out first. Leighanna's blood boiled urgently in her veins, knowing the longer she stayed in the room, the more questions she might have to endure. When August finally reached the door, Leighanna on his heels, her mother called her name.

"Yes, Mother?" Leighanna asked, forcing herself to smile.

Her mother stared down at the note she was writing.

"Next time your brother threatens his life, can you stop him or at least warn me first?" Her mother walked to the window, peering outside before she settled into her armchair, picking up her fan and waving it in front of her.

"Of course, Mother. Next time, I'll be sure to inform you before he tempts death."

"See that you do. And take that note to Etta. Have her call Dr. Thompson."

Leighanna took the note from the table and turned to leave. But then, she hesitated. Victor's words at the warehouse came back to her. He might not have been able to tell her the gossip he'd learned, but she knew someone who might.

Rosalind Lewis.

"Mother?"

Her mother looked up. "What now, Leighanna?"

"Rosalind Lewis—" Her mother arched a brow, so Leighanna hurried on, not wanting to waste the opportunity to ask for something she'd agree to. "—she invited me to tea. May I call on her after we visit the modiste?" She couldn't help the burst of hope that spread through her.

Her mother waved her off with a flick of her wrist. "Better than the commissioner himself."

"Thank you, Mother!" Leighanna said, running back inside and kissing her on the cheek, excitement flooding her veins. Her heart thundered in her chest, and it felt like a step in the right direction, and one her mother couldn't argue.

Leighanna stood off to the side in her brother's room as the doctor leaned over his form and placed his stethoscope on August's heart three hours following his accident. After listening and making a few notes in his notebook, Dr. Thompson had announced August would make a full recovery with at least five days' rest. Luckily, her brother hadn't suffered any broken bones or internal bleeding.

"Though it was a close one," the doctor said, closing his medicine bag at the foot of August's bed, "I wouldn't advise making anyone angry for a few weeks. You wouldn't want to suffer a brain injury."

"I'll be on my best behavior," August promised, and the doctor laughed.

"Thank you, Dr. Thompson," her mother said. "Leighanna, would you please show him out?"

"Of course." Leighanna and the doctor didn't speak on the trip down the stairs and to the front door, and her skin prickled beneath the silence. She felt as if he was waiting for something, but she didn't know what.

When he stopped on the front step, she got her answer.

"You've healed quite quickly, Miss Pauley. Do you have any lingering effects from the illness? I haven't had many patients . . . well, excuse my bluntness, but you're one of the few patients I've had to survive tuberculosis. Your mother hasn't called on me about any lasting effects, and you didn't seem to be out of breath as we walked down the stairs."

Leighanna froze. She hadn't considered what the illness would have done to her body, but somehow she felt she could breathe better now than she'd been able to before she'd nearly died.

"I feel wonderful, actually," she told him with a small smile.

"Splendid. That's marvelous, Miss Pauley." His brow furrowed. "I wonder why you were spared any lasting effects."

Leighanna chose not to answer the doctor's musings, for it felt rather impossible to explain what being caught between the grip of life and death at the same moment did to a person. She gave him a brief farewell and watched him climb into the waiting carriage.

The next day, her mother was ready to go to the shop as soon as the town was awake. Leighanna's conversation with the doctor still rang in her ears as the first day of August's bed rest took full effect.

"Are you ready to go to the modiste?" her mother asked, as Leighanna stood on the front stoop with the sun beating down on her. "While we're there, we'll be getting you a new dress, as well as a new reticule."

Leighanna huffed and pushed aside every desire to push back against the dress. Things had been tense enough as was. "Yes, Mother."

Mrs. Pauley's face lit up with her daughter's compliance. "Good. I'll have Miles look after your brother while we're gone."

"You mean make sure he stays in bed and doesn't try to crawl his way back to the docks?" Leighanna asked, taking her damaged reticule from her mother's extended hand.

Her mother sighed, though she seemed in better spirits. "I think your brother has been properly threatened. He won't be leaving the house."

Leighanna followed after her mother as they made their way to the waiting carriage. "What did you threaten him with?"

Her mother waved a dismissive hand. "Nothing with which you need concern yourself."

Leighanna pursed her lips but remained quiet.

Today, the sun shone high in the sky, the air brisk and filled with scents of spring as they fell heartily into March. She wouldn't let the doctor's words haunt her like Jessilyn Caine, or her mother's threats stop her from living.

After all, the note she'd received from the clockmaker that morning had already crushed her hopes once today.

Miss Pauley, he wrote.

I have phoned my acquaintance in London and jotted down his records. It is with great disappointment, however, that I am sending you only a half completed list of names. The comprehensive list of names of those who purchased the watch is no longer in his possession. However, he did have the most recent names.

Benedict Williams

Alvin Simmons

Lord Marques Barrington

There was another name listed, but only in part. I have included it as well, but I do not know how much assistance it will be to your inquiries.

N. Arthur B.

If you have any more concerns, you can send a note to the shop. I will try to gather any more pertinent information.

Ronald Jameson

The contents of the letter gave her a sliver of hope, but also more confusion. She struck Alvin Simmons off the possible list, but the other three could conceivably also be the moniker associated with the engraved *Papa B* on the inside of the pocket watch.

If only she knew who *Papa B* was. Maybe one of the mothers in society might recognize the names, but she feared showing the list to the wrong person.

"You're quiet," Mrs. Pauley said, jerking Leighanna out of her thoughts. She supposed it was rather unusual for her to be so quiet, but Leighanna's mind had been . . . occupied by more important matters than the niceties discussed between Etta and her mother.

Leighanna sighed. "Are you asking if I have anything untoward planned for this outing?"

She laughed. "I don't think you ever plan it, which is why you always end up in trouble."

"It would ruin the surprise," Leighanna agreed with a small smile. "I don't have anything on my calendar, so don't fret."

Something passed between mother and daughter that neither of them had felt in a while—something almost akin to peace and contentment. Leighanna knew, deep down, that she drove her mother to her wit's end. She also knew that if she did not do the things she did, she would drown beneath a false sense of self.

Before Leighanna's brush with death in December, she had hidden the girl she wanted to be. She had pushed her down deep inside her and crossed all her T's and dotted all her I's the way her mother had taught her. Almost dying had shown Leighanna she needed to write in her own font, not someone else's. But the wedge it drew between mother and daughter had suddenly gone from being a crack in the cobbles to a chasm.

However, the way her mother looked at her in this moment, with a soft gaze and an almost grin . . . Leighanna felt the way she used to, like her mother was proud to call Leighanna her daughter instead of angry at every choice she made. It was accompanied by an echo of profound sadness. She turned back toward the carriage window and watched the world slide past for the rest of the short trip until they pulled up to the modiste.

When they stepped inside, her mother already had a list of fabrics and colors. Too many of which included shades of pink Leighanna did not care for. She and Etta shared a look. "I can suggest some other colors to the assistant, if you would like?" Etta whispered, tugging on her jacket and straightening her clothes after the ride in the carriage.

"If you don't, I'm afraid I'll look like the prized pig at the rest of the balls this season," Leighanna whispered back.

Etta laughed, quickly hiding it behind her hand. "I'm sorry—"

"No, it's quite a funny picture. I'd be the first one they'd slaughter. Please, something in blue."

"Up on the dais, miss," the seamstress said, breaking up their conversation. Instead of the usual modiste, Madame Aubert, the seamstress today was a woman with dark hair and a pinched face. A lone freckle sat just above her lip. It twitched when Leighanna stepped onto the podium.

"Where's Michelle?" her mother asked as Etta walked up to Leighanna with three different reticules. Leighanna picked a purple one.

"Sick, ma'am. I'm happy to help you today."

Mrs. Pauley nodded, but Leighanna could tell her mother preferred the shop's owner over the dour substitute currently measuring Leighanna's waist.

"Would you like some tea, Mrs. Pauley?" a maid asked her mother.

"Your waist has expanded some since you last came in," the seamstress said. "According to the measurements Madame Aubert left."

Leighanna rolled her eyes. "Well, almost dying and then *living* really works up one's appetite."

"Have you heard of rib removal?" the seamstress asked.

Leighanna jerked free, anger churning in her belly. "I beg your pardon. I am a fine size," she said. "Rib removal is only a rumor! To do so for a smaller waist is too high a cost."

"What's the matter?" her mother said.

"She suggested I get my ribs removed!" Leighanna spat, letting her disgust for the practice shine through.

Her mother's face turned puce. "If you're going to comment on my daughter's figure, then we can come back after Madame Aubert ends your employment."

The seamstress gaped and threw down her measuring tape, stomping from the room. The maid rushed to pick up the abandoned tape, spouting off apologies. "I'm so sorry, Mrs. Pauley. She's only a temporary hire from London."

Mrs. Pauley straightened her skirt. "I think it best—"

"One dress, on the house. I will speak to Madame Aubert. She will surely take it from her pay. And the reticule your daughter picked is also included."

"Leighanna?" her mother asked. "We can go, if you want."

Leighanna shook her head. "No, it's fine. Can we try something in green?" she asked the maid as she stood atop the dais.

"Green?" her mother asked.

She knew her mother hated the color, even though Leighanna would love to have something in green to wear. She would've preferred blue, but she would take what she could get.

"Blue would suit you much better, miss," Etta said from the side.

"Blue?" Mrs. Pauley asked the seamstress. "What shades do you have? Nothing teal!"

"Of course not. The last dress that was ordered in teal . . ." The maid shook her head. "Well, it was for Miss Caine," the maid whispered. "She never picked up the dress, and Madame Aubert refuses to make anything in teal now."

"Jessilyn Caine bought a dress here?" Leighanna asked.

The maid shook her head. "I've said too much—"

"Leighanna, leave the girl alone."

"What dress?" Leighanna whispered when the maid got close

enough to finish her measurements. "Just the teal one?"

The maid looked back toward Mrs. Pauley. "No, ma'am, she ordered the dress she died in from Madame Aubert. But please don't tell anyone!"

Leighanna shook her head. "Of course not. Your secret is safe with me. Did Miss Caine say anything about the party when she was here for her measuring?"

The maid stretched the tape from Leighanna's shoulder to the tip of her finger. "She wasn't looking forward to the party, miss. She was going to see the man whose heart she broke. Was to be the first time they'd seen each other since it happened."

"Leighanna, let her do her job," her mother scolded, and Leighanna said no more.

The rest of the trip went as planned, and Leighanna walked away with three dresses ordered, only one of them in pink, and a new reticule in beautiful lavender.

"They'll arrive in time for the midseason ball at Lady Carmine's," the maid informed her mother. "Madame Aubert will put yours first on her list. I'll make sure of it."

"Mother, may I take Etta to the tea shop to meet Miss Lewis?" Leighanna asked as her mother billed the estate.

"Yes, that's quite all right." Her mother waved her away. Leighanna grabbed her maid's wrist and pushed out onto the street and toward the tea shop before her mother could catch up with her.

Leighanna walked into the tea shop with her new reticule and a mission. Victor noticed her from behind the bar and nodded toward the back hallway, where rooms reserved for private parties were situated.

"She reserved a room," Victor said. "Want me to bring you

anything?"

"Some macarons," Leighanna requested and walked back into the hallway, tugging Etta along behind her.

Gilded mirrors lined the long hallway, three doors on each side to break up the wall. She looked in every doorway before reaching the last door on the left where Rosalind sat beneath a window with a cup of tea angled toward her lips. She wore a jade dress and a matching hat, her gloves a soft cream.

"Miss Lewis," Leighanna said in greeting.

Rosalind turned to look at her. The white bandage from the accident at Morven Manor was no longer wrapped around her wrist.

"Hello, Miss Pauley. Care for a cup of tea?"

Leighanna took the seat across from Rosalind. Sunshine filtered through the window and shone down on the delicate tea set. Leighanna poured a cup and added some sugar and a dash of milk, the sound of her spoon hitting the porcelain the only thing filling the space. Victor came in and placed some macarons on the table before leaving them alone.

"I'm sure you're wondering why I called you here," Rosalind began.

Leighanna looked up and met her gaze. "Well, I have caused you harm and embarrassment, and I did use you for information."

A smile sprang to Rosalind's lips. "When you put it like that, even I question why we're here." The openness of her posture invited a laugh from Leighanna.

Rosalind opened her mouth to respond, but a gentle knock at the door stopped her. Both women turned to see Katrina standing in the doorway.

"Your mother said I could find you here," Katrina said in greeting.

Can I not get any time alone?

Rosalind's face turned reserved. "Miss Murray," she said, standing in greeting.

"May I join you?" Katrina asked.

"I have a private meeting with Miss Lewis." Leighanna stood and walked over to Katrina. She grabbed her arm and tugged her back toward the exit. "Are you sure you want to be part of this, Katrina?"

"Like I said, I'm not letting you do this alone anymore. I may not entirely agree with what you're doing, but I won't allow you to sink on your own." Katrina pushed around Leighanna and took a seat in front of Rosalind, fixing herself a cup of tea with the empty cup left sitting on the tray.

Leighanna sat in the remaining empty chair, turning away from the windows and toward the other girls as she picked up her tea cup. "Well?"

Rosalind raised a brow. "Are we sharing our information with her?"

Katrina pursed her lips.

"I suppose we are," Leighanna said into her cup.

Rosalind frowned. "Your fathers have been very vocal in their support of the police. Offering my knowledge to protect you is the least I can give." She paused and then whispered, as if in a room full of people, "I do not care who you involve, but no one can know this information came from me. You must promise me that."

"We understand," Leighanna said. "I was surprised to hear from you again. After . . ." Leighanna motioned toward Rosalind's wrist. Embarrassment and regret burned her cheeks.

Rosalind flexed her hand. "I thought about it a long time," she said. "But then I realized you were right. In your heart, anyway. That's why I'm here." Rosalind glanced toward the door before she pulled a folder from under the table and slid it across the surface to Leighanna.

"What is this?" Leighanna asked, hopeful it would be information from the police.

"The official police report. The very thing you were looking for the first time you called upon me. Were you in on that?" Rosalind asked Katrina.

"No."

Rosalind *hmmed* and picked up a macaron from the tray in front of her. "My father is not actively pursuing the case, and he's even talking with some people in London about turning the whole thing over to them since they dealt with the Ripper killings."

Leighanna opened the file.

"He would do that?"

Rosalind nodded. "Stornshire is too small. The community at large does not like to be reminded of what happened. It's something more apt to take place in London." She sipped her tea. "They say the murderer left a note," Rosalind said, moving on.

Leighanna arched a brow, and Katrina leaned in closer to Rosalind. "What did it say?" she asked.

"Well, I didn't read it verbatim, but Father's notes said the killing was very personal for the murderer. She was already dead when they found her," Rosalind said, drawing Leighanna's attention back to her as she dotted her lips with her fancy lace. "The stablehand saw someone rushing from the carriage house, but by the time the police came, the killer was already gone. They're struggling to create an image of the killer for the officers to search with. There wasn't much left at the scene. However, they do believe the killer to be male, based on the way he killed her. It was . . . personal."

"Can I keep the file?"

Rosalind laughed, the sound jilted and nervous, her eyes jerking toward the door once more. "A kind rookie officer was all too willing to give me the file, but I don't want his head on a pike. He's already bound to catch trouble for allowing me access to the file."

"Am I allowed to take notes?" Leighanna asked.

"Of course."

Leighanna pulled a small notebook from her reticule and flipped through the file, writing down all the information she could. The scratch of her pencil against paper filled the space and danced next to the awkwardness for a good five minutes before she looked up.

"The murderer mentioned his family and friends not seeing him for who he truly is, though he never said their names," Rosalind continued. "It said he had been hurt by the woman in question, turned down one too many times. Apparently, she had made a fool of him."

"*Hmm.*" Leighanna twirled her pencil. "The seamstress's maid said Jessalyn was meeting a man whose heart she'd broken."

"So that would match, yes. The lack of support from his family had driven him to this end." Rosalind took a sip of tea. "Father did tell me one thing when I questioned him on the matter—" Rosalind paused and added, "The letter isn't in there," as Leighanna began to flip through the contents of the file. "At the end of the letter, he said, 'I silenced one voice that saw me beneath the rest, and it was beautiful.'"

"How did she die?" Leighanna asked.

"Her throat was slit. Absolutely horrid."

Hearing it from Rosalind, even though she had seen Miss Caine's ghost twice now, made the ghost's memory even more vivid in her mind.

Leighanna returned her focus to the report, flipping through its pages as she took notes. "It says here she was visiting Stornshire for personal reasons, but they weren't clear on why. That matches what you just said, *and* what I learned at the modiste. The maid said Jessilyn was nervous about seeing the man whose heart she broke," Leighanna said. "But she wasn't from here, was she?"

"She's from up north, near Scotland," Rosalind answered. "Also, Mr. Abercrombie—that's the coroner, you see—said she had not been in the stables long. One of the stablehands found her when he went to get the carriage for a guest wishing to leave the party. The Carmines paid him handsomely to keep quiet."

Leighanna's throat was thick, words barely audible when she whispered, "Do they have any suspects?"

"Father doesn't have any names, but they suspect someone close to Jessilyn's family, though they can't be sure. She had many friends here, even though she was from Scotland and lived there most of her life. She used to stay in Stornshire with an aunt every season before she passed away a few years ago."

Leighanna nodded, half listening to Rosalind but mostly focused on what she was reading in the report. She paused and pointed at a line near the bottom. "It says the police found a hat at the scene. And a mask. A lion's mask that didn't belong to Miss Caine. Her mask was a deer. So the killer definitely *was* a guest at the party." Leighanna had assumed as much but it was a helpful confirmation.

"That's my understanding," Rosalind said.

"It leads straight back to the man Jessilyn told the seamstress about," Leighanna whispered.

If she hadn't already marked Victor off her suspect list, she could now. He had worked during the party, not been part of it and wouldn't have had a mask.

"They handed out masks to guests at the door with numbers to keep track of who had which," Katrina said. "I had a tiger's mask and was number fourteen. Instead of orange and black, the stripes were gold on a white fur."

"Yes, it matched the theme of the party, didn't it?" Leighanna asked.

Katrina nodded. "Yes, it was a white and gold party."

"Lord Carmine," Leighanna began slowly, sharing a look with Katrina, "he was once known to keep records of all events held on the estate. If that's true, then there will be information about the Christmas masquerade. We could obtain it. At the next party."

Rosalind nodded. "His wife is the one responsible for the record keeping now following his passing."

"Then we have a ball to attend," Leighanna said, a smile on her lips as she shut the police file and took a sip of her tea.

CHAPTER FOURTEEN
The Evidence Thickens

ARE YOU ATTENDING the Carmine ball?" Leighanna asked Jeremiah a few days later in her family's parlor. Sunlight filtered in through the open drapes and left trails of yellow and gold on the plush carpets beneath her feet. She fretted with the navy skirt and matching vest her mother had given in and bought her. Accompanied with a striped cream and gray blouse, she felt almost like herself, even if the sleeves were very puffy. She only wished she had worn a pair of August's trousers, like she did while gardening, to make her pacing less loud.

He looked up from his most recent sketch, the crinkle between his brow settling as he schooled his features and comprehended what she said. He wore a vest and no jacket, the sleeves of his shirts pushed up his forearms and his muscles flexing with each movement of his pencil.

"You are?" he asked, more curious than accusatory.

Leighanna nodded. "Of course I'm going." Her boots slapped

against the wooden boards of the sitting room floor. Her mother would be incensed to discover Leighanna's most recent *traipsing* around Stornshire. After learning the chosen mask of the partygoer who had killed Jessilyn Caine, Leighanna spent the following days searching all the reputable shops, trying to determine the one who had supplied the Carmines for the evening. Her boots began to feel too tight on her feet.

So far, her search hadn't been fruitful.

When she wasn't asking all the shops in the city for information, she was getting Katrina to ask other members of society, particularly the mothers, if they knew anything about whose heart Jessilyn Caine broke before her untimely demise.

Jeremiah brushed a loose strand of black hair from his face and tapped the end of his pencil in his sketchbook. Leighanna stopped pacing and walked over to where he sat on the other side of the coffee table. "We haven't talked in a few days. What are you working on—"

He pressed his sketchbook against his chest and out of her eyesight. "Nothing," he muttered, cheeks growing red.

"Oh, come on Jeremiah. Show me!" She tugged at his sketchbook.

"No. It's not ready yet." When Leighanna didn't let go of the book, he snapped, "Leighanna, I said no!"

She jerked back as if slapped. "I'm sorry. I didn't mean—"

He ran a hand through his hair and forced a laugh. "No, no. *I'm* sorry. I didn't mean to offend you, Leighanna," he said. "I'm—" He shook his head. "My apologies, truly. I'm under a lot of pressure to finish this sketch for my tutor, and I would hate for this one to be damaged before it has a chance—" He winced and stopped.

Leighanna's stomach knotted and her cheeks heated. She couldn't fault him for not forgiving her for what had happened at the conservatory.

Jeremiah cleared his throat and added, "And Casper is being . . . well, Casper."

Leighanna, grateful to shift the conversation to focus on someone else versus her failure as a friend, rolled her eyes and jumped at the chance. "You need not explain your cousin to me. He spends all his time at the warehouse with my brother, much to my mother's chagrin. At least it diverts her attention away from me. She hasn't pushed me to pick admirers this season." Embarrassment flooded her, and she found it difficult to look at Jeremiah. Her determination concerning the case hadn't given her enough time to think about Jeremiah and the affection she'd started to feel toward him before she grew ill.

She'd considered approaching her mother to suggest Jeremiah as a suitor, even if he was second in line to inherit the Barton estate, after Casper. Mother most likely wouldn't approve, but if Mother understood Jeremiah could make her happy, she might agree. But then Leighanna had fallen ill, and now finding a husband mattered a lot less than finding herself first.

Jeremiah smiled shyly, his worry washing away. "No suitors, truly?"

"Not yet," Leighanna said. "I've given her enough to worry about. Embarrassing her in front of eligible bachelors is the last thing she wants." She paused. "What of your aunt? Has she tried to set you up with any eligible ladies?"

"My aunt has been more focused on Casper, especially since the woman he was going to marry changed her mind. My aunt would rather society not know."

Leighanna gasped. "Casper was engaged?"

Jeremiah shifted in his seat. A wrinkle formed between his brow. "He'd been betrothed since we were children. They didn't choose one another. It was done quietly, a business deal, truly, to help her family get out of debt. Casper cared about her, but only after years of friendship." Panic overtook his features. "But you can't tell anyone, Leigh. I'm not supposed to mention it at all."

"I won't say anything." She shook her head. "The girl broke it off?" Leighanna asked.

He seemed to think something over for a moment before speaking. "Her father invested in a Californian Railroad in 1885. He paid back our family with interest using the money he profited." Jeremiah swallowed and looked down at his sketchbook. "Which is all information I only recently found out about. I didn't want to tell you before because it may make Casper look bad, but . . . with how much effort you've been putting into this case . . . I've been inspired that justice should be had, even at the expense—"

The butler walked in. "Miss Leighanna, you have a visitor."

Leighanna's heart raced. Was Jeremiah about to tell her that Casper had been engaged to Jessilyn Caine, and that the connection made him a suspect? Her skin prickled at the new information, though it wasn't yet confirmed. She forced herself to smile at the butler. "Thank you, Miles. Who is it?"

"Miss Murray."

Hopefully, Katrina would have information to rival what she had been about to learn. A door in the home slammed, and Leighanna jumped. She began to pace around the room once more. Katrina's voice echoed toward them, and Leighanna glanced at Jeremiah. He kept quiet around Katrina instead of speaking the way he did to Leighanna. If he had been hesitant to tell her about Casper's betrothal before, he wouldn't do it now.

But she needed to know if her assumption was correct.

Katrina walked in a cloud of sweet smelling perfume and fabric. Her crisp cream shirtwaist boasted sleeves with the proper amount of puff, and her hair was piled on her head in an array of curls that perfectly supported a small lavender hat that matched the skirt of the same color. Stan trailed after her, and Leighanna frowned. He mewed up at their new guest, and Katrina leaned down and picked him up. He immediately started purring.

"He likes you more than me," Leighanna said.

Katrina smiled, but it didn't quite meet her eyes. "Good afternoon, Mr. Barton," Katrina said.

Jeremiah raised his pencil in acknowledgement. "Miss Murray."

Katrina lifted a brow in Leighanna's direction, as if to ask, "Can he be trusted?"

"Miles?" Leighanna said, catching the butler before he could leave. "Can you bring us a fresh pot of tea? Maybe some more of those little cakes?"

"Of course, miss," he said with a small bow.

Katrina walked over and took the empty seat next to Leighanna. "Do you want me to tell you now?" she whispered.

"Once we get a fresh pot," Leighanna replied.

"What are you whispering about?" Jeremiah mock whispered in return. He closed his sketchbook and arched a brow at them. He looked eerily like his cousin in that moment, and it sent a chill down Leighanna's spine. Could Jeremiah be trusted? Or did his allegiance lie with his cousin? She didn't think he cared for Casper particularly, but sometimes Leighanna didn't care for August. However, only she was allowed to go against her brother. When others were involved she'd fight them tooth and nail. But would Jeremiah have told her about the betrothal if he was on Casper's side? Where did Jeremiah's loyalties lie?

Leighanna tutted at him to distract herself from the discomfort washing over her. Miles brought a fresh tray of sandwiches and a warm pot of tea. He refilled Leighanna and Jeremiah's cups and filled a fresh cup for Katrina before exiting with another swift bow.

As soon as he disappeared, Leighanna focused on Katrina. Since their conversation at the tea shop the week prior, Katrina's focus shifted from worrying about Leighanna's place in society to gossiping with the same people for information. When Katrina and Rosalind were around one another, which happened more now that Rosalind was giving Leighanna information from the police, the conversations were . . . interesting.

Tense.

Katrina pursed her lips at most things Rosalind said that didn't pertain to the case.

Rosalind rolled her eyes at society news not applicable to finding the killer.

It made Leighanna uncomfortable, but solving a murder seemed easier than broaching the subject of their distaste for one another.

"Well?" Leighanna motioned to Katrina. "What news do you have?"

Katrina sighed and pursed her lips, the same way she did when Rosalind was in the room.

"I didn't find out much, but I spoke to Grandmother."

"The best person to speak to, naturally." *If she corroborated the truth, even better.*

Katrina nodded and sipped her tea. Katrina's grandmother, Mrs. Williams, scared Leighanna, in the best way. She had old money but new ideas. She was the perfect balance of society and progression. She loved gossip, and she loved Katrina more. Since Katrina's stepmother couldn't have children, and Katrina was from her father's previous relationship, Mrs. Williams placed all of her interest in her granddaughter and finding her the best match.

Mrs. Williams's son—Katrina's maternal uncle—may have

married last season, but she remained ingrained in the culture of husband finding. Katrina's stepmother regularly spoke of her mother's interest in the women's progressive movement as distasteful. Mrs. Williams talked about it more to spite her. And seventeen years ago, when her daughter's husband brought a half-Black child with him, Katrina's grandmother began speaking out on equal rights in America. She was one of the best people Leighanna had ever met, and it made her sad she hadn't been there to hear her talk about what she knew regarding Jessilyn Caine's murder.

"Naturally," Katrina said, bringing Leighanna's mind back to the matter at hand. "She told me to tell you she misses you and you should have asked sooner, though she didn't know much."

Both Leighanna's brows lifted. "She didn't know?"

"She knew Jessilyn was from society," Katrina said. "But she didn't realize Jessilyn was marrying someone in Stornshire's society. She did learn, however—and much to her disappointment—Jessilyn was part Scottish."

"It amazes me your grandmother can be so progressive but still hates the Scots."

"She still has the memories of her grandfather speaking about the Battle of Culloden."

Leighanna sipped at her tea. "She realizes the English won, does she not?"

Katrina laughed through her nod. "Not that it matters. Anyway." She schooled her features. "She gave me a list of eligible men who might match the criteria for her betrothed, from the ages of sixteen—"

"Sixteen?"

"It's a list on parchment, not stone."

"Wouldn't sixteen be quite young, though?" Leighanna took the proffered paper and scanned the fifteen names. "Your cousin is on this list, Jeremiah."

The open door she needed.

Both women turned accusatory gazes on him. He took a sip of his tea, eyes averted.

Leighanna rose to her feet, and Stan's fur stood on end. He jumped from Katrina's lap, his back claws taking threads of her dress with him.

"Jeremiah . . . who was your cousin betrothed to?" Leighanna asked.

Jeremiah shifted in his seat. "I, uh, my aunt doesn't want us to speak of it—" He glanced at Katrina. Leighanna had been certain he'd been about to tell her before Katrina walked in. Her friend was making him uneasy.

Katrina cleared her throat. "Leighanna?"

The same uncertainty in Katrina's voice was mirrored in Leighanna's mind.

"Jeremiah," Leighanna began in a measured tone, "was Casper betrothed to Jessilyn Caine?"

Jeremiah looked behind her where Katrina had also risen from her seat. She backed away, as if terrified of the answer to the question Leighanna had posed. Leighanna didn't know what to think.

"He was . . ." Jeremiah said slowly.

Leighanna's head spun. The confirmation she needed, but no one would believe her, not over a man. She had to have concrete evidence before she went to the police. "And he had been at the Carmines' Christmas party, correct?"

Jeremiah nodded slowly.

Leighanna swallowed the knot in her throat. "Jeremiah, do you know what mask Casper wore that night?" She felt her heartbeat pounding in her ears. *Please don't say lion. Please . . .*

Jeremiah worked his jaw, thought for a moment, and then said, "A lion's mask."

Leighanna's stomach twisted into a thousand knots, and bile rose in her throat. As much as Casper annoyed her, the thought of a family friend being the murderer tore her insides to shreds.

Rosalind's words from the tea shop rang in her mind.

It said he had been hurt by the woman in question, turned down one too many times.

Before Leighanna got her family friend locked away, she needed to prove, without a shadow of doubt, that Casper Barton had killed Jessilyn Caine.

CHAPTER FIFTEEN
A Night at the Ring

LEIGHANNA KNOCKED on her brother's door after dinner the following night. March was quickly fading, and the truth still evaded her. She needed concrete proof outside of just Jeremiah's word that Casper had been wearing a lion mask at the party. Since others had worn it, it was possible he wasn't the one who killed Jessilyn Caine. She didn't *want* Casper to be guilty, but she did want justice. She didn't care if Casper was her brother's best mate, not if he had killed his betrothed.

Police were closing the case and sending all they had to the officials in London. Officially blaming the Ripper and encouraging society members that they were safe from the Ripper's clutches.

She'd said some words that would make her brother proud and her mother incensed when Leighanna read the newspaper. Luckily, only Etta had been around to hear her. It's why she needed to go to the docks tonight, not only because August was finally returning to the warehouse after his disastrous fight and could take her, but because she needed more answers. She suspected some of those answers might be found on the less than savory side of town. Her brother had the access she needed. She knew she'd need to go to Morven Manor to find the list of mask wearers, but hopefully she would find even more evidence to either point toward or away from Casper. The ball at Morven Manor was still days away.

Leighanna was lost in her thoughts when the door creaked open. It swung on its hinges, screeching, and the sound shot a spark of terror through her.

"August!" she gasped. "How are you?"

"Tired of Mother hovering and waiting for another wound to appear," he said.

She studied her brother. The bruises around his right eye and cheek were healed, and he stood straight as a line. He flashed her a grin, waving a hand down his torso. "I'm standing, aren't I? No broken bones. Only a broken spirit if I have to listen to her worry over me any longer."

Leighanna rolled her eyes.

"Are you well, Leigh?" he asked, gripping the doorframe. "Why are you wearing that?"

She glanced down at the skirt and blouse August had gotten her from the shop across from the warehouse. The blue blouse and brown skirt were a less conspicuous than her normal clothes. "Well, since you've seen me, I might as well tell you. I'm going with you to the warehouse."

He let out one sharp laugh. "No, you're not. Mother is already watching everywhere I go and everything I do."

"Then she has less time to watch me," she said.

"Not if you're following me around Stornshire." He walked out into the hall.

Leighanna found it easy to keep up with him as he walked

slowly down the stairs, the house all but silent other than their footsteps. It was the only night Leighanna could successfully sneak out with August because her mother was occupied with a society event, and she wasn't going to let him steal this chance.

"Mother is busy all night with the other mothers. This is the perfect night for me to go with you," she said as he grabbed his coat. She reached for his spare one, but he yanked it from her hands and placed it back on the rack.

"You can't go, Leigh. The carriage is full. I'm going with Casper, and your personalities suffocate me when in the same place."

She stiffened. "You can't go with Casper." She blurted out the plea before she had time to settle her features. The chances of him being a killer were as likely as him not being one, and Leighanna didn't want her brother around him.

Her brother turned on her with a confused smile. "I know you don't like him, but that doesn't mean I can't keep his company. He's coaching me tonight."

"Did you know Casper was engaged to Jessilyn Caine?" she blurted out in an effort to cause him to pause.

He huffed. "Yes, I did."

"You didn't think it pertinent to tell me?" Leighanna rested her hands on her hips and her forehead wrinkled with irritation.

He rolled his eyes and tapped the end of her nose. "Why would I tell you a man you dislike is no longer spoken for? Do you secretly harbor feelings for my dear friend?" He smiled wickedly, as if he had just got caught with cookie crumbs on his cheeks but had been able to steal the whole jar anyway.

"Don't be daft. I would be chuffed if he was off the market. One less man for Mother to try to force me upon, especially since I so dislike him."

"Casper is—"

"Why do you spend time with him, Auggie?" She hoped use of his childhood nickname might tap into some kind of familial connection they had, but he only rolled his eyes.

"He's my best mate."

"He dropped out of Oxford to do what? Pick fights with ragamuffins?"

August smiled. "I finished at Oxford, but I'm 'picking fights with ragamuffins' now, aren't I?"

"You also take care of Father's business."

"So I get an excuse because I completed my studies? Casper is only nine and ten. Do you even know why he dropped out of university?"

Leighanna opened her mouth to respond but closed it soon after, brows pinching.

"You should consider the cause before you judge the effect, dear sister," August said.

Stan walked up to them, meowing. He rubbed against Leighanna's skirt, and August leaned down and patted him on the head.

"I can't stay locked up in the house," Leighanna complained.

"Why do you want to come?"

She crossed her arms over her chest as August picked up Stan, and the cat began to purr.

"I have my reasons. None of them concern you."

He looked at her while he continued to pet the purring cat and said, "Your safety is my concern, and I cannot keep you in my sight while I'm in the ring—"

"I'll bring someone with me."

August placed Stan on the ground. "Have a good night, Leighanna," he said and opened the door, letting in the night air, the door closing behind him with a click.

Leighanna wasn't going to let her brother's orders to stay at home keep her there. After August had been gone for half an hour, she changed into a pair of black trousers, a striped gray vest, and a shirtwaist from the back of her father's closet. She stuffed her hair in a newsboy cap August had never seen her wear and smudged her face with dirt to try to hide her feminine features. She needed answers, and what better way to try and determine Casper's guilt or innocence than going to the place he spent most of his time.

Etta caught her as she tried to slip out the back door.

"Miss Leighanna?" she asked. "Where are you going?"

Leighanna's hand froze on the door handle and she slowly turned to face her maid. "Out, Etta," she said.

Etta's eyes widened. "Goodness gracious, Miss Leighanna, did you use the dirt in the flower pots to paint your face?" As if realizing she'd spoken out of turn, Etta covered her mouth with her hand, but Leighanna smiled.

"Yes, I did. Should I have used the dirt in the garden instead?"

Etta mumbled something under her breath and tightened her robe. "You can't—I would advise you not to go out alone, Miss Leighanna."

"Then put on some trousers and come with me. I'll wait."

Ten minutes later, two women dressed like men walked down the gloomy streets of Stornshire toward the warehouse. Leighanna hoped to find information either confirming or denying Casper's innocence or guilt. He spent most of his time at the warehouse, so it would only make sense for there to be more clues there, if she ran into the right people.

On foot, the five minute carriage ride took around fifteen minutes, but it was nothing Leighanna wasn't used to, and they made good time. The gas lamps lighting the warehouse created an eerie glow that rose around the muffled sound of men's voices. They went to the main entrance, but Victor was standing outside, so Leighanna tugged Etta to the back side of the warehouse facing the Thames. She didn't need anyone to recognize her, even if he might be on her side.

"Do the constables not police this area?" Etta asked, straightening her bowler hat.

"When gentlemen are involved, the rules are more relaxed."

"And what are we doing here, miss?" Etta asked when they stopped outside the back door, Leighanna's hand hovering on the handle and ready to pull it open.

"Looking for clues about Casper and his connection to Jessilyn Caine's death. I think . . . I think he may know something he's not telling us. That maybe he's . . . the one." Her words fell away, and Etta's eyes widened.

She grabbed Leighanna's wrist and squeezed. "Miss Leighanna, if you believe him to be the . . . to be involved . . . you can't—well, you shouldn't get involved. Your brother isn't around all the time. What if he's dangerous? If he is responsible, you don't know what he's capable of."

Leighanna had considered this, but it was more important to her that someone try to stop the killer from murdering again, especially if Casper was guilty and she could do something to prevent another death. The commissioner and his men weren't going to do it, but someone had to. She had to—but no one would listen to her without evidence.

"You don't have to join me, Etta. I don't expect that of you."

Etta huffed. "You do what you must. I will keep an eye out."

Leighanna wanted to reach over and wrap her maid in a hug, but she offered her a wide grin instead. "Thank you," she whispered and opened the warehouse door.

The roar of voices reached down the long back hallway. The two girls followed the sound to one of the three sets of double doors leading into the main area where the fights had already commenced. Leighanna peeked in the first doorway and found her brother in the ring. Sweat soaked his brow, and he wore a thin sleeveless white top. His suspenders hung from his belt loops, and he bounced on the balls of his feet as he circled his opponent.

But Leighanna turned her attention away from her brother to find Casper. He stood off to the side of the ring, around the rope barricade, yelling instructions at her brother. She slipped through the doorway then with Etta on her heels.

The girls shared a look and a nod before breaking apart and disappearing into the crowd. Leighanna studied the men around her as the fight picked up urgency, but her eyes always found their way back to Casper. She kept her ears open, but the only conversations she heard were about the men in the ring, not the man outside of it coaching. A cry rose from the crowd, and she stood on the tip of her boots to see August's opponent fall to the ring floor.

A countdown began, and Leighanna moved around the crowd. Casper shouted above the rest, but as the uproar reached seven, a man stepped up beside Casper and whispered in his ear. With his hair hanging over his brow, a look of immense concentration took over Casper's face.

The count reached ten, and Casper stepped down and disappeared into the crowd.

Where is he going?

Leighanna pushed through the crowd, heading in the opposite direction of the excitement. She made it through the melee as the rightmost set of doors swung shut. Her hand wrapped around the handle and pulled it open slowly enough to dampen the sound of the creaking hinges.

She peered down the hall and saw no sight of Casper. The echo of voices behind her made it impossible to hear anything else, so she slipped down the hall, toward the open doorway on her left.

When she was a few feet away, two voices sounded in front of her.

"Thank you." Casper's familiar voice sent shivers down her spine. "Did you find anything else?"

"No, sir," stuttered a small voice.

Leighanna stepped closer, peered in the crack between the door and the frame, and saw the blond pageboy, Charlie, from the day she visited the clockmaker. He stood in front of Casper, hopping from foot to foot.

"You're sure?" Casper asked the boy, voice sharp. "If there was anything else—"

Charlie fiercely shook his head. "I promise, sir, there was nothing else."

Casper remained quiet. Leighanna studied him through the small slit and watched as he stuffed something in his pocket and tossed the boy a coin in return. Someone or something slammed against the door at the very end of the hall, and Leighanna almost jumped out of her skin. She searched for a place to hide, trying multiple doors before she pushed into a darkened room.

Heart pounding against her ribs, she peeked into the hall in time to see her brother come with a few other men slapping him on the back and pushing the doors shut behind him.

"Casper!" her brother yelled. "Where have you run off to?"

The pageboy dashed down the hall, straight past Leighanna's door, and back out into the night. Casper started to talk, but before Leighanna could hear the entire sentence, she was grabbed from behind, a hand clamped over her mouth, and dragged into the room.

CHAPTER SIXTEEN
Secrets Between Siblings

L EIGHANNA YANKED BACK HER ELBOW and landed a blow in her captor's ribs. They let go of her with a grunt, and she dashed toward the door, only to find it jammed shut.

"Leighanna," someone coughed, and she turned around to see Jeremiah hovering in the corner. "It's me!"

"Jeremiah! What are you doing here?" she demanded.

He straightened and took a few deep breaths before coughing out, "I followed you here."

"You followed me?"

He nodded. "Why are *you* here?"

She glanced at the door. "How did you get in here?" she asked without answering his question.

He nodded toward the window. "I saw you come in, but I—I didn't want my cousin to see me. The window was open, and he could have heard. Sorry about grabbing you."

She ignored his apology and asked, "Why did you follow me?"

"You never said why you were here."

She straightened her vest and adjusted her hat on her head. "I think . . . well, I think Casper might have killed Jessilyn Caine, and I'm trying to find proof of his guilt or innocence, whichever is the truth."

Jeremiah cocked his head to the side as if he hadn't heard her. "Pardon?" he asked.

"Don't make me repeat it," she rushed to say, stepping closer to him. "It all fits. He was at the white and gold party with a lion mask, he has a motive, he's missing a pocket watch, and now he's talking suspiciously with pageboys. Something isn't right, and I'm going to prove it. If it's not him, the signs are sure pointing toward him."

Jeremiah frowned. "Do you suppose Casper capable of that? The killer has bypassed the police. It would take someone smart—"

"And Casper *is* smart. I know he dropped out of Oxford, but August said something tonight that made me think: why did your cousin drop out? What happened at Oxford?"

Jeremiah shook his head. "Leigh, he—"

"Do you know?" she demanded. If he had a pattern of behavior, then it would only be more evidence against him. To know he had done something similar before, even if not killing, but harming others. It made her stomach turn.

"It was nothing important. He doesn't need Oxford," Jeremiah said with a mild sneer. "He's got the family name on his side."

"Then why drop out? If he has the family name—"

"It saved his reputation," Jeremiah interrupted. "But it couldn't save his spot at the university. He was caught in a compromising position with one of the professor's daughters. He demanded my cousin either be expelled or leave on his own. If he hadn't been a Barton, he wouldn't have had a choice between the two. Could he have—"

The door flew open. Leighanna barely held in a yelp and spun around to see Etta slide into the room. Her maid's cheeks were flushed and her clothes wrinkled. Leighanna's hand flung to her chest, and she said, "Etta, you gave me a fright."

"I think your brother saw me," she said, but before they had time to make a plan, the door was yanked wider, and a very disgruntled August stood on the other side.

He reached into the room and grabbed Leighanna by the wrist. "What are you thinking?" he barked in her ear as he pulled her close.

She tried to pull away from him, but his grip was too strong. Jeremiah stepped back and tried to speak over her brother's grumbling, but August shouted, "Silence!"

Leighanna turned back toward her friend in time to see him pause. August pulled her out of the way and nodded to the door. Jeremiah took that as his order to leave and slipped into the hall.

"August," she said. She tried to pry his fingers off her wrist, but he wouldn't let go. "You're hurting me!"

He looked at his hand on her wrist and loosened his grip, but it was still too tight to yank herself free. Her boots scraped against the floor as he dragged her down the hall and out the back door of the warehouse. She wanted to scream and fight, and with every step, anger at her brother continued to simmer until it was threatening to boil over.

"August!" she shouted again, but he didn't stop.

She stumbled down the back stairs toward the street, a carriage already waiting. The March wind ruffled her hair beneath her hat, and she had to grab it with her free hand before it fell from her head. August ripped open the carriage door. When he waved at her to go inside, she stomped in and sat on the bench. Etta climbed in meekly, and he followed, slamming the door behind him.

They rode in silence for a few minutes, Leighanna chewing on the angry words she wanted to spew at her brother. But she counted to five hundred and felt her blood start to cool.

"Are you going to tell Mother?" Leighanna asked softly.

Her brother only shook his head. He rubbed the stubble beneath his chin and muttered under his breath. His knee bounced incessantly, and the only sounds that filled the carriage were his disgruntlement and the carriage wheels hitting the cobblestones. She had never seen him so upset.

"Please don't, August—" she found herself saying.

"If I tell her," he said slowly, "then you'd have to marry Jeremiah Barton by the end of tomorrow, and I won't have that. The only reason I found you *alone* with him is because I followed Etta. If she didn't force you to marry, she'd send you away, and I think I've already made it clear I don't want that either."

Leighanna wasn't ready to marry, but she bit her tongue and let her brother continue speaking.

"I told you not to come tonight, Leigh, and you did anyway. You almost caught yourself in a compromising position, and the only reason we're not rushing you to the altar is because anyone within reach will think they saw two"—he glanced at Etta—"three boys in the room. You've got to be more careful."

"I'm sorry, August. I didn't mean—"

"I'm not trying to tell you to abandon this mission you've set yourself on," he said with a wave of his hand, "but there was a reason I didn't want you to come tonight."

He paused, and when it looked as if he wasn't going to continue, Leighanna said, "Well? What is it?"

"Casper heard rumors that the man who attacked us last time was going to send someone to complete the job if I didn't win the fight tonight."

"August! You don't need to be on this side of Stornshire, much less getting mixed up with men who—"

His laughter silenced her words. "I handled it by telling the commissioner. They picked up the men before the fight started, Leigh, but you're one to talk about safety."

Instead of being angry about her brother's chastisement, her lips tugged into a small smile. "I suppose you have a point." She and Etta shared a look, and the maid hid a laugh behind her hand.

The carriage came to a halt in front of their home, and August sighed. "I won't tell Mother," he said. "But you have to promise me one thing . . ."

Leighanna was slow to ask. "What is it?"

"Next time I tell you not to come, trust me."

She nodded. "Very well. Can you answer something for me?" He waved his hand for her to continue. "Why was Casper talking to the pageboy, Charlie, after your fight?"

"What Casper does is not my concern, and it isn't yours either. You have such high standards for the man, and he falls short every time. He's a decent fellow."

It was on the tip of her tongue to tell him that Casper Barton might not be a decent fellow at all. That he might, in fact, be a murderer. But she couldn't, not without all the facts. Especially now. Not before she discovered what he was hiding—the information he received from the pageboy.

It gave her a new goal to pursue in her search for justice: she had to find the boy. "I have a bad feeling about him, August. I wish you could see reason. Would you at least tell me what Casper told you about leaving Oxford? You told me not to judge the effect without knowing the cause." Jeremiah had supplied the reason, but failed to give details.

August sighed and leaned against the carriage seat. "He left for personal reasons, Leighanna. Reasons he didn't want to share with me. However, he's in charge of his father's estate and keeps the books quite well. Father has done business with him, and he has no complaints, and that's a high endorsement."

"His family works in textiles. Father owns ships and railroads. He needs him for a multitude of things. Working with Casper is a *necessity*, not an endorsement."

August tapped her chin with his knuckle. "Father chooses to continue to use the Bartons for business, and I trust his judgment as much as I trust my gut. Let it go, Leigh."

Leighanna's hand hovered on the handle of the carriage door when he suddenly rested a hand on her arm. "And please, don't get caught in a compromising position with a man you're not willing to marry the next day."

Her mouth dried, even though he wasn't as serious as he was before when he mentioned it. Still, the idea caused her to pause. She felt affection toward Jeremiah, but her brother had a point. She wasn't ready to marry and wouldn't be for a while. She enjoyed her life as it was now, and August was correct: she needed to be more careful where men were concerned. Jessilyn Caine certainly hadn't expected to die at the hand of someone who supposedly cared for her, and Leighanna wouldn't put her life in the hands of anyone who didn't have her whole heart.

"I won't," Leighanna said, and this promise she meant to keep.

CHAPTER SEVENTEEN
Riding Pants
and Writing Lists

LEIGHANNA STOOD IN FRONT of her wardrobe, the floor-length looking glass next to it reflecting her in a plum skirt and vest, with a cream shirtwaist beneath. She straightened her hat, smiling to herself and nodding. The sleeves puffed at the shoulders, but they hugged her arms in a comforting way. The lace gloves added an extra touch, and she liked them more than she would admit to her mother.

Thinking of her mother, the absence of her in the home today filled all three floors with a welcomed silence and reprieve from her constant hovering.

Much to her mother's chagrin and Leighanna's pleasure, the women of society invited the former for tea toward the end of the week to discuss the progress of the unsuspecting eligible bachelors and bachelorettes they had tried to match. Leighanna hadn't been one of the girls they had focused on, but she'd heard her mother whispering about Katrina. When Leighanna asked, her mother had stopped talking. It was the first time she had seen her mother go silent. Not wishing to risk her mother turning the questions on her, Leighanna quickly found a reason to take her leave.

Now that her mother was occupied at the tea shop, and August at her father's offices, Leighanna found herself alone at home once again. She would not squander the opportunity.

She packed her carpet bag with a pair of trousers and a shirtwaist and vest combination, and Stan climbed into the bag when she turned her back to grab a pair of boots.

"Stan, you can't come with me this time. I'm looking for clues, and I have to stop by the clock shop." He meowed in response, and Leighanna's heart softened. Then a thought occurred to her. Maybe Stan *should* come. He seemed to notice . . . something Leighanna didn't. Could that help more than harm her chances while sneaking? Especially if he could see Death.

A chill ran through her. She didn't want to waste any of her cat's nine lives, but he might be a good alarm if danger was near. "Fine," she said, scratching behind his ears. Stan purred happily and settled at the bottom of her carpetbag. She placed the boots next to him, and he moved over the top of them, his paws stretching and claws extending.

"But you can't cry for sardines when I'm trying to find answers. Look for the guy with the hat and scissors instead."

He meowed again, and Leighanna took that as a yes.

Etta knocked on the door as she was zipping the bag up enough to allow Stan to peek through.

"Miss Leighanna, the carriage is ready."

Leighanna glanced over her shoulder and smiled, picking up the carpetbag and slinging it over her shoulder and walking out of the room. "Thank you, Etta. I'll grab my coat—"

"Miss Lewis and Miss Murray are also here."

Leighanna almost dropped Stan. "What are they doing here? I told them I would meet them at Rosalind's later today," she asked in a hushed whisper.

"They mentioned that," Etta agreed while Leighanna leaned over the staircase to try to see the girls. "Rosalind said her mother was meeting your mother at the tea shop. She didn't believe you would wait until the set time to go searching."

"I'm assuming Katrina agreed with her," Leighanna said.

Etta smiled apologetically. "I didn't know they could agree, but when it comes to you, they seem to have similar ideas."

"Lovely," Leighanna muttered. "Do you think I could escape out the back?"

"I believe Rosalind sent her driver to watch the back entrance."

Leighanna cursed and hefted the bag higher on her shoulder. Stan mewed in protest, and she reached back, patting him on the head. "Very well. Let us go and face whatever terror they are fraught with."

Etta handed Leighanna her reticule, which she wrapped around her wrist. The hum of voices she hadn't noticed before was eclipsed by a deafening silence. She stepped into the foyer and both girls turned to look at her. Rosalind wore a dress skirt and jacket the color of moss, and Katrina was dressed in a maroon dress that made her skin shine with a warm glow. Or maybe it was the anger rising in her cheeks.

"To what do I owe the pleasure?" Leighanna asked.

"Oh, please, spare us," Katrina said.

Rosalind turned to Katrina with a raised brow and an approving smile. No, this was not good. Leighanna couldn't have them both against her. It worked well for her when they were tense and sharp with each other, but if they started agreeing, then she would have to do something crazy, like find new friends, and it had been difficult enough to find them.

"Spare you what, Kat?" Leighanna asked.

Katrina rolled her eyes. "Whatever lies you are crafting. You have your carpetbag. You have Stan. You're up to something, and you don't need to go alone."

"I wasn't going alone. I have Etta." She turned to smile at the maid, who raised her hands in innocence.

"Miss Leighanna," she began, but Rosalind interrupted her.

"Don't worry your maid," the commissioner's daughter said. "We only wanted to join you. No need to change your plans."

Unlike Katrina, Rosalind didn't scoff. In fact, Leighanna hadn't noticed her hands behind her back until she pulled out a package wrapped in brown paper. "We brought you something."

"To try to get me to not go out?"

"No, to make going out easier," Rosalind said with a little laugh and held out the package.

Stan poked his head out of the carpet bag when Leighanna placed it on the floor. Leighanna untied the string and ripped through the package. She didn't know what to expect when she opened the box, but a new skirt wasn't it.

Two rows of buttons, one on each side that cut through the middle of each thigh, ran up the brown skirt.

"A new skirt," Leighanna said. "Thank you?" She didn't mean for the question mark to tag along because she was grateful, she supposed. The skirt wasn't a dreadful color, and it had a small pocket on the outside to store little things.

Rosalind laughed and took the package from her. She set the box down and pulled out the skirt. "I got your measurements from the modiste. She was more than happy to oblige. She said you wanted something in blue, but she thought brown might be more practical."

Rosalind placed the skirt on the table next to the doorway and began to undo the buttons on the left. "This way," she said, undoing one button at a time, "you won't have to wear your brother's trousers when running around Stornshire looking for clues."

Leighanna's jaw dropped. The skirt was no skirt—well, it was on the outside. But when Rosalind undid the left row of buttons, in the middle of the skirt was a pair of trousers.

She looked down at Leighanna and smiled. "You pull the fabric to the right side. My aunt lives in the country. She started wearing split skirts this year to ride horses. She said side-saddle is for ladies, and she is not. Not to say you aren't, but we know your mother would most likely prefer this to a pair of your brother's old trousers when walking the town."

Leighanna was so thrilled she reached over and hugged Rosalind. "Thank you!" she said. "I love them. Let me change."

It felt like Christmas. Though considering how well her last Christmas had gone, she had a lot of room to work with. She changed into her new—she didn't even know what they were called, but she loved them. The fabric was soft and light. The wooden buttons that lined both sides of her legs clicked against her thighs when she swooshed from side to side. She had never worn anything like it.

For the most part, her wardrobe was something to be tolerated. Like the color orange. It wasn't her favorite, but she learned to live with it. But this skirt was better than orange. To her, it felt like the brightest blue that always lifted her spirits. She could run in this skirt.

Admittedly, she might have to do some running if she ran into complications like she had at the warehouse.

She dashed down the stairs with a smile on her face. Her

stockings would have to keep her warm now that she lacked the same layers as Rosalind and Katrina.

"What do you think?" she asked the girls.

Rosalind smiled at her. "I've never seen a skirt fit anyone better. Now, are you going to tell us where we're headed?"

Leighanna wished her friends had trousers hidden in their skirts, as they slowed her down a little. But at the end of this journey, she would have to be the one to take the most steps.

And she did. Right into the alleyway across the street from the clockmaker's shop.

"You're going there again?" Katrina asked her.

"I need to talk to him about the list he sent me a while back. I asked him for an update. I'll only be a moment." She dashed across the street, carpet bag against her side and Stan meowing in protest, and into the shop before either of the girls could reply.

Neither of them followed, probably because the level of traffic on the cobblestone streets today exceeded others. The weather was nice and sunny, and Stornshire society took advantage of it.

Across from the clock shop, the windows of a second floor apartment building were being replaced with new glass. The shouting of the construction team echoed across the cobblestones. The sound deafened as she pushed into the clock shop, and then the door shut with a click behind her.

She walked to the counter and rang the bell. Stan poked his head out and meowed. Mr. Jameson popped up behind the counter, and a squeal escaped Leighanna's lips. He wore the same magnifying goggles he had the last time they had seen one another, but this time on his head and not on his eyes. His curly brown hair stuck out in all directions, and the grease stains on his apron traveled to his cheeks.

"Miss Pauley," he said. "A pleasure. A friend, I see." He nodded toward Stan.

"Mr. Jameson," she said in a slightly breathy voice. "I didn't realize you were right behind the counter."

The bell on the door rang, and another customer entered the shop.

"Be right with you!" Mr. Jameson called out. "Yes, I dropped my wrench. Now, what can I do for you today? Are you here to collect the information I found you?"

She nodded. "Thank you, Mr. Jameson," she said as he dove back under the counter.

The rustle of papers and the clanging of gears sounded behind the counter. He mumbled to himself—at least Leighanna assumed it was to himself because she couldn't understand a word—before reappearing with a folded piece of paper in his hand.

"Here you are, Miss Pauley," he said. "The information you asked after in your letter. I could only find three of the men mentioned, and they all have the watches in their possession. I've written their names and contact information below if you have any questions. I also included the name of the man I could not find."

Her fingers itched to open it and read, but she forced herself to wait. She needed to have all her clues sitting in a nice, neat pile in front of her before she jumped to conclusions. The girls would no doubt also like a say.

"I sincerely appreciate it, Mr. Jameson. What do I owe you?"

He tapped the end of his nose. "Not a thing. Think of me when you find another missing watch."

She smiled and walked backward to the door as the other customer stepped up to the counter. "Of course, Mr. Jameson," she said, and ran—at the speed of a lady—back outside.

Gray clouds rolled overhead. Leighanna felt the storm in the air, but that did not make her heart jump as much as the pageboy running away from the nearest carriage after catching a pence from its owner.

"Hey! Wait!" she shouted. She *knew* that boy—Charlie. He was the one from the warehouse.

Stan hissed, and jumped from the bag, darting in the opposite direction. Leighanna cursed under her breath and decided Stan was smart enough to find his way home. She took off after the boy.

Charlie paused and glanced back, blue eyes widening at the sight of her.

Then, he bolted.

Leighanna dashed after him, pushing through the crowd. She dropped the bag and released two buttons on her new skirt, stumbling as she did. Irritation threaded through her, but it was drowned out by determination.

The pageboy took the moment to glance back at her, with a smug grin that boiled her blood. While Leighanna continued to fuss with her buttons, Charlie ran straight into a cart of apples.

The last button came undone, and Leighanna gained on him at a sprint, careful to avoid the apples. Charlie rolled over and struggled to his feet, slipping on apples as the cart owner yelled in a thick South London accent. Ignoring the angry shouts, Charlie pushed through the crowd and into the open space in front of an apartment building. Up above, several men hung suspended in ropes, working to hoist a window up to the second story.

Suddenly, Stan darted up the street and stopped short, the hair on his back standing on end, and his eyes trained on a shadow near the alleyway.

Someone called Charlie's name, and he hesitated. At the sound of raised voices, Leighanna looked up. The window began to fall.

She charged toward Charlie. He didn't see her until she knocked him to the ground. The window fell and crashed where he had been standing moments before. Glass rained down on them, and Leighanna felt a few shards cut through the fabric of her clothes. She rolled over onto the cobbles, her breath coming in hacking coughs. Stan's whiskers tickled her face, and Charlie laid with his arms sprawled wide and his eyes round.

"You . . ." he huffed. "You . . ."

Leighanna sat up as Stan climbed into her lap and looked over her shoulder. She glanced back where he looked but no longer saw the shadow from earlier.

"I need to talk to you, Charlie," she told the boy, out of breath.

Charlie sat up with a groan. People rushed over, and Leighanna feared she would lose him in the melee. With one arm she grabbed Stan, and with the other she yanked the boy from the center of the crowd. They broke off into another run, her lungs burning. She ducked into an alley, Charlie's wrist in her firm grip and Stan squirming in her arm. She let the cat jump from her grasp, and he sat down at the lip of the alley, licking his paws and waiting for her to decide what to do next.

Leighanna propped her hands on her hips. Charlie's eyes roved from side to side, trying to find an exit, but determination weasled its way into Leighanna's chest. She would not let him pass.

"Miss—"

"You spoke to Mr. Casper Barton a few days ago. Why? What did you give him?"

Charlie's eyes continued to dart back and forth. A sheen of sweat shone near his hairline, and he brushed his hand through his dusty blond curls. "I didn't give him nothin', miss. Nothin'!"

She took a step closer. He flinched. The flap of her skirt

swayed near her leg, drawing the boy's attention. "I'm not here to hurt you. If I wanted to do you harm, I would have let that window fall on you."

He sniffed. Shrugged. "Why did you save me?"

"Because I could."

Charlie narrowed his gaze. "Now you want somethin' in return?" His fists clenched and unclenched.

"That's not why I saved you." Leighanna chose her words carefully. "You can go if you want." She swept a gloved hand out to show he could leave if he truly wanted. "But if you'll oblige me, I just need to ask you a few questions. I don't want to use you, but I do need your help."

"Why do you want to know what I gave him?" he asked.

"I believe it is a matter of life and death."

Fear widened his eyes. "I—why?"

"If you tell me what you gave Mr. Barton, I can answer that question myself."

He let out a deep breath. "He wanted me to steal something," he said.

"What did you steal?"

"He told me where it was. I didn't look at it."

Leighanna's brow furrowed. "Who did you steal from?"

Charlie backed away. "I can't—I can't tell you that. I could— no, I can't tell you."

"If you fear Mr. Barton—"

"I can't, miss," he said and broke into a run, rushing past her and disappearing around the corner before she could catch him.

CHAPTER EIGHTEEN
Trying to Spill the Tea

"L EIGHANNA! YOUR DRESSES ARE HERE!" her mother shouted from the first floor.

Stan purred in her lap as Leighanna wrote at her desk. The broken pocket watch sat next to her, taunting her, with the list of names from the clockmaker, as well as the list of men who still had possession of their watches. Only one name appeared on just one list.

N. Arthur B.

How was this name connected to Casper? She didn't know any Arthurs, which she assumed was the name of the man who originally had the watch, though it might not be the name he was given at birth.

Her mind wandered back to the pageboy and what he had stolen, but she couldn't make sense of the situation. What on earth could Casper Barton possibly need to steal? She shook the thought free and focused back on the list. Was Casper connected to N.

Arthur? Had he stolen the watch from the man? Did the B stand for Barton? How had he obtained the watch?

Not a single name on that list meant a thing to her. Or Katrina. Not even Rosalind knew any of the men listed. So, they decided Katrina and Rosalind would talk to Katrina's grandmother and the rest of the women in society. Leighanna would search for more clues. Someone had to know the entire name. It could very well be connected to the killer. Connected to Casper.

She didn't want it to be true. Her stomach turned at the thought, but if it was . . . it meant something had to be done.

But she couldn't take her assumptions to the police before she knew for sure if there was any connection. First, she needed to get her hands on something else: the assigned mask list from the night of the Christmas Ball at Morven Manor. If she had physical proof that Casper wore a lion mask, it would be one more mark against him.

"Leigh!"

A throat cleared behind her. She turned and faced Etta. "Sorry to intrude, miss—"

"Leighanna."

Etta laughed at the reminder. "Leighanna, then. Your mother said she needs you downstairs."

Leighanna sighed and rose from her desk. Muted sunlight pierced her lace curtains and created intricate patterns across her notes. She slammed the leather-bound book closed and secured it in her desk drawer before sliding her boots on and walking downstairs to her impatient mother.

The excited woman stood in the center of the sitting room with packages surrounding her. "Ah, darling. Your dresses are here." The butler held another small stack.

"I'll take those, Miles," Leighanna said, but her mother tutted.

"You'll do no such thing," she said, turning to the butler.

"Please take those into my room. Leighanna, I want to see at least one of them on you before you go back upstairs."

"Why can't I try them upstairs?"

"You may think I'm interested in nothing but presenting you in the best light to society, but I am not ignorant. If I send you back upstairs, I will lose you to your notebook and whatever schemes you are currently concocting."

It almost brought a smile to Leighanna's lips. "I'm concocting no schemes. I'm only searching for the truth."

"You are not to make trouble with whatever truth you are seeking," her mother said in a tone suggesting her daughter was nothing but a wayward lost cause, though the smile on her face hinted at affection. "Promise me?"

"Yes, Mother," Leighanna said. "I will not make trouble. I'm excited to attend the Carmines' ball and wouldn't want to ruin it for anyone."

Her mother nodded once, appeased. "Now, the ball is tomorrow, and we need to make sure the dresses fit perfectly. We might have time to go back to the modiste if we get there when she opens."

"Mother—"

Her mother narrowed her gaze. "Go try one dress on. You have to have something to wear besides that dreadful skirt Rosalind Lewis bought you. I don't care what the suffragettes say, women do not belong in trousers. I doubt that trend will still exist in the coming years. It's unseemly."

"I don't intend to wear the skirt Rosalind bought me, though it would please me more than anything," Leighanna said. "Even so, I don't understand why I can't wear one of the dresses I already own. The modiste wasted precious fabric on me, I fear."

"Please, Leighanna," Mother said.

Leighanna walked to her mother's room without another

complaint as the butler handed the dresses off to a maid. She sighed and stared at the three boxes lined up on her mother's desk. Etta trailed in after her.

"Which would you like to try first?" Etta asked.

"Open them all, and I'll pick the one Katrina would like the least."

Etta laughed under her breath and took the tops off all three boxes. Leighanna walked over to them, surprised that she liked what she saw. She liked them, actually. The one on the far left was a light green like the leaves in early spring. In the middle was the blue dress she had asked for. And lastly, on the right, a dress that took her breath away.

"It looks like a million pounds," Etta whispered.

Leighanna grazed her fingers over the high collar. White fabric, almost like a faux shirtwaist, rose from the neck and down in a sharp V at the front of the dress. It gave the appearance of a jacket, without having to wear one. Pearl buttons decorated the front, and the silver sleeves were only slightly puffed.

She pulled the silver dress from the box and let the short train brush against her boots. Etta took the dress from her and laid it across the loveseat in the corner. Leighanna's eyes locked on the sleeves, where they ended in lace, matching pearl buttons holding them together. Something about the dress seemed familiar, but she couldn't place it. Maybe it was a popular style she'd seen at parties.

"It's a bold piece," Etta said. "It would draw attention to you, for sure."

"But unlike the pink dresses, I actually like this one," Leighanna said. It reminded her of the woman in white she'd seen in her dreams when she'd nearly died so many months ago. Something about it tugged her back to that place of perseverance and fighting for her life. A shiver ran through her, and something crossed her mind she had never thought about—the touch of a cold hand and the brush of a warm one, at the same time.

"No," she whispered now, half certain she had whispered it then.

"Did you say something, Miss Leighanna?"

Leighanna's brow furrowed, and she turned to Etta. "Does the party have a theme?" she asked.

"Not this time," she said. "Would you like me to call upon Miss Murray—"

Leighanna waved off the suggestion. "Let's try on the blue dress," she said, tearing her eyes away from the other gown, almost feeling as if she were now the ghost in the room.

Leighanna stood in front of the looking glass in the blue dress the night of the party, its fabric not too light and not too dark. It had ivory buttons up the front, modest puffy sleeves—thank Heavens her mother hadn't insisted on too much puff—and a long skirt that ended right about the tip of her toes. She did a little shimmy in the dress, evoking a laugh from her maid.

Etta twisted her hair into a knot at the base of her neck. She pulled a few framing curls out of their hold and applied only a slight rouge to her cheeks.

"You better be glad I allowed any rouge, Etta," she said as there was a knock on her door.

Etta chuckled and ran to answer it. "You have a visitor, Miss Leighanna," she said.

"Who?" Leighanna asked, grabbing her shoes from their spot in the wardrobe.

"Mr. Barton," Etta said.

Leighanna's emotions went berserk. She didn't know whether to feel fear or relief. Her heart pounded against her ribs, and the dress suddenly felt too tight. "Which one?"

Through a grin—unaware of her mistress's distress that a possible murderer could be in their home—her maid replied, "The one you like."

Leighanna's pulse slowed, and she forced a mask of calm. "Perfect. He had mentioned riding with us to the party, but being so busy, I forgot to confirm with him. At least one of us hadn't forgotten."

She glanced in the looking glass one more time before sliding out of the room and down the stairs, where August held a glass of brandy in one hand and peered at Jeremiah. Her friend, however, held a cup of water between his forefinger and thumb, twirling the glass so the lemon floated around.

"How's the art life?" August arched a brow, and Jeremiah shifted from foot to foot.

"Fine. We've been practicing with live models recently."

August's eyes widened as he sipped his brandy. He smacked his lips after taking a sip, and Leighanna wanted to toss the rest of the glass in his face for bothering Jeremiah. Through a smirk, he asked, "So what do you draw with live models? People in the nude?"

At the moment August went to ask the question, Jeremiah lifted his cup up to his lips to take a sip. The sip of water stuck in his throat, and he choked. Leighanna lifted her hands to her lips to stifle her gasp as the butler rushed over and slapped Jeremiah on the back to steady his coughing.

August leaned in with a concerned pinch to his brow, and Jeremiah waved the butler away, coughing out the word, "Thanks."

Leighanna stomped over to the group. "Was asking him that really necessary?" she said behind gritted teeth and placed a gentle hand on Jeremiah's elbow. "Are you all right?"

Their eyes met, and a spark of happiness went through her. She felt as if she hadn't seen him in more than a few days. He was so occupied with his art, and she was determined to catch a killer.

He still coughed but was able to offer an encouraging smile. "Yes, I'm all right. But, no, I don't usually draw people . . ." He glanced at Leighanna. "Like that. There are some people who focus on those . . . *aspects* of the body . . . but I tend to be more drawn to a person's face. You can tell a lot about a person by their face." He turned to Leighanna. "Many people carry all their emotions here," he said with a hand to his cheek. "It's exciting to get a glimpse into that."

"That sounds wonderful, Mr. Barton," Leighanna said. She turned an accusing look on her brother. "Are you going to quiz him all night, or are we going to have a wonderful evening?"

August's smirk turned lethal, and he placed his brandy on the cart next to him. "I'll be on my best behavior, little sister."

"I'm sure," Leighanna muttered as a knock at the door alerted them to another guest.

A few seconds later, Casper and Katrina walked in. Leighanna's meal threatened to make an appearance at the sight of Katrina so close to the man she thought capable of murder. The same fear mirrored on Katrina's face. Her lips were stretched into a tight line, the gloves on her hands straining across her knuckles. Jeremiah shifted beside Leighanna.

"You took the carriage when I told you to wait on me, Jeremiah," Casper said, a scowl on his face. "Luckily, Miss Murray was kind enough to let me join her."

"Our carriage is already full," Leighanna said. "It looks as if you'll have to find another mode of transportation."

Casper's brow rose, and he took off his top hat and stared at her. "Would you have me walk to the party?"

"A carriage can only carry four—"

Casper smiled. "No bother. I'll ride next to the driver." He then turned and walked back outside.

Leighanna joined Katrina, lifting up her skirts to flash her the worn leather boots she wore with a smug smile that she knew Katrina would hate as Miles walked in with a tray of tea. Her stockings were white and in front of the whole world, and Katrina rolled her eyes. In the same moment, Stan came running in the room, on the tail of a mouse, with Etta's screams of distress trailing after him. Stan ran through Miles's legs and sent the tray of tea flying into the air. It landed with a thud and broke into a million pieces before Leighanna, splashing onto her exposed stockings.

"Ow!" Leighanna screamed and stumbled back. The hot tea sizzled through her white stockings and burned her skin. Katrina caught her before she fell, and Leighanna winced in pain. A curse that would horrify her mother if she had been able to hear her over the noise escaped her lips.

Her mother ran in, gasping with a hand clutched to her chest.

"Stan!" Katrina yelled, and the cat hid behind the curtains.

"It isn't his fault," Leighanna said, her legs prickling where the hot tea had landed.

August rushed to Leighanna's other side and helped her sit down on the couch next to the window. Etta rushed in with a wet cloth and a glass of milk. "This will help with the burn," she explained, as Miles stood off to the side, apologizing profusely before her mother dismissed him with a wave of her hand.

Mother sat down next to Leighanna. "Oh dear, this is not good at all. Are you all right?"

"I'm fine, Mother," she said, wincing when Etta took off her shoes and stockings and applied the wet cloth directly to her burn.

Another maid handed Etta a bowl, and she placed Leighanna's feet inside and poured the milk over the red area. "Better?"

Leighanna nodded. She studied the bottom of her dress. "Oh, just bloody wonderful."

"Leigh!" her mother chided.

She ignored her and continued saying, "I'll have to change—"

"Miss, I don't think you should go tonight—" Etta began, but she cut her off.

"No, I'm going. I can wear one of my other dresses."

"Leigh—" Katrina started to say.

"I'm going!" she interrupted. She had to go. If she didn't get the party guest list, then who knew what Casper would do, especially if he was the guilty party. There hadn't been another death. Would another soon take place? Did he need to kill again? Was it like a festering wound? Had the first kill broken the skin and infected him? And if so, how long until he was septic? She shuddered at the thought.

The information she had managed to discover had already taken long enough. "I'll go upstairs and change—"

Her mother stood and said, "Don't be silly. Going up the stairs will only make things worse. Etta, bring the dresses we bought down to my room."

Leighanna stood to her feet, the pain on her legs from the hot tea diminished now that they had cleaned it off. In her mother's room, Leighanna slipped out of the blue dress and waited in her undergarments, minus the stockings, as Etta went back out for a balm to rub on the burned part of her legs. If it hadn't been for her boots, more of her legs would have been injured, and then she'd never have been allowed to attend tonight.

Etta rushed back in with a lime-water liniment and bandages, wrapping them around Leighanna's ankles before helping her into the alabaster dress and fresh stockings.

"Did you decide on this one?" she asked her maid.

"You loved it, and you have a chance to wear it now."

A laugh escaped Leighanna as she slid into the dress. She stood in front of the looking glass and held up both sides of the skirt. A knock sounded. "The others have left, Leighanna," her mother called. "You'll ride with me."

Leighanna winced and answered. "I'm almost ready!" She turned to Etta. "I wish you could come with me."

Etta laughed. "I'm sorry to say this time you are on your own."

CHAPTER NINETEEN
In the Dead of Night

THEY WERE SILENT ON THE WAY to the party, other than her mother constantly asking her how her legs felt.

"Fine, Mother, like they felt when you asked me three minutes ago. We're almost to Morven Manor. Can you not mention the mishap when we get there?" Her mother rolled her eyes, and Leighanna smiled before saying, "Now, Mother, is rolling your eyes very ladylike?"

Before her mother could reply, the carriage came to a halt in front of Morven Manor. The driver swung down from the seat and opened the door for them, extending his hand to help Leighanna down first—though she was slow because of her legs. Her mother stepped down after her. The party was already in full swing, music and chatter wafting through the door. The windows were alight with the new gas lamps installed in the home.

They entered the home together, Leighanna limping slightly. Anxiety and uncertainty knotted in her gut. As soon as her feet hit the marble floors, she said, "I'm going to look for Katrina."

"Don't make a scene!" her mother snapped as Leighanna hobbled down the long, curving hallways leading to the ballroom.

The fabric of her skirt against the freshly injured part of her legs was irksome, even if her stockings had hindered complete burns and the ointment helped with the rest. The closer she got to the party, the louder the music became. She entered as another dance began. Freshly blooming flowers decorated all available surfaces, as beautiful as the guests' finery. She searched the crowd for Katrina. Even through the ache in her legs, determination rooted her to her mission.

Find Katrina.

She didn't notice people whispering and looking her way until she spotted Katrina in the corner with Rosalind.

Both of them turned to look at her, and Katrina's eyes widened. "What are you wearing?" Katrina asked.

Leighanna glanced down at her dress as if she had forgotten. She pushed thoughts of the ache in her legs away and flattened the skirt. "It's one of the new dresses my mother bought me. I actually liked this one, and—"

Katrina grabbed her wrist and pulled her to the corner of the ballroom. Leighanna winced as the skirt brushed against the burns again. "Do you have any idea what you're wearing?"

"A new dress—"

"Don't be daft, Leigh!"

Rosalind caught up to them with a glass of lemonade in her hand. "What's wrong with her dress?" she whispered.

"Do neither of you know what Jessilyn Caine was wearing at her death? It's all the mothers have been talking about."

They shared a look, and a sickening feeling began to turn Leighanna's stomach. "You're not saying . . ."

"The dress you're wearing is an exact replica of what Jessilyn

Caine wore the night she died, except for the color."

A nervous laugh bubbled up in Leighanna's chest and echoed down the long hall. After all she had been through, finding the watch, her brother almost being stabbed after one of his matches, and *seeing the ghost of a dead socialite*, the dress only made things worse. She could feel the burning gaze of the partygoers as she stood in the corner. To them, this dress was not small. This dress meant something. Unease wiggled its way between her ribs, and her skin prickled.

"You've got to be joking," she spat, wincing as she shifted on her feet. "That cheeky seamstress covering for Madame Aubert must have done it."

Katrina's face showed no humor. "You weren't at the party because you were—you were ill that night, but this is the *exact* dress, except in silver. If the seamstress *did* do this, you should report it!"

"To who? The police don't care about our wardrobe choices. But it's quite devilish of her to make me a replica of a dead girl's dress." The thought sent a chill from the tip of her head to the soles of her shoes.

Katrina said, "You're going to be the talk of the party, which means—"

"—I've got to get that list and leave. Soon."

"People will notice if you disappear after walking around wearing *that*," Katrina said. "You've made an entrance no one can ignore."

"Have you never heard of the word *distraction*?" A sly smile spread on Leighanna's lips.

Causing a distraction in the middle of a ballroom was something Leighanna would have been better suited to do than Katrina, considering Leighanna tended to make a scene wherever she went. The distraction became a necessity since she had yet to have a moment's reprieve from the guests' eyes following her.

They walked arm and arm to the center of the room, Leighanna with a slight limp. "You know what we have to do, don't you?" Leighanna whispered.

Katrina gulped. "We have to get into an argument?"

Leighanna bit back a smile. She glanced over her shoulder to where Rosalind hovered in the shadows, waiting to be their lookout as they slipped away for the diversion Leighanna had in mind. She glanced around carefully, taking in the lay of things. Lady Carmine sat in a chair at the head of the room, watching the dancers, whispering with her friends. They all focused on the girls as they stood in the center.

"Are you ready?" Leighanna whispered.

Before Katrina could complete one full nod, Leighanna ripped her arm away and said in a voice a little too loud to be considered polite, "How could you not tell me?" She stumbled at the sudden movement away from her friend, and gritted her teeth against the uncomfortable slice of pain on her legs. But she continued to play her part and stared at her friend.

If all eyes hadn't been on her before, they were now. Katrina played her part well. Her brown skin darkened at the cheeks, and she glanced around the room. "You didn't need to know, Leigh," she said, but not nearly as loud as Leighanna had.

"Of course I did! You're my friend. I should know these things," she said.

"We didn't want to upset you and—"

August pushed his way through the crowd. "You told her?" August asked Katrina.

Told me . . . what? She looked at Katrina then and saw horror cross her friend's features.

"August—"

"August?" Leighanna repeated. Her mind spun. Katrina's features were set, and the truth of Katrina's words wasn't shared between the girls. Katrina had a secret, and *August* knew it. How had Katrina and August—why did they—Leighanna shook her head, trying to make sense. "Since when—"

"We wanted to tell you, Leigh," August whispered, stepping closer to her. Leighanna looked for Jeremiah somewhere close by but didn't see him, nor did she see Casper. She stepped away from her brother, legs still stinging, but now her heart did, too. Did everyone know this *secret?* Was she the only one who was getting the shock? She wasn't even sure what to be shocked *about,* but secrets between her best friend and brother . . .

"Tell me *what*?" Leighanna asked, turning toward him.

Katrina and August shared a look. "You didn't tell her." Realization widened his eyes.

Katrina mouthed, "No." Either because she had tried to speak and no sound would come or because a part of her still hoped Leighanna couldn't hear her.

But Leighanna had indeed heard.

"What is he talking about?" she asked Katrina. A ringing began in her ears, and she turned to her brother with clenched fists and on weak legs when her friend still didn't answer her. "What are you talking about?"

"We—we'd like to—"

"We're courting, Leigh," Katrina said. "We spent time together when you were sick, and we wanted to court then, but with you sick . . .   But now, we haven't had much time, not with your . . . interests, and I've been trying to be understanding of it."

"Pardon?" This couldn't be true. Katrina and *August?* A crush was one thing, but to *court her brother*? Of all the men in Europe, Katrina chose *August*?

"We wanted to tell you—" Katrina began.

"How serious?" Leighanna interrupted. The couple—Leighanna couldn't believe she was thinking of them as a *couple*—shared a look. "Well?"

"We would like to explore where this goes, but we've all been so busy lately and haven't had time to—well, be together," August said. "Mother—I asked Mother not to say anything to you. She's said nothing to anyone. But Katrina and I have talked, and we want to continue to court, but Katrina was worried about you."

"Mother agreed? For everyone to lie to me? Everyone agreed that was *best*?"

August scoffed. "You have no time for anything other than your sleuthing. Of course she agreed," he whispered. "I gave Katrina the opportunity to talk to you." August glanced at Katrina, a look of disappointment spreading over his features.

Leighanna blinked and took a step back. Her brother had harbored an affection for her best friend. The pain in her legs didn't feel as stark now. "When did this happen?" Her voice rose to a pitch.

"You were ill, and we spent a lot of time together," Katrina explained. "I came to visit you every day. When you fell ill, he asked me to tea to update me on how you fared. We've been seeing each other since. Oh, don't look at me like that," she said when Leighanna made a face. "You didn't have time for me. I've only seen him a few times, and I was going to tell you, but—"

Leighanna laughed and stepped up to Katrina so the conversation was kept between the two of them. "You're blaming me for your betrayal? I almost died! You've had plenty of time to tell me before now." Her skin felt hot and sticky, as if her anger was rolling over her. The room grew stuffy, and she looked back at Rosalind in the shadows. Her eyes were as wide as tea plates. Leighanna took a step back and said, "You shouldn't have lied to me."

"All you do is judge me and everyone else! Of course I had to lie to you! All I want is your approval, and you thought August saw me as nothing but a little sister."

Silence hung over the room, and Leighanna blinked at Katrina. "I—Excuse *me*?"

Katrina's face was red, and she brushed her hair behind her ear. "Don't look at me like that, Leigh. You *know* you're like this. We never would have heard the end of it, and I didn't want to complicate my life any more. Having August was something *good*, and I didn't want to hear all the ways it wouldn't or shouldn't work."

Leighanna's mind reeled. "You're my *friend,* but you lied to me about courting my *brother*. Don't make me the one who should seek forgiveness."

"Things have been different since you got well," Katrina said quietly. "I'm sorry, Leigh."

Leighanna didn't want to deal with this anymore, not right now. Not when she had things to do, clues to find, and a murder to solve. Her mind spun. How could her brother and best friend do this to her without even speaking to her about it?

Stop it, she told herself. *Focus on the plan.*

She looked around the room, anywhere but at her friend and brother in front of her. Neither Jeremiah nor Casper were in sight, but she didn't have the luxury of finding either of them before proceeding the the next part of her scheme. She needed to get out of here, both to find the list and also because she didn't want to be around anyone right now, least of all August and Katrina. She started to leave the room on wobbly legs, but August stepped toward her.

"Don't follow me!" she said as the eyes of most of society

followed her as she limped out of the room and down the hall.

Her heart thundered in her ears, and she barely noticed Rosalind saying her name until they were back at the front of the manor. The pain in her legs was overshadowed by the betrayal burning her inside.

"Leighanna," Rosalind repeated. She grabbed her arm and pulled her to a stop.

Leighanna let out a tight breath. "Did you hear them? Courting! What . . . What is happening?" She placed her hand on her forehead.

"We don't have long to sneak up to Lady Carmine's study," Rosalind said. "Do I need to do it for you?"

Leighanna shook her head, trying to clear her mind so she could focus on finding the list and not the current predicament of her brother and Katrina *courting*. "No, I can do it. Do you know where the study is?"

Rosalind nodded. "My father questioned her in her study and one of the constables told me where I could find it."

Leighanna cracked a smile, and some of the anger and anxiety running through her veins subsided. "Lovely. Show me."

They turned toward the staircase and walked past the few older members of society wandering around the manor. Once they reached the top of the stairs, there were only a few people on the second floor, and by the time they made a few turns, they didn't see anyone else. Rosalind led Leighanna to the end of the hall on the back side of the manor. The large oak door had a gold handle shaped like the head of a lion, and a sense of foreboding rose the hairs on the back of Leighanna's neck. It almost distracted her from the scene downstairs.

Almost.

"I'll keep watch while you look," Rosalind said.

"If anyone comes, we need a signal."

"Am I supposed to caw like a bird?" Rosalind asked with a furrowed brow.

"Something!" Leighanna said. "A word, maybe? Like, bloody cat."

"Bloody cat?"

"Who's to say the Carmines don't have a cat?" Without waiting for Rosalind to come up with another idea, Leighanna slipped inside the study. The curtains were partially open, and the light from the new street lamps installed a few weeks ago created interesting shadows on the floors. Leighanna stepped farther into the room and almost ran into a piece of furniture she hadn't noticed.

A small yelp escaped her lips, and she winced as she stumbled. The door creaked open, and she jumped, but heard Rosalind ask, "Are you okay?"

Leighanna turned to the sound of Rosalind's voice and said, "Keep watch!"

The door slipped shut, and Leighanna walked to the desk with more care. Only the top drawer was locked. She searched through the others for a key, but with no success. Disappointed, she rustled through the papers in the open drawers, but all she found were receipts for Lady Carmine's wardrobe.

She crossed the room to the wall of books. The upper half was shelves and the lower half supported a small counter with drawers beneath it. The top two drawers were locked, so she tried the bottom one.

A gasp fell from her lips. There were boxes filled with files. She opened the first and found receipts with items most likely used at any of the Carmine's parties. With the date of the party in her mind, she riffled through the receipts until she found the file she was looking for. The list of masks was stored in a folder wrapped closed with a string. She untied it and read the pages. It listed who got what and which ones were returned.

"Why didn't she give this to the police?" she whispered, but then she knew why.

The information was only half complete. Instead of names, each person was given a number at the party. Not all the numbers were present.

Leighanna huffed under her breath. It was *just* like the Carmines to make things as complicated as possible. But considering they were the sort of people to hire Victor to spy on their guests, perhaps they had other misdealings going on that required them to make the guest and mask lists so complicated. She would need to figure out what names corresponded with which mask number.

The constable who had gotten Rosalind information hadn't included the fact that some numbers were missing in the report. They blamed the Ripper and ignored all the other evidence. Leighanna couldn't ignore this, and when she found the truth, she wouldn't let them continue to ignore the other evidence either.

She used the nearest pencil to write down the missing numbers on a scrap piece of paper before stuffing the files back inside the box. She shut the drawer as quietly as possible. As she stood to leave, voices sounded outside the door.

She froze and waited for Rosalind's cue, but it never came. In a few more moments, the sound of footsteps leading away from the office filled her ears, and a curse slipped past her lips. With her heart in her throat and beating so fast it drowned out all other sound, she moved to exit when the door cracked open. She ducked beneath the desk and pulled the chair in front of her so the expanse of her skirts were tucked up around her, her spine pressed firmly into the front of the desk.

Someone moved into the room. It wasn't Rosalind. She would

have announced herself with their code word.

Could it be the killer? Why did Rosalind leave her post? Leighanna covered her mouth with her hand to try to dampen the sound of her breathing. She didn't want to assume the person on the other side of the desk was safe. Movement next to the window caught her attention, and she turned and saw the man with the top hat—Death. Their eyes met, and he held his finger up to his lips. Fear pulsed in her veins, and she curled in on herself under the desk. Her legs ached, but the urgency coursing through her took care of most of the pain.

The floor creaked with every footfall, and a line of sweat started to drip down her spine. Death walked around the desk so she could no longer see him. She swallowed the lump in her throat and bit the inside of her cheek to keep from speaking. Every bone in her body fought against the instinct to pop out of hiding and run. Something about the way the figure moved into the room, in the cloak of darkness, seemed sinister.

She itched to look up and see the face of her visitor. She didn't know for sure whose face she would see, but it could be that of a killer —and she was a woman alone in a room where she shouldn't be.

A shadow passed over the desk, and if it weren't for the chair hiding her, she would easily be caught.

Like she had, the intruder fiddled with the desk handles with the same level of success. The shadow moved farther away, and Leighanna's shoulders dropped only slightly. She heard the ruffling of papers and knew the intruder was looking through the same information she had. It grew quiet for a long moment, almost long enough to convince her the intruder had left, when the sudden crack of the drawer being slammed shut sounded around the room. There was a loud crash, as if he was kicking the wall.

He's angry.

She bit down on her tongue until the pain kept her fear from revealing her hiding spot. Her legs burned again, as if all the blood was rushing to the injury to remind her she was still alive. For now —while in the room with a possible killer. The footsteps rushed toward the door, and the thud of the door shutting drew a yelp from her.

But whoever had interrupted her search was gone.

Leighanna waited a few more minutes before climbing out of her hiding spot. Both Death and the intruder were gone. She searched all corners of the shadowed room for signs of anything out of place before going back to the drawer. She opened it and peered inside. The papers looked nearly the same as they had when she had put them back. A stack with information about the Christmas party was near the top. Her fingers flipped through the papers. Everything was still where it should have been.

Except for one sheet. Now, the remaining paper listing the numbers that correlated with the masks was gone.

Leighanna didn't stay at the party much longer. She found Rosalind downstairs with a worried tilt to her lips outside the ballroom.

"I'm so sorry, Leighanna. One of the maids asked if I was lost, and I didn't want to give you away—"

She grabbed her wrist to quiet her. "Casper was just upstairs, looking through the files I found in a drawer."

Rosalind froze. "You saw him?"

"Well," she whispered, "someone was in that room, and it could have been Casper. Do you see him now?"

They peered into the ballroom as another dance began. Katrina and August stood off to the side in a deep conversation while Casper and a young girl stood in the corner. Casper's entire body was seized with tension, from the pinched purse of his lips to the tapping of his foot against marble. His chest rose and fell rapidly . . . as if he'd just ran back to the party.

"There," Rosalind said. "You don't think he'd hurt the girl next to him, do you?"

"Not in front of everyone," Leighanna said. "But we need to leave."

Anger pulsed through Leighanna's veins. The new courtship was impeding her investigation. As if she needed something else to stress about. However, the unwanted news was a temporary balm to the fear of being in the same room as Jessilyn Caine's killer.

"Have you seen Jeremiah?" she asked.

"I haven't. I saw him in the hall looking for Casper when the maid was leading me back here, but not since then."

Leighanna shook her head. "Whoever was in that office was upset. The list was incomplete. The Carmines used a number system to keep up with the masks."

"Do you think we could get a copy of who had which mask from one of the servants? Maybe she stores her files somewhere else," Rosalind said.

"Or I can ask your father if he knows?"

"I doubt he'd tell me. I can try, but if I can't, what are we going to do?"

"I'm not sure," Leighanna said. "We can't do it tonight. Meet me at the tea shop next week? Maybe you can get the list that's missing from your father so we can check to see who had the lion masks."

"Very well, I'll try. Are you ready to go? I can ask my driver to take you home."

Leighanna searched the crowd for her mother. She hovered at the lemonade table and turned her sharp gaze to Leighanna as if she had felt her eyes on her. Anger bloomed in her mother's cheeks, and it didn't take much of a guess to know Mrs. Pauley had seen the argument in the center of the ballroom.

Leighanna nodded and said, "Unless I want to be stuck in this crowd all night." She found Katrina's gaze among the partygoers. Their eyes locked before Leighanna broke the hold. "And I most certainly do not want to get stuck here. My mother looks ready to leave, anyway. Or yell at me. Whichever comes first."

Rosalind disappeared around the corner and asked a nearby maid to fetch her carriage. Leighanna trailed after and caught the end of their conversation.

"I'm sorry, miss, but you'll have to wait a moment for them to fetch your carriage. They've been having trouble with the horses at night, and the stablehands just went around back to calm them so as not to disrupt the party."

"What kind of problems? Are they still getting spooked?" Leighanna asked. Her mother walked up behind her and took hold of her wrist.

"I trust you're ready to leave," Mother said, her grip a little too tight, but now Leighanna's attention was on the maid.

The maid looked at her with wide eyes. "Yes, miss. About the same time every night they go mad in their stalls. No one knows why," she said.

Leighanna's mind spun. When she had come to Morven Manor and found the watch, the horses had spooked then, too. Before she could share her thoughts with anyone, she turned toward the back of the manor and ran as fast as propriety—and her burning legs—would allow. Even her mother's cries didn't slow her down. She cut around the ballroom and back toward the kitchens. She ran through the bustling servants going in and out of the swinging doors with trays of food and almost ran into the nearest waiter.

Déjà vu overcame her as the clock in the hallway struck midnight, and the world around her began to slow.

"Miss!" someone shouted, but she kept going until she broke through the back door of the manor facing the stables.

The frantic neighing of the horses in their stalls grew louder as Leighanna ran across the grass and toward the sound. A horse burst from the stable, galloping toward her, but then it stopped, eyes white and wide, frozen in time. The breath from its snout curled suspended in the air. Time stood still all around Leighanna.

A woman covered in blood stepped out from behind the still horse. Leighanna had never noticed the details of the dress before since it was so bloody and torn. But around the tears and through the stains, the sleeves looked similar to her own. The rest was red.

"He's here," the ghost said in a choked voice. Her eyes bugged from her skull and she stared at Leighanna for a full minute before running toward her. Leighanna froze and waited, but Jessilyn Caine didn't stop, not even when she ran *through* Leighanna and back toward the manor. An icy cold gust passed through Leighanna's body and shook her to her marrow. She fell in the grass and looked back over her shoulder. She expected to see Jessilyn in her ghostly glory, but instead, her dress was now absent of blood and her hands hovered around her neck.

"You're going to catch him. That's what Death said," Jessilyn told her. "You will stop my killer."

Leighanna nodded, pride and determination swelling in her core. Jessilyn let out a breath, a small smile on her lips. Next to her stood a woman with wild red curls in trousers and a shirtwaist without sleeves. The redhead looked at the ghost, then at Leighanna.

"Interesting," the redhead said before snapping her fingers.

Time started back up again, and air rushed into Leighanna's lungs. The horse that had been frozen resumed its run, then slowed until it stopped completely. Both the ghost and red-headed woman disappeared. Leighanna's heart threatened to break through her ribs, almost more painful than the tuberculosis had been. Questions spun in her mind.

Did Death really believe she could catch the killer? Was Jessilyn able to act more normal because Leighanna was close to the truth?

Rosalind and Katrina ran from the house and through the grass. Relief warred with disappointment in Leighanna's core. Any chance at getting answers from these supernatural people she kept seeing was gone—for now, anyways. Would they even be able to give her answers at all?

"Leighanna," Rosalind shouted and ran over to her with Katrina on her heels. "Leighanna, are you all right?" But Leighanna couldn't speak. Her mother came rushing out, face redder than the blood on the dead girl's body, and fussed and scolded. But Leighanna didn't really hear her.

All she could think about was the ghost and a woman who had restarted time.

CHAPTER TWENTY
Another Murder

EATH HATED ATTENDING A MURDER. He knew the sentiment to be selfish, because as difficult as it was for him to bring the deceased over after such a gruesome end, it was exponentially more difficult for the one being murdered. In a perfect world, violence would not end lives. But perfect worlds did not exist.

Instead, he took some of their pain in himself and wore it. The shadows followed him for eternity.

He could smell the anger wafting down the alley. He'd hovered in the darkness, watching Leighanna Pauley as she looked through the Carmines' records. He shouldn't have, but he felt the murderer on her heels. The killer wouldn't end Leighanna, not yet. She knew too much, but the killer didn't know how much.

Death knew how close the killer had been to discovering Leighanna under that desk. He felt the tug of her strings pulling him into the dark office, and he held his breath as he watched the killer open the same drawers Leighanna had. The killer's face was masked in the shadows so even Death himself could not discern who he was.

What Leighanna must have heard, but did not feel like Death could, was the anger that followed.

The anger led the killer here, to this alley. To kill again. But there was also a hunger, a yearning that hadn't been there when Jessilyn had died. The desire hung like a fog over the dead girl's body.

The teenage girl died in an alleyway near the Thames, leaning against the nearest wall with a ring of red around her neck where the life seeped from her and onto the cobblestones. However, something about the way he placed her on the wall showed care, an attention to detail. It chilled Death to see how much she looked like Leighanna. He knew the killer could sense Leighanna growing closer to the answer of who had ended Jessilyn Caine's life. This girl, this kill, was nothing more than a burst of anger and impatience.

Anger directed at the girl the killer could not touch.

Not yet.

He was still too much of a coward for that.

Remnants of Death's unexpected friend, Life, clung in the air, as if she had wanted to be called but there wasn't enough of a pull. The police would not arrive for some time, and the girl had already suffered long enough. Death felt it when he drew closer.

The ghost of the girl turned her eyes toward Death, and he took off his hat and set it on the ground beside her. The collar of her gray dress was soaked in blood, and the train was covered in mud and muck from the street. Her nails were half ripped from their beds, and remnants of her killer's skin clung to them.

"That will leave a mark," he told her.

Death held out his hand, and her soul reached for him. As soon as they touched, the rest of her was ripped from the already decaying body, and the ghost-like soul stood next to him. The dead girl let out a long breath. "Thank you," she said.

"You needn't thank me."

But a soul's first words after death mattered, and this girl, brutally taken from the clutches of life, had chosen to thank him rather than curse her killer. It made the exchange, Death's presence at the scene, feel all the more sad.

This death reeked of Jessilyn Caine's end, though it lacked the personal touch Death assumed would have been there if the victim had been Leighanna Pauley like he suspected the killer desired. But the killer had laid the body against the wall with the same care and attention to detail he treated the society girl with. She had the same slice in her throat as his first victim. The way he'd hidden her was as if her death was for his eyes alone. People would remember it when the papers plastered the story across the top of the Stornshire Gazette. But one thing remained different—the killer had simply been angry when he'd slaughtered Jessilyn, but he'd been *hungry* for Leighanna when he ended this girl.

Leighanna was right. The Ripper killings in London made the Ripper infamous. Some remembered the women he murdered, but not in the same way they remembered the man who did the killing —even if his true identity hadn't been discovered. But Death remembered. He remembered every name. Every word they said as they grabbed his hand for the first time.

The ghost of the dead girl, Rachel Martin, turned away from her body, looking up at him. In this new form, she did not retain the evidence of death, not like Jessilyn Caine. This girl had already said goodbye to the memory of her murder, whereas Jessilyn clung to it and demanded to know answers. This girl's neck was whole, and she had a light in her eyes that hinted at where she would go once Death pushed her into the place beyond the inbetween.

"Do you remember?" Death asked Rachel.

"Remember what?" she asked, a slight smile on her lips.

"Who did this to you?" He didn't look at her body when he asked the question, but she did.

"I don't . . . I don't think I want to," she answered. "I would like to go, please." It made her different from Jessilyn Caine. Jessilyn had run after her murderer, and that's why he couldn't push her over into the next life. She had wanted to stay here, to search for the answer to the question she could never ask through the gurgle of blood.

Rachel didn't want to know why the killer had chosen her. She wanted to escape the pain and enjoy the life beyond.

Death, never one to refuse a dying wish, released Rachel's hand, and she disappeared as smoke does when a brisk breeze blows past. Acceptance settled in Death's chest, and he bent to pick up his hat and place it on his head, grimacing to himself.

Leighanna's life, which should have been snuffed out on Christmas night nearly a quarter of a year ago, bothered him. It made him question not how he did his job but why. He was helping them, yes, but could he—no, could this girl who accidentally cheated him —do something more for those gone too soon? Would it help make others' lives longer? Because Death wouldn't mind taking his hat off at houses filled with love and years a little more often.

He glanced back at the girl's empty body once more, noting the piece of paper gripped in her palm. He couldn't move it, but curiosity drew him closer. Whatever the killer had written inside was smudged with blood, but he recognized the paper.

"Life?" he whispered, wishing she could respond to his call, but knowing she never would. They were opposites, but it didn't stop him from wondering if she could read the paper in Rachel's hand.

She didn't appear.

Not when he called. He had no life to tempt her with.

Only death remained in this place.

So, Death stood once more and answered the call of another, suddenly wishing he had never stopped to look back.

CHAPTER TWENTY-ONE
Thicker Than Thieves

L EIGHANNA WAS SITTING AT HER DESK when her mother rushed into the room, still wearing her dressing gown. The bags under her eyes showed she hadn't slept the night before. None of it surprised Leighanna, though she had expected her mother would fuss about the spectacle she had made at the party.

"I've been up all night, Leighanna," her mother said, pacing the floor next to the bed. "All night thinking about how this could have gone differently. How I"—she placed a hand on her chest—"could have done better as a mother. But I cannot fathom where I went wrong."

"Mother—"

She raised her hand. In the other was the day's paper. "I'm done, Leighanna. I've had enough. I told you to stop making such a spectacle of yourself, and the first party you go to you end up sprawled in the Carmines' backyard where all of society could see you. I don't know what you consumed besides utter disregard for any of my rules and wishes."

"I didn't mean—" Leighanna stood and took a step toward her mother, but she slashed her hand through the air, cutting off her words.

"You never mean it, Leighanna." She didn't shout. Leighanna almost wished she would. Instead, she spoke softly, dejectedly. "But I do mean this. Pack your things. You have one week, and then you are going to live with your aunt."

"Mother!"

"Say your goodbyes, but I've had it. We are done pretending like you ever listen—"

"So you're sending me away?" Leighanna shouted.

Stan ran out from underneath her bed and out of the room. He passed her mother, tail thwacking against her calves. Her mother let out a little yelp of surprise and threw the paper in her hands at her daughter's feet.

Leighanna picked up the paper, the black writing on the front catching her gaze. Her throat went dry as she read the words. At her mother's sniff, Leighanna glanced up and saw her wipe moisture from her eyes. Tears of her own threatened to fall, but she held them in until her chest ached; these were not tears of sadness but of anger. And fear. The killer had struck again—why? The thought sent ice dripping down her spine.

"Another girl has been murdered," Leighanna whispered.

"Exactly. More the reason to send you away," her mother said, and Leighanna stepped closer, grabbing her mother's wrist.

"Please, Mother, please don't send me away. This is the reason why I have to stay!" She waved the paper in her mother's face.

Her mother yanked it away and made a show of ripping it down the middle and throwing it on the floor. "I am sick of hearing about this case of yours, Leighanna. I let you have your fun, but this is not fun or a game. This is real life, and you are risking yours.

You've made a mess of your reputation, but I will not have you end up dead."

The two stared at each other for a long moment. Her mother's shoulders sagged, and she rubbed her eyes with her manicured fingers. "Your aunt is expecting you," she said. "You can take Stan."

Then before Leighanna could plead her case any further, her mother left the room, slamming the door shut behind her.

Leighanna's mind whirled as she rode in her carriage to Katrina's home. What had happened between them the night before haunted her as much as Jessilyn's ghost did, and she wanted—needed—to talk to her longtime friend. Her best friend. If only she could get her mind to slow down and stop repeating the missive a pageboy had delivered from Rosalind.

Father refused me the list, Rosalind wrote in her neat script. *But I fear asking Miss Murray to obtain the list from Lady Carmine would only cause more strife between you two. I can ask another.*

Leighanna hadn't bothered to write her back. If one constable said no, then all the others would. So Leighanna had made a decision; she needed to not only apologize to Katrina for her behavior, but she also needed her help.

Another thought plagued her: One week. She only had one week to prove Casper's guilt before she was whisked away to the country.

She arrived at the Murrays' home as the clock struck nine in the morning and was ushered in by a maid into the Murrays' sitting room. A cup of tea sat on the table in front of her spot on the faded patterned couch, steadily growing cold.

Katrina's home always felt more welcoming than Leighanna's own, in a way, because of the trinkets from the family's travels. It told the story of a family that spent time together and presented that in everything they did. When Leighanna's father had brought her back a cornhusk doll made by a Cherokee woman from his trip to the mountains in the southern states, her mother had made Leighanna keep the toy in her room alongside all the rest rather than letting her play with it in the sitting room. "The guests don't need to be distracted by your toys."

"It's not a toy, Mama," she'd told her. "It's from Daddy's travels! Don't you want the world to see it?"

But her mother had places for everything, and toys did not belong in sitting rooms. The same style doll sat on the Murrays' mantle, asking someone to question where it came from. Every piece had a story, like the people who lived here. The walls were a pale cream and welcomed the sunlight on even the rainiest of days. The couches were in the last decade's fashion, but they spoke of comfort and use rather than style. The curved back of the couch Leighanna currently sat on was the same couch she had jumped over and busted her lip when she was seven.

The Murrays had more wealth than Leighanna's family, but they filled their home with memories rather than trinkets.

Katrina entered the room and broke Leighanna from her thoughts. "I was surprised you wanted to meet," she said and took the seat across from her. Her presence was cold and stiff, and she tilted her head high.

They had ventured far from the girls who used to tell each other everything.

Leighanna had come here fully intending to ask for forgiveness, but upon seeing Katrina's haughtiness, she was forced to be all business instead. "I need you to ask Lady Carmine for the guest list. I couldn't get the wearers of the lion mask from Rosalind."

"You came here to ask me that?" Katrina asked in disbelief. "I take stealing it didn't work?"

"I stole nothing. The paper is still safely in her desk. Don't act as if you didn't take Miss Lucille Thompson's fan during our first year at finishing school. Who was the thief then?"

Katrina gasped. "She kept quoting Revelations to me, and it was warranted. It was your idea!"

Leighanna rolled her eyes. "You didn't have to do it! We will both have our day in the lake of fire if I'm as bad as you say. Besides, I could have pretended to forgive you and then asked."

Katrina huffed. "I don't even know you anymore."

Leighanna jumped to her feet and glared at her. "You don't know me? The Katrina I knew wouldn't have started courting my brother without telling me! August, of all people."

"You're a different person, Leigh!" Katrina rose. "You have no time for me or our friendship. You could have died, and I—it would have killed me to have lost you, but I lost you anyway."

"You were fine without me!" Leighanna threw her hands in the air. "You had August!"

"August is not a replacement for you," Katrina said. "No one could be a replacement for you."

"But you want me to be the Leighanna I was before," she said. "And I can't be her anymore."

"Why? What happened to you?"

One week. She shook the thought free and instead said, "I almost died, and it showed me that I wasn't living, not the life I wanted. Jessilyn Caine had her whole life ahead of her, but she doesn't get to experience it because someone stole her chance."

Katrina sat down again, and Leighanna saw it as the moment she'd long needed. The moment to finally let out the words that had been eating her alive.

"I have no desire to be someone important only because of

who I marry," she said. "Do I want a husband? Yes, one day, but first I want to help Jessilyn. We're taught to sit above everyone else and let things get solved for us. I don't want that! Someone killed Jessilyn Caine, and if I can figure out who, I can make sure that no one forgets her name. I can make sure everyone knows."

"Knows what, Leigh?" Katrina asked through a sigh.

"That we are not women to be married and put on a shelf. We have purpose and passions and the ability to be so much more. She could have been much more than a victim. I will make sure she is."

Katrina stared at her for a long time. "That's how you feel? Truly? Like we are nothing more than future wives? Leighanna, that's a sad way to live."

"If it weren't true, then my mother wouldn't be sending me away in a week." The blood rushed in her head, and she could barely meet Katrina's gaze, but she forced her eyes upward.

Katrina's face paled. "You can't leave, Leigh." She sounded like the Katrina she knew.

"Well, if I don't solve this case in less than a week, I'll have no other choice. But if I can convince Mother it was all for a good reason and there's no longer a murderer on the loose, she might change her mind."

Katrina nodded. "I will get you the list," she said with newfound determination in her eyes.

Leighanna blinked twice. "Thank you," she said.

"If..."

Leighanna huffed, and Katrina cracked a grin.

"If," she repeated, "you let me meet this new Leighanna. I should have said something earlier because I miss you, Leigh. I miss not being the person you tell all your schemes to."

"That's what I've been doing—trying to anyway," Leighanna said. "Though I may have done so quite ... abruptly."

"I could have been more accepting," Katrina said. "This time, I promise I will give her—*you*—a chance."

Leighanna smiled. Her throat felt thick. She held out her hand, and Katrina looked at it as if she had never seen a hand before. "You shake it, Kat."

"Is this part of the new you?"

She smiled and nodded. "Yes, the new me shakes hands." They shook, and when their hands fell, Leighanna said, "I hope August doesn't do anything stupid to lose you."

Katrina laughed, and the fractured pieces of their friendship fell back into place.

CHAPTER TWENTY-TWO
Storm in a Teacup

LEIGHANNA STOOD ON KATRINA'S DOORSTEP and rapped her knuckles on the large oaken door. The week deadline her mother had imposed on her daughter weighed heavily on Leighanna's shoulders. Katrina had promised her the completed list of mask wearers from Lady Carmine when she'd sent a missive the evening before, though it would "take some kind of agreement," her note read. Lady Carmine, unfortunately, would not hand it over willingly. However, anticipation crept up Leighanna's spine as she waited on the door to open. Knowing she was one step closer to zeroing in on Casper as the guilty party drove her forward.

Her head was woozy with knowledge. Could Casper really be capable of murder? All signs pointed to him. August and his reaction filled her thoughts. What would he say when the truth came to light?

Mrs. Murray answered with tight lips and red eyes. "She'll be down in a moment," she said. "Would you like some tea?"

Leighanna rubbed her gloved hands together and fixed her hat on her head. "We have an appointment—"

Mrs. Murray took a step toward her. Leighanna's breath caught in her throat. Katrina's stepmother knew Leighanna about as well as her own mother did, though that wasn't a glowing assessment, considering Katrina and their strained relationship lately. A disapproving wrinkle formed between her brow.

"Do you think you can help anyone by doing what you're doing? You've roped Katrina into this game, and someone is bound to get hurt."

Leighanna swallowed the lump in her throat. "I need to know what happened to Jessilyn Caine."

"There are people whose jobs are to answer the questions you have. Leave it to them."

"They aren't answering them, Mrs. Murray, so if I don't, no one will."

Mrs. Murray's throat bobbed. "You are a woman. It is not your job to catch a murderer."

Even though the words hit the part of her that doubted everything she had learned, all the information at her fingertips and ready to reveal the truth, Leighanna held her head high. "Maybe not. But I'm the woman to do this."

Katrina appeared behind her mother, the picture of grace, her blue dress the vibrant color of the sky in spring.

"I'm giving a dead woman back her voice," Leighanna said. "Because if we don't remember her name, then who will? I'll be in the carriage." Leighanna turned and walked down the steps.

Katrina climbed into the carriage and handed her a leather folder. "The lists, as you asked."

"Was it difficult to get?"

Katrina nodded. "I told her I would let her spread the word of my future engagement, though that's to be years away," she rushed to add. "You know she loves to be on the forefront of gossip, and I may or may not have given her some information on some of the other eligible women in society."

Leighanna chose to remain silent. She wasn't ready to talk about Katrina and August as a couple, or anyone on the marriage market. It wasn't the fact that August and Katrina were together that truly upset her, but how long they kept it from her that still stung. Katrina didn't have a ring on her finger, at least, and Leighanna doubted August would rush their relationship with her father outside the country.

"I have something better for you," Katrina said, breaking the silence.

"What?" Leighanna arched a brow, curiosity curling in her gut.

Katrina dug into her bag and pulled out another piece of paper, the edges worn and the information wrinkled. She held it out for Leighanna, and she took it from her friend. "What is it?" she asked, opening it.

Katrina wiggled in her seat, a smile on her face. "Open it and find out."

Leighanna did and understanding slowly dawned on her. In her hands she held a family tree—the Barton family tree. "Where did you get this?"

"Would you believe that my grandmother has a copy of all eligible bachelors' family trees?"

"I would," Leighanna whispered, her eyes roaming the paper until they landed on a name.

Nicholas Arthur Barton.

N. Arthur B.

Nicholas Arthur Barton was Casper's grandfather and the owner of the broken pocket watch.

"Kat, this is bloody brilliant! This ties Casper to the pocket watch!" Leighanna leaned over and hugged her friend. "You have gone beyond my wildest expectations."

Katrina let out a small laugh as Leighanna situated herself back on the bench across from her. Worry wrinkled her features and she chewed on her bottom lip. "Your theory is starting to look more reasonable."

Heavy silence settled over them. If they could prove the mask had belonged to Casper, it would truly tie him to the murder.

Katrina eyed the files on Leighanna's lap. "What will we do now?"

"We're going to go over it with Rosalind and then . . . well, I made a promise to Etta," she said. "Now that I have the list *and* this family tree, I'm going to give all my evidence to the police."

"And what if they ignore it?"

Leighanna shrugged and felt her mother cringe from blocks away. "Then I'll stop him myself if I have to."

The street in front of Stornshire's local police station was alive with people at ten in the morning. "What is our plan exactly?" Katrina asked, giving a cursory look around the bustling crowd.

Leighanna turned to Katrina and waved a hand in front of her face. "The smog is horrible today," she said through a cough. "Rosalind needed to meet us in the police station to walk her to the tea shop. Her mother doesn't approve, and she used the excuse of visiting her father's workplace."

"It seems to be a common thread, disappointing our mothers."

"Did your mother speak to you?" Leighanna asked.

"Of course."

Leighanna blew out a puff of air. "We'll worry about making it up to them after this matter is settled, and not a minute before."

She took a step forward, but something caught her eye. On the opposite side of the street, under the police station's sign, stood

Jessilyn Caine. Leighanna shuddered at the memory of Jessilyn Caine running straight through her body, and the face of the redheaded woman who'd resumed time. Leighanna's chest ached at the sight, and she couldn't tear her eyes away until Katrina shook her arm and pulled on her.

"What is it, Leigh?" Katrina whispered as carriages continued to drive past.

Leighanna looked back at the spot where Jessilyn had been standing, but the ghost had disappeared. In her place stood two other figures, a white haired woman in a white dress similar to the ones her mother wore and a man in a black suit with a top hat. They glowed with their own respective colors—the woman shimmering gold and the man being hugged by shadow.

She blinked, and the figures disappeared. "Nothing," Leighanna said. "Let's go. Rosalind is probably waiting."

They lingered on the sidewalk until the last carriage had passed before crossing the street and walking into the station.

The only other woman in the room was Rosalind. She hovered in the middle of the men's desks wearing a green dress with gold embroidery. It made her hair appear even more red in its half-updo, a simple style that would make Leighanna's mother choke. She had the attention of most men in the room, her smile bright and contagious. The loud raucous group of men stole any chance of them getting her attention without wandering through the crowd or calling out. And they, as women not related to the commissioner, had already drawn the attention of a nearby constable.

"You ladies aren't supposed to be in here," a policeman said.

Leighanna turned a bright smile toward him. "We're friends of Rosalind Lewis. We're meeting her here today. Could you please inform her of our arrival?"

The policeman's face pinched. "I'm afraid I'm going to have to ask you ladies to leave. Only Miss Lewis is allowed—"

Rosalind turned at the sound of her name, the call rising above the other voices in the room. She walked toward them and placed a gloved hand on the policeman's shoulder. In her other hand she held papers, and Leighanna's body buzzed with excitement. The constable startled, heat rising in his cheeks.

"Pardon, Constable Parker," Rosalind said sweetly, deftly moving through the crowd. "I was waiting for my companions to arrive before heading for refreshments at the tea shop across the way. We can show ourselves out."

The policeman made a disgruntled noise in the back of his throat and nodded. "Very well."

Rosalind looped her arm through Leighanna's and led them back outside.

"Rules of society really are ridiculous," she said.

Leighanna and Katrina shared a look, struggling to hold back a smile. "Said rules do not apply to you, it seems," Katrina said.

"My father has power over their jobs, so they turn a blind eye." Rosalind tossed them a grin. "I've reserved a private room in the tea shop."

"Perfect," Leighanna said. She held up her folder and the new papers. "Katrina got the guest list from Lady Carmine, as well as a family tree that ties the pocket watch to Casper. N. Arthur B. stands for Nicholas Arthur Burton!"

"Marvelous!" Rosalind said, tossing Katrina a smile. "Good work, Miss Murray."

"Thank you," Katrina said, cheeks darkening.

"I wrote down the numbers who were given lion masks based on what I found in the Carmines' study," Leighanna said. "We're going to compare the lists at the shop."

Rosalind walked into the establishment and led the girls to one of the back rooms. They settled into a room with soft blue walls and one large round table. A pot of tea was swiftly brought to them.

As soon as the waiter left, Leighanna laid the files and papers out on the table.

"The constable you met at the door is the one I can usually convince when I need information," Rosalind said.

Leighanna laid out the list Katrina had gotten from Lady Carmine. The parchment crinkled under her fingers, and excitement pierced her core.

"Really? That constable?" Katrina asked, sipping her tea.

Rosalind nodded. "He's less scary than some of the men you might have run into. He acts like he's going to enforce the rules, but he won't, not when I'm involved."

Leighanna cracked a smile at Rosalind's sway over the constables as she read the list.

The girls spent the next few minutes pouring over the two lists. The list Katrina acquired showed the numbers each guest was assigned. The list Leighanna had scribbled down in the Carmine's office showed what mask correlated to what number. They had to compare the numbered lion masks to names, but they eventually had it narrowed down. Now, written out by hand on a fresh piece of parchment, they stared at the seven names of those who wore a lion mask.

Henry Griffith
Ernest Fitzpatrick
Oscar Durant
Whitlock Lewis
Casper Barton

Leighanna and Rosalind's eyes met across the table, and Katrina swallowed hard before picking her teacup up with a shaking hand.

"Casper," Leighanna whispered, heart thundering in her chest. She didn't want it to be true, but it stared her in the face. Her stomach knotted, half relieved and half dreading the truth laid out before her. Casper had worn a lion's mask.

Leighanna shifted in her seat. "They were betrothed, and now we have proof beyond just Jeremiah's word that Casper was at the party, that he wore a lion mask, and that the watch belonged to his family."

"Are you sure the police didn't see this?" Katrina asked.

Rosalind worried her bottom lip. "Casper Barton was never a suspect, according to the constable. The only possibility they came up with was Jack the Ripper."

"And the police gave up investigating once they decided it was the Ripper, so I doubt they even got this far, right?"

"Possibly? I don't know—" Rosalind began.

Katrina tapped her chin in thought. "There's one more missing piece to all of this. We have it on Jeremiah's word that Casper was betrothed to Jessilyn, but just like we needed proof of the mask beyond just Jeremiah's word, we need proof about the engagement, too."

Rosalind nodded. "Someone's word only goes so far. Any ideas?"

An idea slowly formed in Leighanna's head, even though her stomach turned at the thought of her brother's closest friend being responsible for Jessilyn Caine's death. She thought of her brother, and the close friendship and business dealings he shared with Casper and how this would turn her brother's world upside down. It would destroy her to know someone so close to her, even if not her favorite person, to be guilty of such a crime. However, if he was guilty, he deserved whatever was coming at him. "Leave it to me."

CHAPTER TWENTY-THREE
Like a Sneak in the Night

THE NEXT MORNING, after August left for a meeting with Casper at the warehouse, Leighanna seized the opportunity. She put on her best dress and snuck out before her mother or Etta could stop her. If anyone caught her sneaking inside the Barton house, it would ruin her already bruised reputation, but the week deadline her mother had imposed on her pushed all concerns to the dark recesses of her mind.

She needed answers.

Now.

The home was much like Leighanna's family's residence, though closer to the Thames. Today was a good day, but still the stench of the river stung her nostrils. She rang the bell and waited, foot tapping impatiently. After a long five minutes, the door opened, with a maid on the other side.

"Good morning, Miss Pauley. Neither Mr. Barton nor Mr. Barton are here at the moment, I'm afraid." The maid glanced behind Leighanna, no doubt looking for the chaperone that would not appear.

"That's quite all right," Leighanna said. "I was actually coming to check to see if I had left something in the library the last time I was visiting with Jeremiah."

The maid's brow furrowed. "I don't believe so, but I'm happy to check—"

"Do you mind if I look myself?" Leighanna interrupted. "I don't want to inconvenience you, and I think I remember where I last saw it."

The maid slowly nodded. "Of course. Let me show you to the library—"

"I know the way, and I don't want to bother you," Leighanna said. "Please, really!" Then before the maid could say anything else, Leighanna dashed into the home and up the stairs. "I'll only be a moment!"

The maid was on her heels, so Leighanna walked straight into the library. The rows of shelves to the left of the room created weird shadows. Sunlight streamed in through the window in front of her overlooking the street, and the dying embers of a fire on her right settled in the bottom of the hearth.

Unlike Rosalind's small library, this one was the size of a small ballroom. They had five freestanding bookshelves to Leighanna's left and another wall covered with books behind them. It was like a maze of reading material, and Leighanna wished she could be here under different circumstances. Some of her fondest memories of this place had occurred here, standing amongst the shelves and reading a new novel while Jeremiah sketched a shelf away.

The maid was quick to follow, and Leighanna's mind whirled with ways to get rid of her. Her eyes scanned the library, and she saw a half filled tea cup and an abandoned breakfast tray on the table beneath the window. She reached inside her reticule and pulled out a hummingbird pin, hastily tossing it near the table before the maid could see what she had done.

Leighanna made for the fallen pin and knocked into the table with a little more force than necessary, but the damage was done. The tea splattered on her dress, and she shrieked in surprise.

The maid rushed over, an apology already forming on her lips. "Miss, let me—"

"It's fine, it's fine. I found my pin." She retrieved it from the floor. "Is there a place I could freshen up?" Leighanna asked, pasting on a grin.

"Of course. The first door on your right. I'll clean up here," she hurried to add when Leighanna made out like she was going to help.

"Are you sure you don't need my assistance?" Leighanna asked, but her blood quickened at the opportunity she had to snoop in the house.

"Yes, miss. First door on your right," she repeated, and Leighanna didn't make her say it again.

She sped into the hall and walked past both the first and second doors to the right, around the bannister, and into Casper Barton's room. The room was a mess, much like Casper after a bad fight. Clothes were strewn across the chair underneath the window on the far side of the room. Sunlight streamed in through the curtains, catching dust particles in the air. The bed was left unmade, covers hanging off the end of it. Leighanna's cheeks burned at the impropriety of her standing in a man's room. Alone. But she shook herself free of the thought and began her search.

She started with the dresser perpendicular to the entrance and looked through the top and bottom drawers with little success. The armoire to the left side of the room was no better, and neither was the small desk under the window.

"Blast it all," she muttered, knowing her time was limited but having no other ideas. With a sigh, she walked back into the hall.

As Casper was coming up the stairs.

Not wanting to get caught in his room, she reached for the nearest door and ended up with her back against the back of the attic door, staring up at the rickety steps that led to the top of the house. From behind the door, she heard Casper's low baritone asking the maid if anyone had stopped by, and Leighanna held her breath.

"Not to see you, Mr. Barton. Miss Pauley stopped by to get a forgotten pin . . ." Her voice trailed away. Leighanna heard the washroom door open and close, and then the maid said, "She seems to have slipped out."

Leighanna shifted on her feet, and the floorboard creaked. She cursed inwardly and waited to be found out. Footsteps headed her way and she rushed up the attic stairwell. Darkness engulfed her as she made the climb. As she turned the corner in the attic, she heard the door below open. A few moments of silence passed, followed by Casper muttering something, and the door closing.

Leighanna took a deep breath and scanned the attic. It took a few moments for her eyes to adjust to the light. There were dozens of boxes stacked in the corner, and she wondered if any clues may be inside them. She started with the easiest one to open. Not finding anything of consequence, she went to the spare desk they had stored near the window and dug through the drawers. It also had nothing she could use.

She let out a tight breath and stared at the mess around her, wondering how she would get out of the attic and back onto the street, when a flash of sunlight lit up a locket that had fallen on the floor from a nearby box. She walked over to it and opened the inside, finding a familiar face.

Jessilyn Caine.

And right next to her picture, a lock of hair. A shiver ran down Leighanna's spine. She now had proof of his connection. She glanced over into the box and found what she had hoped: letters, and a lot of them. She opened the first one, scanning the contents.

We were never meant to be, Casper, the last line read. *You have to let me go.*

Leighanna clasped the letter in her hand, confusion warring with triumph in her chest. She had all the proof she needed.

The last time Leighanna had been in Commissioner Lewis's office, she'd stolen police files from his briefcase. This time, she sat on the small couch in the corner, with Katrina on one side and Rosalind on the other.

"Mother said to give him a few minutes," Rosalind whispered.

Voices in the hall silenced any more words the girls might have produced, and the door to the commissioner's office creaked open as he stepped through. Leighanna's spine snapped to attention, and she rubbed her sweaty palms on her creased skirt.

Commissioner Lewis's dark auburn hair was gray around the edges, and his freckled face was creased with worry lines around his mouth. He wore the shadow of a beard on his face and bags under his eyes. His broad shoulders strained against a wrinkled suit, and he almost had to duck entering his own office.

"Miss Pauley," he said in a gravelly voice, "my daughter says you have something you'd like to talk to me about." He walked past them and sat behind his desk. He picked up a cigar and lit it with a match.

"Papa! Mama said no more smoking in the house," Rosalind said, cheeks red.

It brought a smile to Leighanna's lips. Commissioner Lewis tossed his daughter a disgruntled look and continued to breathe in the smoke from his cigar.

"Your mother needn't know, Rosa." He waved his hand at Leighanna. "Now, care to explain why my daughter asked a favor of me, Miss Pauley?"

Leighanna stood and held the leather folder to her chest. "Commissioner, over the past few weeks, I've been gathering information pertaining to the death of Jessilyn Caine—"

"Miss Pauley," he began, leaning his elbows on his desk and holding his cigar in one hand.

"With all due respect, Commissioner Lewis, I think you need to hear this before you stop me," she rushed to say. "Your police force has blamed the Ripper for the murder, but I've researched the Ripper, and not only do the killings not match—"

"Miss Pauley," he said a little louder, but Leighanna wasn't finished.

"—but I think I know who killed her! Another girl has been murdered—"

"This is not business for a lady, Miss Pauley," he said in a booming voice. He pushed away from his desk and rose to his feet.

Leighanna swallowed her fear and said, "Commissioner Lewis, in this folder, I have evidence that proves Casper Barton as the murderer of Jessilyn Caine."

She didn't know what to expect, but he sighed as if she was a child in need of coddling when she got the answer to a question wrong. "Miss Pauley."

"Here are my findings!" She held out the leather folder and waved it a little as if it would convince him to take it. She needed him to take it—to believe her.

He glanced at his daughter. "I don't need your findings, Miss Pauley."

"But this proves—as much as one could without the help of

the police—that Casper Barton had something to do with Jessilyn Caine's murder. He had a motive since she ended their engagement. He was at the party, and even at the scene of the crime. We have the list that proves he was given a lion mask. We know the killer is part of high society, and the killings don't match the Ripper's patterns."

"Mr. Barton was never a suspect, Miss Pauley, and this case is no longer ours to investigate. Leave it to the police in London."

Leighanna froze. "But that's impossible. Why—why would he be gallivanting around the city and asking pageboys for information? Why wouldn't you tell the police in London about him?"

The Commissioner's brow furrowed. "They don't need to know about him, Miss Pauley. Besides, I can't tell you what Mr. Barton does in his free time, but we have already spoken to him, even if that information wasn't given to my daughter by one of my constables."

She glanced at Rosalind and saw her cheeks reddening as bright as her hair.

"I'm not sure what you mean . . ." Leighanna mumbled. Commissioner Lewis laughed, and the sound curled Leighanna's toes. Anger pulsed through her, but she sat the folder on his desk calmly. "I think you should reconsider Mr. Barton as a suspect."

He eyed the folder before picking it up and opening it to the first page. His eyes skimmed it, but before Leighanna could get her hopes up, he shook his head, snapped the folder shut, and placed it back in front of her. "Miss Pauley, you need to leave the murder of Jessilyn Caine alone. My department has been working tirelessly to make sure that Stornshire remains safe, and the London police have it handled—"

"Is that why another girl was murdered? Do you think the Ripper killed her, too? I also have—"

Her hand was on the watch in her reticule when the commissioner exploded. "I won't be spoken to this way by someone whose only business inside of a police station was to stop by to take my daughter to tea! I have tried to be patient, Miss Pauley, but you need to remember who you are speaking to. I've told you Mr. Barton is not a suspect, and what my department is doing is not any of your concern."

Leighanna's fury stole her tongue, and she could do nothing except shoot a glare in the commissioner's direction. Her hand released the watch, thankful she still had that in her possession.

"Your safety isn't a concern, so you shouldn't worry yourself about the case," he added firmly.

"But, Commissioner—"

"Rosalind," he said. "Please see your friends out."

"Can you at least tell me why Mr. Barton was never a suspect?" Leighanna asked.

He held a hand out toward the door and nodded toward his daughter. "Now, Rosalind."

"Let's go, Leighanna," Katrina whispered.

"He should at least tell me why my findings are wrong!" she said. Anger pulsed through her and boiled her blood, and even when Rosalind pressed a hand on her lower back and tried to steer her out of the room, she still turned back toward the commissioner with pleading eyes.

"It's part of the investigation, Miss Pauley."

"Then can I have my folder back?" She spun out of Rosalind's grasp and reached for the folder, but the commissioner yanked it away.

"I'm sorry, Miss Pauley. Even if you had it in your possession for some time, that does not change the fact it is police property, as are all the notes you added to the margins."

"Bloody—"

"Leighanna!" Katrina snapped. "Let's go!"

Leighanna stormed out of the office. She saw red all the way down the stairs and out the front door of Rosalind's home. The sound of the city greeted her as she ran down the stairs with her breaths coming fast and her heart beating faster. She cursed the commissioner under her breath and paced in front of his home. Somewhere in the background, she heard Katrina talking to their carriage driver and Rosalind saying something to her mother in the front doorway.

"Leighanna, we need to get off the street before you make a scene," Katrina said.

"A scene?" she yelled. "A *scene*? Someone has to since the police obviously can't be bothered!" A few people stopped and stared, whispers echoing around them.

"Please get in the carriage, Leigh," Rosalind said in a tight voice. "We can talk about this somewhere else."

The street seemed to quiet, and Leighanna stomped toward the carriage.

Once inside, she waited on her friends to join her and immediately said, "I finally tried to let the police do their job, but since they won't, it's my time to catch a killer."

CHAPTER TWENTY-FOUR
Trust, but Verify

LEIGHANNA'S BLOOD BOILED as they rode in the carriage toward her next stop: the Barton home.

She needed answers *immediately*. The deadline Leighanna's mother had imposed on her didn't give her the luxury of time.

"Leighanna," Katrina began, "I think you need to give yourself time to calm down after what happened."

She shook her head and tightened her fists. "I need answers, and if Commissioner Lewis won't give them to me, then I will talk to Casper himself." She saw Rosalind flinch out of the corner of her eye, but she ignored it and steeled herself for the next conversation.

Commissioner Lewis wouldn't listen to her, but Casper would—he must. She wouldn't be ignored. He would tell her where he was the night of Jessilyn Caine's murder if she had to force it out of him. The part of her that wanted to believe his innocence itched with impatience and the hope of relief. The other part, the one that thought him guilty, wanted to vomit.

They were silent the rest of the ride to the Bartons' residence. As soon as the carriage came to a halt in front of the modest home, Leighanna flung open the door and stomped up the steps.

Her gloves scratched against her knuckles as she rapped them against the door. Her foot created an unsteady up and down rhythm as she tapped it on the top step. When the door opened, she asked the maid, "Is Mr. Barton in?"

"I'm sorry, Miss Pauley, Mr. Jeremiah is at the Conservatory—"

"I'm here to see the other Mr. Barton," she interrupted.

The maid jerked back as if slapped. "My apologies, miss. He's in the study. I'll fetch him for you, if you want to wait in the sitting room. Do you have a chaperone with you?"

The maid glanced behind Leighanna, waiting for the chaperones in question to appear, but Rosalind and Katrina were arguing in the carriage. "That's quite all right. I'll see my way to the study. I know how to get there."

"Miss!" the maid called out after her, but Leighanna was already halfway up the stairs. Her skirt was slick in her hands, her palms sweaty with nerves and anger.

She pushed into the library at the end of the hall on the second floor. Casper stood near the windows and turned to look at her, hiding his hands behind his back. He unclasped them and revealed a notebook, the tips of his fingers stained with ink.

"My cousin isn't here, Miss Pauley," he said.

Leighanna pasted on a tight smile and crossed her arms over her chest. "I'm not here to see Jeremiah, Mr. Barton. I'm here to see you."

He fell into the green velvet chair next to the windows. His eyes flashed to the wall of shelves behind the fireplace and then to the hearth before going back to Leighanna. He pasted on a devil-may-care grin and crossed one leg over the other. "Oh? And what have I done to deserve to be graced with your presence?"

If Leighanna had considered him even remotely agreeable, she might have even found the look attractive with his messy brown hair and vibrant gaze. Luckily for her, she wasn't impressed with his charm and sharp-witted charisma. He only irritated her.

"Leigh!" Katrina burst in behind her, cheeks reddened with exertion.

"You and Rosalind were free to wait in the carriage," Leighanna said when Rosalind came in behind Katrina, her face just as flushed.

"And risk the scandal of you two being caught unchaperoned? Then to hazard the possibility of you having to marry this man because society demands it? I think not," Rosalind said and elbowed past Katrina. She took the open seat next to the library door. "I will, however, sit down for this."

Leighanna looked back toward Casper.

The butler took that moment to knock on the library door. Leighanna didn't turn away from Casper when the butler said, "Sir, I'm sorry, but the new maid let them in."

"It's all right, Reggie. Let them get on with whatever they're here for."

Leighanna let out a humorless laugh. She might have been feisty, but she doubted she could take Casper down. Not alone. She looked at the butler, a tall man with graying brown hair, spectacles, and an impressive build. Old, but she imagined with the combined force of her fury and his strength, they could do the job that needed to be done. "Please stay," she told the man.

"Leighanna," Katrina protested, but Leighanna raised a hand to silence her.

"Sir?" the butler said.

"Stay, Reginald."

The butler shifted from foot to foot at the entrance, and

Leighanna finally zeroed in on Casper. Her eyes narrowed. "Where were you the night of Jessilyn Caine's murder?" Leighanna asked.

The grin disappeared from Casper's face and he sat upright, his boots hitting the floor. "Why do you want to know?" he asked. He flipped his notebook over on one knee and leaned forward.

"Because I think you killed Jessilyn Caine."

It was as if all the air had been sucked out of the room. That, or Leighanna had forgotten how to breathe. She watched Casper for any sign of his guilt, but it didn't pass over him like she thought it would. Instead of resignation, she only saw disgust.

"I know we don't get on, Miss Pauley, but do you really think I'm capable of murder?" he asked, hurt shadowing his words.

She stared at him, considering the question. Her mind flashed to him in the boxing ring. She wanted to believe any man who was a friend of her brother's wouldn't swing until his opponent lay dead at his feet. But . . . she had seen him at the warehouse when he'd stopped ushering her to safety to pummel another man.

And that was when another realization came to life. The person Casper had beaten was a man. His opponents were *always* men. Jessilyn Caine was a woman. As much as she disliked him, Casper had never shown violence toward a woman. At least, not in her presence. But there was the question of what he'd done with that woman that got him kicked out of school . . .

Leighanna refused to shake hands with guilt. All signs pointed toward *Casper*. She'd done the work. She'd searched for the true culprit. She had to stand firm in her conclusions.

"You were engaged to Jessilyn Caine," she said. She could feel the butler hovering behind her in the doorway, and it gave her a little bravery. She wouldn't be deterred now.

"Betrothed," he replied softly, almost with yearning.

"She called off whatever you two had," Leighanna answered,

throwing her arms in the air to voice her frustration. "That's motive!"

"No, that was a relief." Casper set the journal to the table next to him and rose to his feet. When he stepped toward her, Leighanna moved back, closer to the butler. Casper's jaw clenched. "Hearing she no longer wanted to follow through with our agreement to wed was the best news I've received in years. We couldn't stand one another in childhood, and if we were to marry, she would have lived a life in Scotland, and I would have stayed here."

Leighanna gritted her teeth. "You were at the party the night she died, and you were given a lion mask—like the killer!"

He ran a hand through his hair. "Leighanna Pauley. I wasn't even *at* that party. I was boxing. Besides, what of the others on that list who also had the lion masks? Did you even consider any of them as suspects before pinning the blame on me?" he asked.

"Not when I found this at the scene of the crime!" She reached into her reticule and produced the watch. "Explain to me how this watch came to be where a girl was murdered. There are only ten in existence. Does this one belong to you?"

He blinked once. He blinked twice. Casper took a step toward her, hand outstretched, but Leighanna jerked the pocket watch back and stuffed it back in her pocket. Her mind spun, but she didn't feel fear. She felt invigorated.

"It was my grandfather's," he whispered. "He gave it to me when I started at Oxford."

"How do you explain it being at the scene of the crime?"

Their eyes met, and her breath caught in her throat. Casper's eyes were wide with confusion. His mouth hung partially open as if about to speak. She had never seen Casper so vulnerable before, and it sent a shot of anxiety through her. His eyes pleaded with her, and his open hand shook. "That watch was stolen from my office weeks before the holidays."

She snorted. "Of course it was."

"You don't believe me, Miss Pauley, but what if I had proof that I didn't do it?"

"It would have to be indelible," Leighanna answered.

"Not only can I prove I didn't do it, I can show you who I think did."

CHAPTER TWENTY-FIVE
Superior Evidence

THE CARRIAGE CAME TO A STOP in front of the warehouse, and Leighanna peeked out from the curtain covering the door. Swift-moving clouds rose in the sky, and droplets of rain began to fall from the heavens. The separate carriage, bearing Casper, had yet to arrive, and she nodded to herself in satisfaction. Time to do some sleuthing of her own.

"Should we go in before it begins to rain?" she asked the other girls.

"Don't you think we should wait for Casper to arrive?" Katrina countered. Leighanna's friend had been nervous throughout the ride but pleased, stating that she'd never been convinced of Casper Barton's guilt. Leighanna was not sure she trusted Casper, but she was willing to explore other options if he did indeed have *proof* of his innocence.

"Mr. Barton said to meet us here because he had proof, but if he's lying, having a look through his office might give us answers he's unwilling to share. Also someone in there might be able to confirm his *supposed* alibi."

"Leigh, are you sure this is the best plan? My father would have spoken to these men, surely—" Rosalind started.

"Rosalind, I say this kindly, but your father has already decided who to blame for the killings. He knew when he spoke to these men who he considered guilty. I need proof Casper didn't do it first-hand, for the sake of my sanity." Without waiting for her friends to comment, Leighanna pushed open the carriage door, jumped out, and ran through the drizzle and into the warehouse.

The warehouse door slammed shut behind her, and the sound echoed into the high ceilings. The two men sweeping the floor around the ring stopped in their tasks and looked toward her.

"'An I 'elp you, miss?" the first one, an older gentleman, said in a thick Scouse accent.

She straightened her spine and gripped the strap of her reticule tighter. "I'm here to see Mr. Casper Barton," she said. The door to the warehouse opened and closed behind her as Rosalind and Katrina joined her.

"Mr. Barton isn't supposed to be coming in today," a younger man told her, a similar cadence to his tone.

"He agreed to meet me here. If you could show me to his office, my companions and I can wait for him there." Her heart beat against her ribs, but she didn't break eye contact, meaning business.

The two men exchanged a look and a few whispered words before the older gentleman grabbed a ring of keys from his belt loop and handed it to the younger. The tightness in Leighanna's chest loosened.

"I'll take you, misses," the young man said. "If you'll follow me."

The girls shared a look similar to the one the men had exchanged before following. Leighanna studied the back of the young man's head and the curl of brown hair brushing his shirt collar. A pageboy cap stuck out of the back pocket of his trousers, threadbare and probably older than most of the clothes in Leighanna's wardrobe.

He took them into the back hallway where she had seen Casper doing business with the pageboy and through to the same door that had been their hideaway.

"You can wait in here for him, but I should probably stay with you until he arrives."

Leighanna plastered on a perfect grin. "That really won't be necessary," she said over the key fitting into the lock. Anxiety shot through her like a train, but she pushed away her nerves and focused on the raw determination. "We can wait for him by ourselves. He told us to act like the office belonged to us," Leighanna lied.

He looked back at her, then at her friends in turn, clearly uneasy. "I don't . . . Mr. Barton is very particular about who he lets in his office."

"Really, we don't want to be a bother, and you looked quite busy when we walked in," Leighanna assured him.

He pushed open the door to the office, and the smell of cedar and cigar smoke drifted into the hallway.

"There's a settee," the man said. "I can bring in another chair—"

"I'll take the one behind his desk," Leighanna said and pushed past him and into the exposed brick room. The large windows were street level, and she could see a line of shops and other warehouses lining the way. A fading rug covered most of the floor, and her boots were silent as she walked behind the large wooden desk and sat in the brown leather chair.

Rosalind and Katrina took a seat on the settee in front of the mostly empty bookshelves.

"We don't have tea or anything. The bar isn't open this time of day, but I could get you all a glass of something to drink."

"Well—" Leighanna said.

"No, thank you," Katrina interrupted, giving her a look.

Leighanna refrained from rolling her eyes and pasted on a grin. "We'll wait here," she said. She leaned her forearms on the desk and winked at him. He shifted on his feet and averted his gaze.

"Oh, yes, of course," he murmured.

"Before you go, I did have one question."

The young man looked relieved. "Of course, miss."

"Christmas Night, Mr. Barton said he was here. Is that true?"

"As far as I know, he fought that night, miss, but I can go get the log to make sure my memory serves me correctly. Mr. Barton and his business partner were holding a fundraiser for the local orphanage. Any bets placed were given toward Christmas for the children."

"Business partner?" she asked. Who would go into business with Casper? Her heart skipped a beat, and she came to the conclusion almost as soon as the man confirmed her suspicions.

"Yes, miss. Mr. Barton and Mr. Pauley own the fight club and are in charge of the membership fees. They employ my father and myself to keep the place clean."

Shock rushed through her. It seemed she was learning something new about her brother as well. It explained why he stayed in Stornshire rather than going to America with their father the most recent time he sailed across the Atlantic for business. She glanced at Katrina. Was her friend aware of August's apparent deep involvement in the ring? The surprise reflected in Katrina's expression suggested she was not. "Were they both here that night?" she asked.

"No, only Mr. Barton. Mr. Pauley's sister was ill and he was home with the family."

"But you know for certain Mr. Barton was here."

"Of course, miss."

"Can I see the ledger?" she asked. The man hesitated for a moment, and Leighanna added, "My brother is Mr. Pauley." He still didn't seem convinced, but he finally relented.

The man walked over to the table sitting beneath the windows. He opened the drawer with a small key from the ring he'd been given and pulled out a large ledger. "Mr. Barton gave us the keys in case any financial personnel came when he wasn't in the office." He sat the ledger on the table and opened it to the middle. The pages crackled beneath his fingers as he flipped them once, twice, and then a third time before stopping.

"Here are the records for that night. All the gamblers signed in and placed their bets on the fights listed on the left. Mr. Barton was the second fight of the night." He pointed to a line with Barton v. Newton scribbled on it. "And then Mr. Barton also placed a large bet on the last fight of the night. The sum funded a third of the money given to the orphanage."

Casper's name was scribbled in ink. The curl of his signature stared Leighanna in the face, and a ringing began in her ears.

Casper couldn't have killed Jessilyn Caine.

It was written in black and white. A sick feeling settled in her gut. How could she have been so wrong?

"Thank you," she said, voice hollow and distant.

He smiled and closed the book. "Of course." He walked over and slid the ledger back in the desk and locked it up. "I'll tell Mr. Barton you're here when he arrives."

As soon as he was out the door, Rosalind rose to her feet. "The ledger was probably the evidence Father saw to prove Casper's innocence."

Leighanna leaned back in the chair, mind spinning. "Is this

what Casper wanted to show us?" she whispered, tips of her fingers pressed to her lips.

"It would have to be," Katrina said as she walked over to the desk.

She nodded to herself. But Casper hadn't just proclaimed his own innocence. He had alluded to knowing who had actually murdered Jessilyn Caine. "There has to be more," she said, pushing to her feet.

The bookshelves were mostly empty, all except for a few leather folders and a handful of books, most of which were resting on their sides. They all looked new. Leighanna wandered over to the shelves on the other side of the settee, hoping something would speak to her.

"We need to wait on Mr. Barton, Leigh," Katrina said, anxiously. "How long do you think August has been in business with Casper?"

"This is a secret my brother and Casper Barton have apparently kept to themselves. No doubt so my mother wouldn't die of embarrassment with her son owning a fight club. She doesn't even approve of boxing." Leighanna turned back to the stack of books at eye level. "But by the looks of this place, and the amount of men I've seen when I've visited, they don't need to worry about turning a profit." She propped her hands on her hips. "So why is this bookcase so bare."

"Maybe he doesn't like to read," Rosalind said.

She shook her head. If she knew her brother, he would have a hive of information at his disposal. Their father had taught them to always have the facts straight. Even if Casper didn't like to read, he would have stored something here to help with his business ventures. Leighanna picked up the nearest book, and a creak sounded from the wall.

Then the wall began to move.

Katrina shrieked in surprise and Rosalind cursed. Leighanna

couldn't help the smirk of satisfaction that crossed her lips as she stepped back and the bookcase screeched open. She slipped a gloved hand in the crack and pulled. The door opened, revealing the room inside. A dim glass lamp shone on a smaller desk inside, and gray light from a long, narrow window lit the rest of the room.

Every inch of the desk was covered in paper and ink. While chaotic, Leighanna could sense order in the documents spread across the desk. Twine was wrapped around a stack of papers on the left side of the desk, and a map of Stornshire sat in the middle. On the other side of the desk was a basket, this also filled with papers.

The wall parallel to the door was nothing but tomes. In the corner sat an emerald velvet chair, and a small wooden table next to it had a folder with a single piece of paper on top. Leighanna walked over to the folder and picked it up. The light wasn't bright enough in the corner, so she turned her back to her friends and walked toward the small window to study the folder. The girls continued to peruse the room, looking for their own clues.

The folder was thick and wrapped with twine, held together by a wax seal. Leighanna wanted to break it open, to find out whatever was hidden inside, but she *could* at least give Casper the chance to explain himself first.

But before she could fully make up her mind about the folder, a voice from outside spoke. "Miss?"

Leighanna cursed inwardly and tucked the folder under her arm. She ran out into the room where the man from earlier held a rain speckled note in his hands.

"We just got word from Mr. Barton," he said. "He's been detained. He asked that you see him another day."

Leighanna yanked the note from the man's hand and scanned the words. The wax sealed folder felt monumental under her armpit. Her brow furrowed. "But—"

"I'm going to have to ask you ladies to leave, miss." He eyed the opened bookcase and raised a brow.

"Are you serious?" Anger pulsed in her veins, and she squinted at the man in front of her. Casper should have been here by now. He was putting her off after he had planted a seed of doubt in her mind. She wanted to throttle him.

The man's face reddened. "'Fraid I am, miss. This is a business—"

"Fine," Leighanna snapped. "Rosalind, Katrina?" she called out. The girls appeared from the hidden office.

"What's the matter?" Katrina asked.

"We're being asked to leave," Leighanna deadpanned, staring the man down as he shifted from foot to foot. She pasted on a waxen smile. "I understand, sir. But I will be taking this with me." She held up the folder.

"Miss—" He started, but she glared at him.

"My brother is August Pauley. He has allowed me to be here. Do you really want to question what I can and cannot take?"

The man stumbled over his words, and a little guilt niggled at her over using her brother and her last name over the man.

"Let's go," she said to the girls and stomped out of the office and all the way to the exit. Venom snaked its way up Leighanna's throat, and she placed a shaking hand on the base of her neck as they stood at the entrance to the warehouse. She looked at the folder in her hand, but something stopped her from breaking the seal without Casper present. Rain beat against the roof, and she didn't hear what Katrina said the first time.

"Sorry, what?" she asked.

"It's raining pretty heavily," Katrina said. "We best make a run for it." Katrina opened the door, and a sheet of rain hid the carriage from view.

Leighanna tucked the folder under her arm to block the rain.

They broke into a run and threw themselves into the carriage. Soaked to the bone, they remained silent as Leighanna's mind whirled. "Mr. Barton wasn't lying. He was at the warehouse the night of Miss Caine's death. Why did he cancel on us?" She put the wet folder in her lap.

"What did you find?" Rosalind asked.

"I don't know," Leighanna said, shaking her head and rubbing the tick of pain starting in her temple. "It's sealed."

What to do, what to do, what to do—ugh!

"Further proof. Records of bets," Rosalind was saying. "Open it."

Blood roared in Leighanna's ears, and she forced herself to appear calm though her heart raced so fast she felt as if she might faint.

The girls shared a look as the rain began to slow.

"I can't," Leighanna said. "I told him I would hear him out. So I will. But I'm not waiting around for answers."

"What are you going to do?" Katrina asked.

"I'm not sure yet, but let's all go home and I'll let you know when I have a plan."

CHAPTER TWENTY-SIX
How to Catch a Killer

ONCE ROSALIND AND KATRINA RETURNED to their homes, Leighanna set off for the Bartons' house. She was fairly certain Casper was innocent, but if he wasn't, she didn't need to risk their lives anymore than she'd already had. She doubted Casper was home, but she had forced her way into his home before. She could do it again.

Her feet moved fast across the payment, and the rain seemed to hit her from all sides. Anxiety pulsed through her veins, and she itched to take off her gloves and cool her damp palms. Electricity sparked in the air, and thunder boomed a far ways off. She knocked on the door, breathless from the brisk walk.

The door opened, and Jeremiah stood on the other side. Relief flooded her veins at the sight of her friend and a shiver ran through her body, which was now soaked through.

"Is your cousin home?" she asked, glancing around him.

"Hello, Miss Pauley," he said. His hair was messier than usual, and he looked tired. "Nice to see you, too."

"Hello, Jeremiah. I don't mean to be rude, but I was supposed to meet your cousin, and he didn't appear. I was worried about you." She cleared her throat. "I was worried you two might have had a spat." She wasn't ready yet to explain all that she had learned over the past few weeks to Jeremiah. First, she needed to find out where Casper had truly gone.

Jeremiah took a step back and allowed Leighanna inside. The door clicked shut behind her before he said, "He went out. He said he was going to see you."

"Oh," Leighanna said. "Maybe I missed him." The lie felt right as it slipped out, even though she didn't believe she had missed him. Where could he have gone? Why didn't he show up? Something was not lining up, but at least Jeremiah seemed well.

Jeremiah glanced behind her, and she turned to look. "Are you expecting someone, Jeremiah?" Leighanna asked, a foreign sensation prickling her skin. She rubbed her damp arms and then sneezed.

"Bless you. And no," he said. "Keeping an eye on the weather. Hoping it clears up soon so I can take a stroll." He looked her over as water dripped off her dress. Leighanna glanced at the sky through the side windows behind her, and a bolt of lightning lit up the sky, followed by a rumble of thunder. "Please, Leigh. You must be more careful. You shouldn't be out in that. You'll catch a cold or worse." Jeremiah called for a maid.

She nodded, comforted by her friend's consideration. "You're right."

The maid walked in from the hall with a smile on her face. "Yes, sir?"

"Would you get Miss Pauley a dry dress to wear?"

The maid nodded. "Right away, sir. Would you also like a fresh pot of tea?"

"Thank you, Ida. That would be fantastic," he said, voice sharp, grabbed Leighanna's elbow, and pulled her toward the stairs. "You can wait for Casper in the library, if you want, Leighanna. I was working on some portraits for the next show. I'd love to show them to you."

"Do you need a chaperone?" the maid squeaked.

But whatever Jeremiah said in response, Leighanna didn't hear it. Before she knew it, she was ushered up the staircase and was in the library, her dress dripping on the stairs. She really should have stayed near the door to catch Casper as soon as he returned. "I don't know if I should wait this far from the door. I do really need to speak to Casper." She glanced at the clock in the corner. She let out a tight laugh when Jeremiah looked disappointed. "I really did come here to see how you were faring, too."

"You can't stay for a cup of tea?" Jeremiah asked. "The weather outside is dreadful, but if you wait it out, my carriage can take you back home and Casper can call on you later. You can look at some of my drawings I haven't had the chance to show you yet."

A surge of guilt rushed through Leighanna. She had been neglecting her friendship with Jeremiah since her search for the killer had started. Her eyes strayed to the clock once more before she said, "Okay. One cup." A soft smile lit up his face. He took the seat in the same chair Casper had earlier when she accused him of murder. He motioned to the seat across from him.

Leighanna sat, the sealed file heavy in her lap. She looked at the teapot already resting on the desk and frowned. "There's already tea here? But you only just sent the maid for it."

Jeremiah waved her off. "A friend from the Conservatory was visiting. He left before the storm hit. The tea is cold by now."

As if summoned, thunder boomed outside, causing Leighanna to jump.

"All right, Leigh?" Jeremiah asked, a crooked smile on his lips.

Leighanna shook herself. "Yes, of course. Sorry. I don't know what's come over me." She glanced at the clock in the room. Where was Casper?

She had evidence that proved he'd been at the party. The maid came in with a fresh tray of tea and Leighanna a new dress. Leighanna excused herself and changed in the washroom, mind whirring. It didn't take her long to change, and, now dry, she rejoined Jeremiah in the library.

As she sat down, she had the thought, *Casper couldn't have been in two places at once.* Leighanna's brow furrowed. She looked over her shoulder out the window, which was covered in a sheet of rain. *But why did Casper not come to the warehouse? What does he know that I don't?*

The clock struck at the half hour mark. "Can you show me the drawings, Jeremiah?"

He grabbed a notebook from the shelf behind him, half open and bending the pages. Another fell to the floor in front of the fireplace, and Leighanna placed the file in her seat and jumped up to help him. The open collar of his shirt slid to reveal his collarbone. Heat spread on Leighanna's cheeks, but it was quickly replaced by curiosity. Angry red scratches slashed like ink stains across his skin.

"Did you hurt yourself?" she asked.

Jeremiah looked down, ignoring the fallen notebook. "Oh, that. I tried to rescue a cat near the Conservatory. It didn't take kindly to the help." He laughed lightly, placing his notebook on the mantel above the fireplace.

A bout of suspicion spread through her middle. Something about the explanation fell flat. Jeremiah sat back down and she noticed his two fingers tapping on his knee, his telltale sign that he was lying.

The door to the library opened, and the maid, Ida, came in. "Do you two need a fresh pot—"

"Not now, Ida," Jeremiah said, his voice clipped as he got up to head the maid off.

Leighanna paused. She had never heard him sound that way before. As the girl apologized to them both, Leighanna lowered her gaze, embarrassed that Jeremiah was treating her so harshly. He followed the maid out, pulling the door mostly closed, and mumbled something else to her in the hall. His attitude turned Leighanna's stomach.

She reached down for the fallen sketchbook and flipped it over to busy herself from the awkward exchange happening outside. "I really should—" Her eyes skimmed the page, but she didn't register what she'd actually seen until she flipped to the next portrait.

Each portrait featured a beautiful woman, her eyes closed as she faced the artist. But these weren't like the portraits she'd seen featured at the Conservatory. These drawings were angry, violent— red slashes and splatters of ugly red paint marring the cream sheets.

The library door slammed shut, and Leighanna jumped.

"I apologize—what's the matter?" Jeremiah asked.

Leighanna closed the sketchbook before she turned around. "Your sketchbook fell. Which shelf does it go on?" she asked, breathless.

Jeremiah walked toward her, and Leighanna had to stop herself from backing up. Her heart raced in her chest, and a steady ringing had begun in her ears. She couldn't get the image of the violent art out of her mind.

"I can take it," he said and almost snatched it from her hand.

Why had he drawn it that way? Why why why?

But a dark part of her thought she knew why. Her mouth went dry. He took a step toward her, and she searched for something to distract him.

"Is that the tie I got you for Christmas last year?" she asked, forcing his mind away from the journal.

It hung loosely around his neck. He picked up the end and smiled. "So it is." He shook his head. "I apologize about the maid, Leigh. You know how protective I am of my art."

Leighanna forced herself to smile. "Yes, of course." She picked up the sealed file and placed it on the table, scared of what was inside it now. She sat down once more, smoothing her skirt and trying to act normal despite the thundering of her heart. "The night of the party . . ." she began.

Jeremiah looked up at her. "What party?" He said the words as if he truly didn't know, with a layer of innocence that turned Leighanna's stomach.

"The Christmas party at Morven Manor."

Jeremiah returned to the desk. "They blamed the Ripper, didn't they?" he asked.

Leighanna's palms broke out in a cold sweat. "Yes, and they sent all their findings to London, which is already rampant with crime and doesn't have time to investigate one pesky little murder in Stornshire."

His brow furrowed, and he sipped on his tea. "You're not satisfied with that answer."

"I used to believe a few things, but I think I was wrong."

"Wrong about what?" he asked, words a little sharper now.

The room felt too warm, too small, even though this was the largest room in the Bartons' home. The seat of the chair pressed against her calves as she shifted. She clenched her shaking hands.

"I believed Casper was the killer. All the clues led to him, but he told me he had proof he hadn't done it. That's why he wanted to meet me at the warehouse, but he didn't show. I wanted to talk to you—to see what you thought."

He studied her and nodded to the folder next to her. "What's that?" he asked.

"Nothing. Just some business documents I have to take home for August." She added a short laugh.

Jeremiah stepped around her and grabbed the file. Before she could react, he ripped open the folder, finally breaking the seal on the wax holding it closed. His eyes scanned the contents. Leighanna's heart pounded against her rib cage, and the accusation tasted sour on the tip of her tongue, even though she had yet to allow herself to think the words. Jeremiah's knuckles whitened around the file.

Leighanna looked back at the door anxiously, wishing the maid would come back. She should've never let Jeremiah get her into the library alone like this. She needed to escape, but what could she say? What excuse could she make that he would allow?

"Would you like to know where I was the night of the Christmas party?" he asked, and she jerked her attention toward him.

She cleared her throat. "You were out of town at your exhibition."

He gave her a wicked grin, a shine in his eye she'd never seen before. "That's what I told you, Leigh." He shook his head. "I never did like lying to you. . ."

"When will the maid be back?" she made herself ask, afraid to hear what he was about to say. That he was here in Stornshire that night.

"Oh, her? She should stay away." Leighanna had never heard Jeremiah's voice so cold, not even when she'd accidentally put her fist through his artwork. It turned her insides. "We don't need a chaperone. After all, we're dear friends, aren't we, Miss Pauley?"

She had to somehow get the maid and tell her to get the police, and she had to do it *now*.

Jeremiah's eyes met hers, and he tossed the file in the fire. "Just like friends wouldn't tell anyone else that I came home to Stornshire early that week because I knew Jessilyn would be here. *Friends* trust each other."

"What did you do?" she whispered. The words slipped past her lips without her permission.

He reached down for the used teacup and threw it. Leighanna ducked in time to miss taking it in the nose. Jeremiah lunged and grabbed her by the wrist. She brought up her knee and hit him in the groin. He doubled over with a gasp and gave her enough time to yank free and dash for the library exit.

But the door was locked, with no key in sight. There was no way out.

Leighanna's eyes searched the room for a weapon and landed on a vase on a table near the door. If she couldn't escape, she could make enough noise to send the Bartons' household staff running for the library. She snatched up the vase and dumped the flowers and water out in front of her. Jeremiah slipped on the mess, falling to the floor, and snarled at her. Leighanna smashed the vase against the wall, sending a resounding crash.

From the other side of the door, the maid called, "Mr. Barton, Miss Pauley, are you all right?" The handle shook.

"I can't believe you didn't see it before, Leigh, as smart as you are." Jeremiah stood and began to stalk her. She snatched one of the broken vase pieces and edged away from him. Her hands sweated beneath her gloves, shaking.

"Miss Pauley?" The door handle shook once more.

Leighanna's throat felt thick, and she couldn't settle on the words flying through her mind. "Ida, go get help!"

"Stay away, Ida!" Jeremiah shouted.

Leighanna kept backing away, but Jeremiah drew nearer. "You always paid attention when no one else did, took an interest," he said. "At least you used to. I saw you losing interest at the exhibition in March. It made sense, though. Even you were more fascinated by Casper—believed he could have killed Jessilyn Caine." Disgust pinched his features, and fear trickled down her back.

"Your p-professor . . ." she finally managed to stutter. "He talked about how your art had changed. You had a clearer picture of what you wanted to convey."

Jeremiah's grin turned outright malicious, and it curdled Leighanna's blood. "Jessilyn used to be my muse. She would let me draw her when she and Casper were fighting during all those summers we spent in the Highlands with her father's family, but I never showed those drawings to anyone. She and Casper never got along, and when she ended things, she had no time for me anymore." Jeremiah sneered and lunged again.

Leighanna screamed and sliced at him with the broken piece of glass. It grazed against his cheek enough to make him wince and pause. She ran behind the shelves.

"Won't you stop and listen, Leigh?" he asked. The maid was no longer trying to get in the library, and Leighanna hoped she had gone for help. For someone.

For *anyone*.

Leighanna froze behind the middle of the five shelves, peering between the books and catching sight of the top of Jeremiah's head as he stalked her. "How do you think it felt to be ignored my entire life?" he asked.

Leighanna took slow steps backward through the shelves as he advanced, positioning herself toward the door. If she had time, she might be able to break through, if only she could reach the fireplace and grab a poker. But that was on the other side of the room.

Stupid, stupid, stupid, she chided herself, but she didn't have time for it.

She wasn't sure, but she needed something to force her way

out that door. Until then, she knocked as many books off the shelf as she could, creating noise and a barrier between her and Jeremiah.

Keep him talking.

"You weren't ignored."

Jeremiah laughed, and the floor creaked as he moved between the shelves, growing closer to her. She glanced toward the fireplace and readied herself to make a run for it.

"I was always ignored for Casper. *He's* the one who will inherit the estate. *He's* the one who made it all about him when he got kicked out of Oxford. No one even cared that I had just got accepted to the university for my art. And that's why I had to pretend I was Casper the night of the party, to make him pay. Most were too drunk to notice the differences between us by the time I arrived."

Leighanna didn't know this boy. If this was the real him . . . she hadn't known Jeremiah Barton at all.

"But my art is going to pave my way, Leighanna. You heard my professor. It's brilliant now that I've . . . changed my approach."

Bile threatened to claw its way up her throat, but she forced herself to ask, "What is your new approach, Jeremiah?"

"The dead girls, Leigh. Women are the fairer sex, after all. What else would I have drawn? When you stop talking, you become even prettier."

The idea turned her stomach. Her gaze darted toward the fireplace on the other side of the room, her feet inching slowly in that direction. The open floor was so close, but the fear of being exposed chased away all her courage.

You have to do this, Leigh.

"You could've had a woman of your own, Jeremiah." Her voice shook, and she hated herself for it. Another step closer to the fireplace. She needed to run across the open room toward it, but at least Jeremiah was on her other side now. She could reach the poker if she could just get one step closer.

"I had Jessilyn! But when she decided to end things with Casper, she ended things with me, too!" One of the books was wrenched from the shelf. Jeremiah threw the book to the floor and glared at her through the opening. "But if she was dead, no one else could have her. And now, no one else can have you either."

Leighanna bolted.

The fireplace had never seemed so far away, but she refused to look back, even with Jeremiah on her heels. The fire poker was just out of reach when a novel hit her from behind and sent her sprawling. Her knees thudded against the carpeted floor, and she toppled chest first into the ground. She tried to crawl toward the fireplace. Her fingers grazed the brick edge when Jeremiah forced her down, his knee in her back.

"Ah!" The scream scraped at her throat.

Jeremiah turned her over, and her shoulder twisted at an awkward angle. He straddled her, a marble paperweight shaped like a swan from the desk in one hand. His hair was askew, his expression enraged, and spittle dripped from his mouth like a rabid dog. With her arm still pulled back, she tried to reach the poker.

Jeremiah leaned down so his hot breath touched her face. "Stay still, Leigh," he ordered. He wrenched back her free hand, the pain so blinding she thought her arm might pop out of socket.

Leighanna threw her head forward and bit him on the nose. He screamed in pain and released her a little. Managing to wiggle free, she brought up her knee and slammed it into his groin. He groaned and rolled off her. She grabbed the poker and slammed it against his head, sending it snapping backward so that he landed on the ground with a thunk. She took a step toward him, and he groaned.

Without waiting a second longer, Leighanna raced for the door and slammed the poker handle down against the doorknob with all her strength. Finally, with one last wrenching blow, the knob clattered from the door.

She opened her mouth to scream, but she was yanked back, a pressure around her neck. Her hands flew to the—it felt like fabric. A tie. He was using his tie to strangle her. She choked on her next lungful of air.

His breath was hot in her ear. "Can't you just be still?" he asked, yanking harder. Air struggled to fill her lungs, and she stumbled, the hold only growing stronger. She fumbled with the tie, but it dug deeper into her neck. Her feet scrambled to find purchase on the floor, and she writhed against his chest.

The maid shrieked from the hallway, but Leighanna couldn't make out what she said.

Jeremiah cursed but didn't let up, and Leighanna's vision began to blacken around the edges. Her nails dug into Jeremiah's hands, hot blood dripping between her fingers. The air remaining in her lungs screamed to be released.

A figure suddenly appeared before her. A man in a top hat. A man she'd seen before in the stables with Jessilyn Caine. A man she'd seen outside the police station mere hours before. A man she'd seen hovering over her deathbed. He slowly took off his top hat. Death. Death was here.

Panic seized her, and the sight of the figure caused her to fight harder. Next to him stood the woman with white ringlets, tanned skin, and wearing a white dress. She tugged at her vest and glanced at the man in black.

Leighanna wanted to scream at them both to go away, but words failed her. Her fight began to lessen, and her muscles ached to relax, her lungs burning with final breath.

No! She told herself again and again, *No! You will not die.*

But the man in black stepped closer, hat in hand, and he

smelled of frankincense and lilies. Then she heard another shout. The woman in white turned to look down the stairs, at least Leighanna thought she did. She seemed little more than smoke in the air compared to the man of growing shadows. The man in black halted, and they vanished.

Suddenly, Casper came into view at the top of the stairs. Blood dripped down his temple from a cut near his scalp, a nasty bruise on his cheek. His wrists were rubbed raw as if he'd been tied up. He looked as awful as Leighanna felt. He caught sight of her, and his eyes darkened.

"Jeremiah, stop!" Casper thundered and made a grab for the other man but the tie only tightened as Jeremiah jerked her back. Casper let out a roar and slammed his fist into Jeremiah's arm. She heard a snap, and Jeremiah screamed.

Finally, air rushed into her lungs. She fell forward and tumbled to the floor.

Casper wasn't done. His fist smashed into Jeremiah's stomach then his jaw. Blood splattered across the carpet.

"Casper!" Leighanna squeaked, but her throat was raw. "Casper!" she said louder.

His fist paused in the air, blood covering his knuckles.

Jeremiah's head hung to the side, eyes beginning to swell shut. His chest rose and fell in heavy breaths, knocked out cold.

"I ran to the nearest call box and phoned the police." Ida's voice drifted from the doorway. "He cut the lines to our phone."

"I gave him that tie," Leighanna said, and they all turned to look at the fallen tie near her foot, where she had collapsed. Every breath felt like fire in her throat. She closed her eyes to steady her breathing and tried to stand, but the world spun.

Casper rushed over to her and pushed her lightly back down on the floor. "You don't need to move," he said. "Lean against the wall."

She did as he asked and turned to him. "What happened to you?" Leighanna coughed into her elbow.

Casper leaned back on his arms, sitting on the floor next to her. His breath was ragged. "After you left for the warehouse, Jeremiah came at me from behind, then tied me up. Just got away." He touched his forehead and it came away with blood. Casper glanced in her direction. "Are you well?"

Am I?

Leighanna swallowed hard, glancing at Jeremiah's body on the floor, and tears pricked at her eyes. Everything from the last few weeks came crumbling down around her. Nearly dying from consumption. Seeing Jessilyn's ghost. Her brother hiding life-altering information from her. Her mother's threats to send her away. Thinking her brother's best friend was a murderer. And finally: her childhood friend trying to kill her. She wanted to be okay, and she knew she would be, but right now, she was not. Her hands shook as she wiped away the tears trickling down her cheeks.

"No," she croaked out. Leighanna's fingers prodded at the bruising around her neck, and she winced.

Casper wiped his bloodied knuckles on his pants and scooted over to her. Before she knew what was happening, Casper pulled her into his arms. She tensed against his touch before relaxing into it. Why did *Casper* have to be the one to see her fall apart?

"Casper, I'm sorry—" Something out of the corner of her eye caught Leighanna's attention. The woman and man from before stood next to one another. The man placed his top hat back on his head and held out his arm. The woman took it in hers. Then, they turned and disappeared without a backward glance.

Leighanna opened her mouth to speak, but then Jessilyn Caine appeared. She looked beyond Leighanna at Jeremiah, who was still knocked out cold. She spit at him, the ghost phlegm disappearing as soon as it hit the carpet.

"Thank you," Jessilyn mouthed. Then she turned and walked down the staircase.

The police pounded on the door and rushed in, filling the space where the ghost girl had been moments before. And as the police surveyed the scene and dealt with the murderer, Casper whispered in Leighanna's ear, "It's over, Leighanna. You're safe now."

And in his arms, that's exactly how she felt.

CHAPTER TWENTY-SEVEN
The Beginning

LIFE AND DEATH HOVERED IN THE CORNER of Leighanna Pauley's room as they watched her drift into her dreams. They shouldn't have come. Leighanna had caught Jeremiah, and she'd survived his attempt on her life. They weren't needed any longer. Her fate was set; she had time to live.

But they both kept coming back to stare at her and wonder. Why did Death and Life answer the call to her bedside those months ago? What made her so unique? Did the powers above sense something special about this girl? Death thought it possible.

"Her dreams are not of life, not this one," Life said. "She dreams in full color, of a time not like the one she inhabits. Her desires aren't that of a girl in this age."

Death tilted his head to the side and took a step closer to the girl. "Possibly her soul has split, half here and half there. Long term . . ."

Life ignored him, and he had to straighten his features into indifference.

"Do you think we should keep a close eye on her? In case she attracts others," Life asked. "If she can still see beyond the veil, then they will see her, too." She nodded once in answer to her own questions, decisive.

"Life, we can't—"

"You say we can't. I say we must. There are worse things than ghosts."

Leighanna startled awake. She gasped for breath. The cat jumped from the bed and into the opened wardrobe.

"Do you think it will happen again?" Death asked Life.

"We won't know until it does," Life replied.

"She's caught the killer. Jessilyn Caine is at rest."

Death had visited Jessilyn after Jeremiah had been thrown behind bars. He'd walked on the grounds of Morven Manor in search of the ghost of the dead girl and found her at the stables, though the stall where she died remained empty. The stables held memories that were best not forgotten—Leighanna Pauley had made sure no one would forget Jessilyn's name—but handled with care.

"Are you ready to go now?" he asked her when he met her at the stables.

Jessilyn had returned to her previous state, before the life had bled out of her. She stood in the white and gold dress she'd worn to the Christmas party with her hair curled atop her head and a small gold hat on top.

He asked the question he'd been longing to ask: "Why did you stay?"

Jessilyn looked off into the distance, as if searching for her killer. "He needed to be caught."

"So you picked the most stubborn girl in Stornshire to help?" Death asked. Jessilyn only smiled, taking his hand briefly. And as she crossed over, Death smiled back.

The sunlight shone in through Leighanna's curtains, and she breathed in the air flowing through the crack in her window, welcoming the new day. Stan mewed in concern as Leighanna got ready in her bedroom.

The door to her room cracked open, and Leighanna's mother walked in. "Mr. Barton is here to see you. Are you almost ready?"

Leighanna pulled at the collar of her dress, rubbing her throat. The ring of purplish bruising where Jeremiah had tried to end her was beginning to fade to a nasty yellow after three weeks' time.

"Yes." The word came out barely a whisper from Leighanna's lips.

Her mother sat on the end of the bed. She reached out, hand hovering in the air for a moment before she pulled it back. "I wanted to apologize."

Leighanna jerked back. "Pardon?"

Her mother choked on a laugh. "I should have seen it. I should have known it was him. A mother should know these things."

Leighanna snorted, and her mother pursed her lips, though she held her tongue. "You couldn't have known any more than I did." She fiddled with the end of her blanket, asking, "Is Casper is in the parlor?"

"*Mr. Barton* is handling his family affairs, and he can't stay long. His mother is, of course, in a state. She'll be leaving for the country."

"Naturally," Leighanna said, frustration at society prickling her skin. People cared too much about what others thought.

"Leighanna," her mother said through a sigh.

"It's what we do in society. Escape our problems. I was only acknowledging that." Leighanna shrugged. "But I—well, I may not particularly care for Casper—Mr. Barton—but no one deserves to have to go through this. And he's staying in Stornshire, to face it head on. I'm glad he isn't afraid to face me, at least." Leighanna chewed on her words. "I'm glad I'm getting to stay, too."

"Well, your heroism made up for your lack of decorum." Leighanna laughed.

Her mother pursed her lips and waved in Etta, who carried a large box. Leighanna went to help her, curiosity curling in her belly, but her mother ordered her back down and helped Etta place the box on her desk.

"Thank you, Etta," her mother said.

"Of course, Mrs. Pauley. Pleased to see you ready for the day, Leighanna."

Leighanna reached over and hugged her maid, and after a heartbeat, Etta did the same. Warmth spread through her, and she clenched her eyes shut, hugging her tightly once more. When she pulled back, tears shone in Etta's eyes. "I'm so very glad you're not dead, Leigh."

Her mother cleared her throat. Etta backed away with a stiff curtsy and left them alone once more.

"What is it?" Leighanna asked, going up to the box and running her hands over the top. She tilted her head to the side, studying the black box, gold writing embossed on the top.

Remington, it read.

"Your father sent you something from New York."

A smile stretched across Leighanna's face, and she was nearly out of her skin with excitement. "Really?" she asked.

"Yes, truly," her mother said. "He said it would arrive before he would, though he's due in a few weeks. He'll be glad to see you."

"What is it?" she asked.

A genuine smile broke out on her mother's face. "Open it and see."

Leighanna removed the lid and gasped. The typewriter's glass letters shone in the early morning light streaming into her bedroom. She ran her fingers over them with reverence. All the things she could say had been forgotten.

"You can use it to communicate with your friends. Katrina, Rosalind . . . Casper." She paused and then added, "Though I wouldn't tell just anyone you're speaking to Casper and—"

"Are you suggesting I don't interact with Casper because of Jeremiah?"

"Leighanna, his cousin is a murderer—"

Stubborn determination flooded Leighanna. "Casper is not a murderer. If it wasn't for him, the police might not have believed the evidence staring them in the face. He made them listen." It's the first time she'd admitted it out loud.

Men wouldn't listen to women when they didn't need to. Casper had given them her evidence and also gave her the credit for the research on the killer when he took his findings to the police. The file, though burned, had contained evidence that Jeremiah was the killer, from drawings he had done of the murdered girl to a letter from the friend he'd swapped tickets with to be in Stornshire the night of Jessilyn Caine's death. Fortunately, Casper had made a copy of the file Jeremiah had burned in the library fireplace. Jeremiah would be behind bars for a long time. That must have been what the pageboy had been helping Casper with.

To think, all this time Leighanna had been opposed to Casper, and he'd been on the same mission as her.

"I won't abandon him. I want to talk to him. May I? I already thought him a murderer. I won't agree to make him an outcast."

"Leighanna—"

"I almost died, Mother. Do I have so little say in who I associate with? I'm not asking to marry him."

Her mother looked ready to argue, shoulders still and brow furrowed. Leighanna chewed on her bottom lip in anticipation of her mother turning down the idea.

Leighanna's fingers twitched. In the corner, she saw two shadows appear—the man in the top hat and the woman in the white dress. They whispered to one another, almost too low for Leighanna to hear.

Not until the man asked, "Are they all like this?"

The woman, Life, narrowed her gaze. "No," she said slowly. "Not all of them are this lively."

At that, Leighanna's mouth quirked in a smile.

"Very well." Her mother's lips formed a tight line, bringing Leighanna back. "You need to send a letter to your father, but I suppose you can do that after you speak to Mr. Barton." She motioned toward the typewriter. "Your father so rarely sends telegrams, and when he does, you've been galavanting across Stornshire, too busy with your newest escapade to reply."

Leighanna focused back on the gift and ignored the jab. "This must have cost Father—"

"A fortune," her mother finished. "His business with the Americans is going well, but you could ruin that by consorting with the wrong sort."

"With enough money, you can buy me a husband. At least allow me friends," she said, running her hand over the machine.

Her mother sighed. "I don't have time for this. Write your letters, Leighanna. Even write penny dreadfuls and sell them to all of Stornshire. But don't threaten to die again."

She walked toward the exit, and Leighanna said, "Mother?"

Her mother turned to stare at her. "Yes?"

"Thank you for not sending me away."

Her mother waved away the thanks and said, "Hurry and speak to Mr. Barton. He has things to attend to." Her mother exited the room with the grace of a well-bred lady. Stan stepped out of his hiding spot and jumped up onto the desk, sniffing curiously at the new machinery.

Leighanna reached out and rubbed her hand along the cat's spine, a chorus of pleased purrs and mews celebrating the attention.

"Let's go, then," Leighanna whispered to the cat, picking him up and walking barefoot through the house.

She felt the two people, Life and Death, follow her down the stairs and to the parlor where Casper stood near the window, looking out on the spring filled streets of Stornshire. She glanced back and they hovered in the doorway. As if sensing her unease, the woman pulled Death back, and they disappeared around the corner.

"Mr. Barton," Leighanna said in introduction.

Casper turned from the window with his bowler hat in hand and the other hand resting on his vest. Leighanna studied him, and something felt off about the man she knew. His eyes didn't have the fire she so readily expected from him, and worry niggled into her veins.

What's different about him? she wondered. Then she thought about the things he'd seen that most humans wouldn't have to comprehend.

"You asked to see me, Miss Pauley?" Casper said.

Leighanna placed Stan on the floor, and he went and rubbed against Casper's trousers. Casper laughed and petted the cat, who then found a spot on the fainting couch with a good view of the street and a nice ray of sunshine to keep him warm.

"Yes, um, yes, I did." Leighanna fretted with the edge of her glove, eyes on her toes before they moved back to Casper. "I wanted to apologize for . . . well, I should have not considered you capable of what Jeremiah did." She flinched, and her cheeks burned.

"It was a mistake, Miss Pauley," Casper said, placing his hat on his head.

Leighanna frowned and took a step toward him. He moved one step closer to the door. She said, "I really—I don't know what came over me—"

"You have never seen me in the most positive light, I will admit. And I'm glad you're well and safe, of course." He paused and swallowed. "However, I find myself shocked at how much your low opinion of me did fracture mine of you."

Leighanna's breath came in a stuttering gasp. "I hope we can move past—"

He raised his hand and took two more steps toward the door. "I appreciate your apology, but I must be on my way. Your brother is expecting me. We have business to attend to." He walked out into the hall, and Leighanna trailed after him.

Life and Death stood near the stairs, and she wished she could ignore their presence. Something about the exchange embarrassed her, and she wished no one else was present for it.

"Casper," she said, voice breaking on his name.

He looked back at her, but the forced distance and dispassionate mask fell away.

"I'm sorry," she repeated.

Casper's jaw tightened and he lifted his head. "As you said, Miss Pauley. I think it best we leave it at that and move on with our lives, separate from each other." Then without another word, Casper walked out into the sunny April morning, leaving Leighanna slack jawed at the door.

She closed the door slowly, her brow furrowed. Stan came and rubbed against her legs. Then he meowed and turned his attention toward the man at the stairs. Leighanna followed his line of sight.

"I can feel you," Leighanna said, and Stan cocked his head, curious. He glanced back at Death and hissed.

Leighanna laughed, but it sounded more like a sob. "Not only have I ruined whatever was between Casper and me but I'm still *feeling* things. Things I shouldn't."

Leighanna walked back into the parlor and watched Casper's

carriage pull away from the curb. "Don't worry. I don't intend to see you any time in the near future, but you can visit if you'd like. As long as Death doesn't hold his hand out for me. Maybe eventually I can make sense of this . . . of myself." She touched her lips and then pressed her fingers to the glass.

Leighanna felt a string tug at her chest as the carriage turned around the bend. For reasons she didn't care to demystify, her eyes burned with tears as Casper slowly vanished from her life, nothing but a ghost of a memory now.

Acknowledgments

Without my Lord and Savior, Jesus Christ, none of this would be possible. It is through Him that I have my passion for writing and have followed the path of this creative pursuit. It is Him that I thank first and foremost for the book you now hold in your hands.

There is a lot that goes into writing a book. Leighanna's story didn't start as an entire novel but a short story. Anne, the publisher of this novel, asked me to write a story about light overcoming darkness for the second edition of her anthology, *What Darkness Fears*. From it came the story of a girl who could see ghosts. A ghost comes to her at midnight, asking her to catch a killer before he or she has the chance to kill again. The story, Ghosts at Midnight, stayed with me long after I wrote it, and I pitched a series of novellas to Twenty Hills. Basically, after reading what I had written, they thought Leighanna's story needed to be longer—which is how *The Curious Case of the Midnight Specter* came to be. I truly loved exploring this story and writing Leighanna's story. Thank you so much to Anne for being the first one to believe in this story and for helping me shape it into what it is today.

Next, I'd like to thank Lara, who also saw my vision alongside Anne and helped it come to fruition. Both she and Anne listened to my ideas over Google Meet for this book and didn't doubt the story for one second.

After writing a novel comes editing it. Thank you to my developmental editors, Anne J. Hill, Sarah Sutton, and Mariella Taylor for finding all the inconsistencies in this story and making it all make sense. To my line editor, Crystal Grant, for making this story flow and become clear on the page. To Sarah Harmon and Anne J. Hill, my copy editors, for taking the final leap and finding all the last minute fixes. Without Sarah Harmon and her abundance of knowledge on history around the globe, there still might be telephone and telegrams where a simple letter would do.

Alongside all the people who help you on the path to turning the first draft into a novel, are the people who have been by your side since it was nothing more than an idea. Thank you to all my beta readers, Kayla E. Green, AudraKate Gonzalez, J. R. Brady, Masheeha Seedat, Kimberly Byrd, and others.

One of the largest parts of making a book look like a book comes in formatting and cover design. A huge thank you to Catarina Book Designs for taking my terrible vision and designing a masterpiece. I adore the cover so much, and it's exactly like I imagined it. Twenty Hills allowed me to be a big part of the cover design process, and I appreciate that immensely. Also to Andrea Renae for doing the inside work on the novel and making it as beautiful on the inside as it is on the outside.

When I started writing this book, I had a vision of the characters in my mind. Thank you to all the artists who brought my vision to life: Almu Costa, Ellie Tran, Abigail Rouleau, Adelyn Belsterling, and Kaitlyn Van Ravenstein.

Finally, to all the people on the sidelines cheering me on.

Writing is not an easy endeavor. Thank you to Amanda Auler, Ellen McGinty, Lorie Langdon, Nova McBee, Autumn Krause, Alissa Zavalianos, Abi Hobbs, and Adelyn Belsterling for always being willing to talk books and to share your stories with me and to read mine in return. I appreciate you all more than you will ever know! And to all of my fellow writers and readers who are always cheering me on via social media, you all are amazing! You make writing much more than a solo sport.

Thank you to my parents for always supporting my dreams. My mom has taken me to book signings since I was in middle school, and it's surreal that I have a table now. To my grandmother, who is no longer with us, for always reading my stories. She read this when it was a short story, but I wish she could have read it in this format. She never got to finish any of my novels, but I know she was incredibly proud of me. To my in-laws for driving hours on a Saturday to attend a book signing nowhere near where they live. To my brother for also supporting my dream—I didn't forget to include you in this book, even though I might have in *Heart of the Sea*.

Lastly, to my husband, the one who reads books about Gettysburg before he does fiction. You have never questioned sitting at the bookstore or coffee shop for hours as I sold books. Thank you for supporting my dream and believing in me when I don't believe in myself. I love you.

– Moriah Chavis

About the Author

Moriah is the author of the three-time Realm Makers finalist young adult fantasy, *Heart of the Sea,* the young adult mystery, *The Curious Case of the Midnight Specter*, and various short stories. She is a two-time graduate from the University of South Carolina with a Bachelor's in Liberal Arts and a Master's in Library and Information Science. It's been said you can find her perusing bookstores, attempting to persuade strangers to read her favorite books, oscillating between watching the *Lord of the Rings* trilogy (her husband's favorite) or *Harry Potter* (hers), and keeping her books from the clutches of her two feisty cats.

If you enjoyed
The Curious Case of the Midnight Specter,
Check out these other books
by Twenty Hills Publishing

She Had Glass Eyes

Princesses, Spies, and Other Modern Lies

There Will Be Wolves

The *Bearers of Hope* Short Story Series

The Forbidden Library

www.annejhill.com/twenty-hills-publishing
Instagram @twenty_hills